Acknowledgments

Acknowledgments go to the Production Team for successfully volunteering to produce an entertaining and educational story about firefighting and forestry conservation, and about what it takes to be a good leader. Thank You.

I0599370

My favorite scene in this chapter was where the girls were first introduced to their firefighting station and the overall environment at the station. — Young Adult

I like the way Sandy and her mom are seeing things. It makes me think back to the family trips I took. — Avid Reader

The Colonel's comments are brief and to the point and fair to everyone. A perfect inspiration and role model to the people around him. — Cartographer

Even an old firefighter like me got caught up in the story line! — Fire Prevention Coordinator

It has been a long time since I have read a novel. A very minor comment, why couldn't the mother wake up young Sandy earlier in order for her to have time for breakfast? — Hiker

It's not a boring lecture about conservation — it's a fun lesson told in a story. — Reader & Conservationist

The description of the pack test was priceless. One of the authors must have experienced the pack test to write such a thorough description. — Firefighter

Good stuff on fire prevention for high school kids . . . putting food in the oven, toaster oven or microwave and then getting distracted is a big problem. — Fire Marshal

— Production Team notes, 2006-2007

Quality Parks is a U.S. federally registered, 501(c)(3), public charity. We are a professional organization sponsoring projects that improve both business and environmental conditions. We balance recreational and economic needs while conserving and restoring the Earth's cultural and ecological biodiversity. We cooperate with and directly support park and protected area managers. We also disseminate information, provide experiential learning opportunities, and support efforts designed to stimulate, encourage, educate and involve the general public in natural resource stewardship practices.

ISBN: 0-9663197-2-9
ISBN13: 978-0-9663197-2-9

HOW TO ORDER

Copies may be ordered online: www.qualityparks.org
Email: info @ qualityparks.org.

All proceeds go to charitable purposes.

Contents

Cast Of Characters

Rick - Company Five's Captain and Kim's father
Sam - US Army Guard Pilot
Steve - Junior Company Captain

Mostly Unnamed Minor Characters

9/11 Planters (social worker, intern, Tony, etc.)
Arson Investigator
Colorado Firefighter & Wildland Fire Academy Incident
    Commander & Georgeann's father
Company Two's Captain
Company Two's Driver & Chief
Fire Chief
Photographer at Water Bucket Training Drill
Pine Barrens Wildland Fire Task Force members
Structural Fire Academy Instructors
Sergeant at Water Bucket Training Drill
Third Assistant Chief
Wildland Fire Academy Instructor
Wildland Fire Academy Planning Chief, Operations Chief,
    Finance Chief, Safety Officer, Public Information
    Officer, and Liaison Officer

Extras

- tree planters, police officers, firefighters, military personnel,
    forest rangers, park officials, family members and friends

The Pine Barrens

Sandy's beach

Sunrise Fire

Long Island was tinderbox dry which, if you think about it, can mean only one thing — fire! A fiery inferno that would instantly transform one naturalist and one naturalist to be.

— Sandy Lewis, summer beach party, 2006

PART A

PROTECTING LIFE & PROPERTY

Chapter 1

Best Idea Ever

Sandy held her firefighter helmet in her hand and gazed up at the large white pine tree before her, thinking hard. *What if we are in the middle of another long summer drought and this large pine tree catches fire?!* From childhood, she remembered the fire engines with their sirens and flashing red lights, the darkening sky filled with falling ash, a woodchuck family fleeing for their lives, and a firefighter who said, "Pine trees aren't just catching fire; they're exploding in bright orange flames."

"Come on, Sandy! Stop daydreaming about the Sunrise Fire," said her friend, Kim, who was equally suited up in firefighter gear. With only her red freckles and a determined frown visible, she said, "That was a long time ago!"

"Not to me!" Sandy protested.

Sandy and Kim lived a short distance away from the Pine Barrens, a fire-prone, coastal forest of pine trees and sandy soils, tucked between the coastal North shore village where they lived and the ocean further south. It was there, in the Pine Barrens, that the Sunrise Fire burned so ferociously. But on this Sunday morning, with few awake at this early hour, volunteer firefighters trained. It was a common occurrence on the village's elementary school grounds.

Sandy brushed her blond hair away from her eyes, and continued thinking about the big fire in the Pine Barrens. "Even though the Sunrise Fire was a long time ago," she muttered, "it's not a matter of if; it's a matter of when, it will happen again." She looked to Kim, but Kim was already on her way to the assembling Junior Firefighters. They were high school students, wearing an assortment of ill-fitting firefighting gear. They stood beside two oak trees. A senior firefighter organized them.

"This is the doorway to the school," the Captain explained. He was a rugged good-looking man with a faint dusting of freckles. His expressive eyes conveyed a sense of concern and seriousness. "Imagine a long narrow corridor that you will need to pull the hose through, between these two trees over to the edge of the school grounds." He pointed to Billy, a handsome young boy who held the promise of being an officer someday, and to another of his daughter's friends, Tina, who at the moment, much to his dismay, was giggling. "You two, take off your helmets and pretend you are victims," he snapped. The two moved to the other side of the two oak trees and stood there waiting. "No, not there. Get further back and act like victims. On the ground. The smoke is bad — you're probably coughing or unconscious!"

He marched the rest of them back to the engines and commanded, "Pull out the hose line. Keep it to the side of the school driveway. Position yourself. You'll be crossing over to the entrance. This is a drill, but I want all of you to get down on your knees when you enter the building. I want you to even do better! I want you to crawl in on your bellies. The search and rescue crew will lead." He stopped momentarily and waited until the Junior Firefighters got into position. "Ready? Good."

Sandy was assigned to be on the search and rescue crew. Crouching down, she readied herself, visualizing the elementary school on fire. Would all the school children get out fast enough?!

"The door's open. Search and rescue go in!" called out the Captain.

Sandy crossed the driveway. She dropped to her belly. Using her elbows and knees to push forward, she entered through the doorway. Imagining the thick smoke billowing through the school, she continued in to search for victims. The hose line crew followed.

With experience gained from attacking real structural fires, the Captain anticipated, "The search and rescue crew won't be able to get their victims out with the hose line crew piling up in the school hallway. Pull the hose in on the right. Let search and rescue exit on the left." His arms moved with each direction he gave, trying to assist those who had already entered the imagined structural fire. "You don't want the hallway all jammed up. Watch where you're going! Those of you rescuing victims need to get out and those putting out the fire need to get in. Keep your wits about you!"

Sandy looked back at him and her blue eyes glazed over The Captain was the firefighter who had said of the Sunrise Fire, "Pine trees aren't just catching fire; they're exploding in bright orange flames."

"Sandy!" the Captain called. "Rescue your victim!"

"Yes, sir!" She crawled over to Billy and pulled hard. "I can't! He's too heavy!" Nearby was a skinny, long armed Junior Firefighter named Jim. He pulled out a heavy rope from his turnout jacket and easily wrapped it around his buddy's chest. Together, they pulled Billy out.

"Jim's such a nerd in school," Tina was thinking until Kim grabbed her turnout jacket and pulled her out to safety.

"Very good," called out the Captain to the boys, glancing back at his daughter and her friends with an amused smile. Kim's determination drained out of her body, and Tina saw her slump. Not minding what Kim's father thought, Tina tugged on Kim's turnout jacket, and said, "Great job at saving me! I couldn't have done it myself. You know, I'm just the girly girl of the three of us." She laughed, easing the tension.

Kim turned her back to her father. Grinning, she said, "I hope I didn't chip your shiny pink nail polish by pulling you out of the fire!"

Sandy joined in on the laughter.

"Hey, wasn't it the best idea ever to do our community service time as firefighters?" Kim asked, catching her breath.

Tina smiled a wide smile, "Totally."

But Sandy wasn't too sure, had it been Kim's wishes for her to be a firefighter or her own?

"Sandy," Kim shouted, several months prior. She dashed about anxiously searching for her friend. The high school hallway was bustling with students making a final visit to their lockers for the day. Kim spotted Sandy wearing the overly large Colorado sweatshirt her father had given her. Seconds before making contact, Kim skidded to a stop; her navy blue sweatshirt hood flopped down onto her vest, revealing her short cropped, red hair.

"How'd you know I was going down to the beach for a swim?" Sandy asked, tossing her books in her locker, brushing her blond hair away from her eyes.

"It's March. I know how you are, always getting a jump on the season." Kim pointed to the beach picture Sandy kept in her locker. "Tina says, being that you're down at the beach so much, you should think about being a lifeguard. Anyway, I saw your winter wetsuit in the back of your truck. Isn't it cool that your mom gave you her old red pickup?"

Sandy walked around Kim, trying to leave. "It's not what you think. I got the truck because my mom has no use for it anymore. She's far too busy going to wildland fire meetings. She bought a small sedan to save on gas, and gave me the truck.

And tell Tina to quit bugging me about being a lifeguard. That's all my mom has to hear now. She's finally gotten over me not wanting to teach environmental education. As for being a lifeguard, she'll latch onto that instead, and have me filling out summer applications."

"At least your mother cares," Kim said, kicking the school lockers in anger. "I wish my father would do the same." Her voice trailed off when she realized Sandy was out of sight. Kim chased after her, remembering what she wanted to tell Sandy. Catching up with her, Kim spun Sandy around and said, "We're gonna join the fire department for high school community service!"

"Oh, great," responded a less enthusiastic Sandy.

"Uh-oh. Wrong approach," Kim thought to herself. Sandy, being the oldest of the three, had to be won over. Kim cleared her throat and prepared an alternative delivery; this one, hopefully, would elicit a better response.

"Hey guys!" Tina appeared out of nowhere.

"Tina!" exclaimed Sandy.

Tina smiled at her two friends. She was an attractive young woman with short brown hair. She needed no makeup to accentuate her natural beauty but always wore some to match her creative outfits, as she called them; the ones she mixed and matched from the sales racks. Full of excitement, she hugged Sandy, "What do you think — us? Firefighters!"

"I just can't picture us doing that," Sandy responded disinterested, gazing out the window at the sky, "though I have seen them at the beach on their practice drills."

"Yeah, aren't they awesome?" gushed Tina.

"Tina," asked Sandy suspiciously, "Why your sudden interest in firefighting?"

Kim couldn't resist. "Billy," she exclaimed in an exaggerated tone, rolling her eyes teasingly. "He's a firefighter. And he's soooo cute!"

Tina gave her such a look, as if to say, "This is no laughing matter," whereupon she spotted Billy wearing a loosely buttoned shirt draped around broad shoulders. His youthful features were framed with dark hair. Pointedly, she ignored his nerdy friend, Jim.

Usually neither of the boys paid any attention to girls staring at Billy. They walked side by side discussing fire business.

"So what was the fire alarm?" asked Jim.

Jim was gawky with long arms, eyeglasses, and acne. He was a misfit from all appearances, except that he equally matched Billy's firefighting abilities and easily surpassed Billy's knowledge of the latest trends in firefighting equipment.

"Huh?" Billy asked distracted.

Jim frowned. Billy was plainly eyeing one of those three girls in the corner. From the looks of it, it was that dreamy blonde, Sandy. Playfully punching Billy in the shoulder, he yelled, "Captain!"

Billy turned back, annoyed, "Don't be calling me Captain. I'm not the Captain of the Junior Firefighters anymore. And don't plan on me being any kind of officer in the future."

"You'll be an officer again, soon enough. You just got cold feet."

"No one ever listened to me," Billy muttered.

"Got your attention though didn't I? Besides, she's kinda short and I've seen better."

"Didn't think you noticed," Billy replied, showing his sly smile. Then with a wrinkled brow, he added, "Now, don't go saying something dumb when we walk by them like, 'Gee, Billy really likes you!' "

Jim laughed. "All the girls have their eyes on you when you're not looking so what's the harm done?"

Billy shook his head and gave him a hopeless glare.

"All right!" Jim snapped. "I'm not going to do anything! Forget it." Jim threw his awkwardly long arms into the air. "We're talking shop, remember?"

"O.K., O.K. It was a structural fire alarm on the bluff, several houses down from yours. We got our gear on, drove up, went inside, and found nothing; nothing until the computer's backup power supply unit sparked."

"Cool. Any fire?"

"Nah."

"How ya ever going to make it as a New York City firefighter if the only action you ever see is a few sparks?" chided Jim. Billy countered with news of a real working fire.

They passed by the three girls in the corner and Kim overheard them. At first she was eager to overhear their conversation, but soon she became fraught with frustration when she realized her father would never let her join the fire department. The closest he'd ever let her get to a working fire was listening at home on her scanner. She turned back to them, "Well?" But Sandy was staring out the window again. And Tina was busy with straightening her white frilled blouse. "Sandy! Tina! It will look good on our college applications."

Tina blinked and looked at Sandy. "That's right it will look good on our college applications. You'll be a senior next year."

Kim nodded and smiled eagerly.

"You two! Quit nagging! I already have one nagging mother, I don't need two more!" In an unfair imitation of her mother, Sandy scolded an imaginary daughter, "You live your life at the beach. You should be applying for a summer internship at a nature center by now. You're quite the accomplished naturalist. Make your mother proud!" Exasperated by her own voice, she added, "All I want is to get a swim in before the sun sets behind the bluff!"

Sandy took off down the school hallway.

"Sandy!" Kim persisted. Sunlight accentuated Kim's red hair, as the three of them left the school building.

"What?"

Tina jumped in, "Kim needs your go-ahead before we can join the fire department for high school community service."

"That's right," Kim nodded, and pressed on stubbornly, "We'll save lives."

Sandy stopped walking, remembering a childhood promise she made. "Would we be saving the animals too?"

Kim reassured, "Yeah, we can save the cats and dogs too."

Wrapped in her own thoughts, Sandy didn't reply.

"Earth to Sandy," Kim said. Slowly waving her hand up and down in front of Sandy's face, she tugged on her sweatshirt sleeve, which fell down. Absently, Sandy yanked the sleeve up again. Her father kept sending her sweatshirts sized for his girlfriend. Sandy's parents were divorced.

Tina tapped her shoulder. "Sandy! It's the best idea ever."

"Oh sorry; I was just thinking about how some people watch hurricanes, and how my mom and I watch fires instead. I love the smell of the Pine Barrens on fire! Maybe I can help put fires out and not just chase black smoke and study fire scars." Sandy grabbed Kim's shoulders, asking "As firefighters, we'd be putting them out, right? Just like our fire department did in 1995 for the Sunrise Fire. I was there. I should know."

Kim looked at Sandy incredulously, "What? Were you like five years old then?"

"No, I was seven," Sandy recalled immediately, dropping her hands.

Billy overheard Sandy as he and Jim left the school. Much to Jim's chagrin, Billy walked over to the three girls and said, "Wow, you were actually at the Sunrise Fire!? I've only heard stories about it from Rick, errr, Kim's dad." He gave Kim a nod, and then turned back to Sandy, continuing, "Anyway, Rick said they had the equipment and the gear to make a stand. He thought they could've run hose south of the highway to stop any flying embers from touching down. But there were just too many spot fires. That's how the fire jumped a major four lane highway. Luckily, no one got hurt."

"My mom and I must've been gone well before that," she paused, then added, "but I did see a woodchuck family. They were running from the fire. I thought it was awful for the animals. They looked so scared."

"Sandy, stop boo hooing over the animals; it's no big deal," Kim said, disdainfully shaking her head as her dad would. She turned to Billy, peeved, "Oh, so now my dad is 'Rick' and not Captain to you, huh, Billy?" Although her comment was directed towards Billy, she was really annoyed at the fact that her father never told her firefighting stories.

Impatient with the chatter, Jim grabbed Billy's arm to leave.

Billy pulled his arm free.

"It was a big deal for the woodchuck family," said Sandy unaware of the conflict surrounding her. Her mind was still on the Sunrise Fire.

"I think it's sweet that you remembered that from when you were just a kid," said Tina.

Sandy thought out loud, "You know, joining the fire department isn't such a bad idea. Back then I wanted to be a firefighter. They say you always keep your first dream. Maybe I should check it out."

This took the boys by surprise. Puzzled, Billy looked at each of them, especially Tina. Jim just started laughing.

Tina blushed from Billy's directly placed attention. Holding on to her pocket book tightly, she squeaked, "Kim! You should ask Billy about signing us up, right?"

Jim asked, "Don't you *girls* have better things to do?"

Billy winced at Jim's attitude toward girls. He knew he was better than that. When they were alone he was a normal guy. But as soon as they were around girls, Jim stiffened and spoke down to them. Billy reached for Jim's shoulder and in an amiable and friendly voice said, "What Jim meant to say was joining the fire department is a big commitment. It eats up a lot of your time."

"Yeah, I guess that's what I meant to say," Jim said pulling out from Billy's grip.

"So you're really serious about joining the fire department?" Billy asked Sandy with keen interest.

Sandy flashed a smile, "Why not?"

Kim was delighted. "OK. So now that we're all decided, how do we sign up?"

"Why don't you talk to your dad, Kim?" suggested Sandy.

Tina placed her hand over Sandy's mouth and quickly whispered, "Shh . . . That's not part of the plan."

"Oh," said Sandy, who now realized what Kim was up to — getting around her father.

Billy offered, "I can tell 'em at the firehouse."

Reluctantly, Jim added, "Sandy, you'll be 18 soon right?"

Sandy tilted her head and frowned. "I'll be 18 at the end of May. What difference will that make?"

"You'll probably be put on as a probationary firefighter," said Jim.

Billy interjected excitedly, "and respond to real house fires!"

Before Sandy could have any second thoughts, the group dispersed with Kim and Tina heading downtown.

"Kim," asked Tina as they walked, "I'm confused about who gets to be a Junior Firefighter and who gets to be on probation?"

"Easy. If you put in a year at the firehouse, you can go on probation at 17. But we haven't put in a year yet. Anyone who turns 18 is required to be put on probation and is too old to be a Junior Firefighter. Probation means you need to finish your training, here and at the Structural Fire Academy before being a firefighter — usually that takes a year."

"I thought this was just going to be a few months of community service?" Tina asked alarmed, nervously fingering the frills of her white blouse.

"You know time spent in the fire service goes by pretty fast."

"What are you saying?" Tina stopped walking and eyed Kim apprehensively.

"Nothing," Kim tugged on Tina's sleeve. "Come on, Tina. Stop worrying! I thought you wanted to check out the sales racks downtown before the stores close."

Tina eagerly quickened her pace.

Sandy honked her horn and waved to them as she headed down to the beach for a swim. Billy and Jim made a left turn off Main Street to the firehouse. Kim looked back at them realizing she'd soon be able to do the same.

"Come on, Kim," said Tina. "The stores will be closing soon!"

Chapter 2

My Helmet Keeps Falling Off

It took two whole months to process the three girls' request to join the fire department. Kim counted the days, but with each day, her father's disapproving looks became more frequent, until they were almost unbearable. Sandy eased into the warmer days. Tina shopped. As the time passed, Sandy no longer needed a winter wetsuit to go swimming. The streets of the village were crowded with tourists. The ferry was running a packed three boat schedule to and from Connecticut. Finally, around Sandy's birthday, the three girls stood at the firehouse's entrance.

"Everyone set?" asked Kim as they stood ready to enter the firehouse, a two story, red brick building not far from the village's center. Sandy wasn't too sure about fighting house fires. Tina wasn't too sure about fighting any kind of fire. Kim, however, didn't even try to hide the grin on her face as she opened the door.

"Ready?" Kim asked for their approval.

"Yes!" the three chimed in anticipation.

Kim took the first step into the firehouse, feeling as if she had just walked into her own house. There were the fire engines all lined up and ready to go as soon as the fire alarm sounded, the loosely hung turnout jackets, the bunker pants rolled down over boots, and the helmets neatly organized on top shelves. All of it was second nature to her, even the faint smell of diesel fuel. As a child, her father used to tell her to go watch television in the lounge when he had his meetings upstairs. But instead of watching television, she'd roam around alone among the engines exploring.

Glancing back at her friends who had not stepped in as confidently, she reassured, "Just go ahead and make yourselves comfortable."

"Easy for you to say," quipped Sandy. Sandy felt closed in by the dark and silent walls of the firehouse, and the diesel fuel stank, far worse than a skunk!

Tina, however, had no trouble making herself at home. She forgot about fighting fire. She couldn't wait until their first Sunday morning drill began. Then, the boys would start looking like firefighters, not just acting goofy. Tina's eyes brightened the minute she caught sight of Billy. She rushed over to Sandy and said, "Oh, Sandy, Billy's here!"

"Honestly Tina," sighed Sandy.

"It can't hurt to give a guy the once over. See, Billy's staring at you with obvious interest."

"What?"

Tina laughed

Sandy blushed.

In the din, Kim heard an Assistant Chief call out an order to the new recruits. Bright and confident, he said to them, "Let's go!"

"Gorgeous," Tina whispered to Sandy. "This is going to be great community service, even if my white frilled blouse lost out to wearing one of Kim's scruffy T-shirts."

As the young man walked over, he introduced himself, "I'm Third Assistant Chief."

"I'm Tina," she gushed. "You must be a great firefighter to be an Assistant Chief."

Sandy whispered in Kim's ear, "She wasn't this boy crazy a few years ago, remember?"

"At least she didn't complain too much about changing her attire — except for her shiny pink nail polish!" answered Kim. With a flair for the theatrics, she pretended to polish her own fingernails with an imaginary brush and admired them.

The Third Assistant Chief smiled politely turning back to Kim saying, "You need to get gear." He signaled for the three of them to follow him. Tina squeezed in right between him and Kim as they walked out of the lounge, across the parking lot to the annex building.

The upstairs walk-in closet was packed full of firefighter gear, from hand-me-down turnout jackets and bunker pants to accessories. There was barely enough room for the four of them. Kim and Sandy stepped out into the hallway to try on their own gear. Kim fitted herself with bunker pants, tightening the red suspenders. Sandy tried on several bunker pants but her small, stocky stature made the fit difficult.

"Does this one fit me right?" Tina asked from inside the walk-in closet. She stared down at her oversized turnout jacket.

"Maybe I can help you find a better fit," said the Assistant Chief rummaging through the rack.

"Oh, thank you," Tina's voice pretended to be shy.

Kim and Sandy rolled their eyes.

Moving away from Tina, the Assistant Chief reached for fire gloves and helmets, a yellow probationary shield, pager and flashlight for Sandy and bright orange Junior shields for Tina and Kim. After fitting them with boots, he was done.

"But my bunker pants are still too long," said Sandy.

"And my boots are too big, "said Tina.

"My helmet keeps falling off," cried Kim.

In his second year as Third Assistant Chief, he was used to such complaints. "We can't go buying new gear for every volunteer. You'll get new gear when you're no longer Juniors and off probation. You'll have to wait your turn." He swiftly led them back, "Go to your assigned company and put your gear on the racks."

Rick stood by the engines talking to Billy. Running his hand over his closely shaven red hair, he said, "The way I look at it is this. You must always train the person next in line for your job, so that when you move up in rank, someone is ready to take your place." Rick had been a Fire Chief several years ago and now, as an Ex-Chief, was going through the ranks again as Company Five's Captain.

"That's how it should be from Lieutenant to Captain, and Assistant Chiefs to the Chief." The Captain glanced up at the firehouse clock. "Now go on and get something to eat. Your Captain will want you to do an engine check in a few minutes." Patting Billy on the back, he grinned.

Billy appreciated the advice, but what Rick didn't understand was why Billy didn't want to be an officer, and how much it bothered Billy when the subject was brought up. Billy screamed the words in his head, "Don't count on me being an officer!" Out loud he grinned back and said, "Thanks for the advice."

"Hi Dad," Kim said confidently. She walked right by Billy in front of her father, wearing her helmet proudly. She carried the rest of her gear in her arms.

"You're going through with this, aren't you?"

Sharply turning to face him, Kim's helmet toppled off her head. She reached down to pick it up and reset it firmly back on her head. They stared at each other until Tina broke the silence saying, "Come on Kim. Let's go find Jim. He's in Company Five, where we should be now!"

"Oh great," she mumbled. She had been assigned to her father's Company.

By the time they stowed their gear, Rick's annoyance subsided. If his daughter and her friends were going to be doing their high school community service at the firehouse, they would be treated just like everyone else. His expressive eyes rallied the Juniors, "No monkey business. We're doing an engine check."

Jim had been resting his long arm protectively on the driver's shiny exterior door, chatting with Steve, the Junior Captain, about tires.

"Jim, go check the engine's lights; front, sides, and back."

"Yes sir!"

The rest of the Juniors scurried around the engine. Each week they performed the same engine check until they knew it by heart. They checked the condition of tools: pike poles used for pulling down ceilings, axes, bolt cutters, fire hose couplings and nozzles. They opened and inspected cabinets neatly organized with flares, rags, tool boxes, shovels, spare air tanks and a spill kit used to absorb radiator fluid at the scene of a car accident.

Kim knew the engine well enough, unfamiliar with only a few items. Tina tagged along, complaining, "Kim, shouldn't this be someone else's job? I mean there are mechanics that are paid to do this, like my brother."

Jim returned just in time to overhear her. He gave Tina an incredulous look, freshly annoyed at the three girls and their intrusion into his world. Worse still, Sandy was assigned to be in Company Two. He was supposed to get that probationary assignment as soon as he turned 17. Turning to Steve, he cracked, "She'd be better off doing something useful like making her brother dinner." Steve wasn't like Billy though. He snorted as he laughed.

Company Five's Captain rallied them once more, including the less motivated. "Tina, why don't you open this compartment, look in, and tell us what you think is inside?"

Tina gave Jim a dirty look as she took hold of the cabinet's latch bar. Staring inside, she studiously answered, "There's a milk carton with a wrench and some hose attachments inside. I think they are the tools for getting water."

Company Five's Captain nodded. "A firefighter will use these tools to attach a supply line from the fire hydrant to the engine." Drawing the Juniors even closer, he instructed, "It's up to us to keep the engine clean and ready. We could be called out on an emergency at any moment," pausing to make his point, he somberly added, "that means it can happen right now."

Tina responded with a newfound dedication to making sure the fire engine functioned properly, but not without giving up her initial preoccupation. Stepping back between two of the Juniors who had gathered around, she asked, "Aren't you two in my Language Arts class?"

They gawked at her.

"Steve," said Company Five's Captain to the Junior Captain, "You team up with Kim. Chris, you with Tina. I want you to show them how to check the packs. I'll be watching. Make sure they're full of air, turn them on, check the regulator for air flow and make sure the straps are pulled out on the masks."

Sandy was doing the same with Billy on Company Two's fire engine, though disappointed to learn that the Brush Truck was in Company Three. She kept staring back at the Brush Truck imagining herself fighting wildland fires. Her newly assigned Captain, a tall and slender man, noticed her distraction and said in a matter of fact tone, "You must learn our engine first."

"I was just thinking about training on the Brush Truck so that I can fight wildland fires," she said in a straightforward voice with her hand resting on the engine.

Leaning over Sandy's smaller frame, he spelled it out this time, "It's unlikely you'll get the kind of experience you want here. Our priorities are different. If you want to fight wildland fires, you'd better go out West."

"Oh," Sandy said, stepping back thinking she had done something wrong.

By noon, their first Sunday morning drill had ended, but not for Kim. She kept quizzing Tina and Sandy on terminology, creating imaginary firefighting drills for them to practice on during the week.

On the following Sunday, they trained in the use of air packs. Walking up and down the firehouse steps and grounds, they placed bets on whose air bottle would run out of air last. Eventually, air packs thudded and vibrated alerts in their ears, signaling that the air packs were empty. Company Five's Captain pushed them on so they would learn how much air and time they really had left after the warning. Air tanks emptied one by one. Tina, unexpectedly, held on the longest!

And on the following Sunday, with just enough time to make her younger brother breakfast, fix her hair, and sneak a necklace under her older brother's hand-me-down T-shirt, Tina quietly closed the house door. Her father being a construction worker, her mother working retail, and her older brother being a car mechanic meant most Saturdays were busy which left sleeping late for Sundays. She ran down the hill, passing the library, post office, restaurants and stores.

Sandy rolled down the fire engine window, calling out, "Hey, Tina! I'm on my way to the beach!"

Tina waved and hurried into the engine bays where the Juniors were already assembled. She fumbled with her gear, slipping into her boots pulling up her bunker pants, putting on her jacket, reaching for her helmet and running off to find Kim. In her haste, she ran out of her left boot, having forgotten to double her socks. Tina pulled out the extra pair of socks she had brought from home. Sheepishly, getting her gear back on, Tina spotted Kim already on the engine. She was too embarrassed to even look at the guys. She heard Jim snickering.

"Jump on," shouted Kim.

"Where are we going?" asked Tina sitting next to her in the crowded engine cab.

"The elementary school for a live water drill!"

The engine strained up the hill to the elementary school, and parked. The Juniors piled out, pulling hose off the engine bed. Her father chose Kim to be first on the nozzle. With determined features, Kim crouched to face an imaginary house on fire, keeping a strong grip on the nozzle. Jim backed her up by holding onto the hose behind her and leaning snugly into her back. Steve was third man on the hose. The hose was limp in their hands as they waited for the line to be charged.

"Water coming," shouted Company Five's Driver, who was operating the pump.

Water from the fire engine crept slowly at first then rapidly until the hose line was fully charged.

"Open it, slowly. Bleed out some air," her Captain said.

Jim and Steve leaned forward in anticipation. Kim slowly pulled back on the nozzle handle, letting the air out, and then more fully. Water shot across the lawn in a great arc.

"Swirl the hose around. Hit the fire first, and then cool the vapors above, then below again," shouted her Captain.

Kim raised the hose, swirling streams of water against imaginary flames.

"Okay, next," said Company Five's Captain.

Kim shut off the water slowly to prevent a water hammer, a backlash of energy that might damage their fire engine. But she had trouble getting the hose to shut off completely. Neither wanting nor expecting any help, she decidedly threw her body into it. Closing down the nozzle handle, her helmet toppled off into a pool of water. Reaching for her soaked helmet, she put it back on. Ignoring her father's critical eye and the water dripping in her face, Kim kept her gaze steady.

Meanwhile, Sandy was looking forward to her Sunday morning drill at the beach. Being so busy with firefighting, she had lost touch with the changing seasons of the beach, especially her favorite past time, rescuing horseshoe crabs. Horseshoe crabs, more closely related to spiders, were marine animals with hard shells and a nonstinging tail. She would find them stranded on the beach, upside down, with legs dangling helpless in the air. Picking them up, she rescued each of them, carefully holding them by the side of their shell and placing them back into the water. They would swim back to safety, but not before, they turned to her as if to say thank you. But the horseshoe crabs had long since finished mating: the female nestled into the sand and the males came near to fertilize the eggs the female laid. They did this near high tide and sometimes ended up stuck on the beach, upside down, in the hot blazing sun.

The beautiful weather also awakened the beach bum in her. But on this Sunday morning, her time spent in the sand was far from relaxing. When she reached to pull the hose off the back of the engine like the other guys did, she wasn't tall enough. When she did manage to climb up higher, she fought with her bunker pants. The fire department's hired female tailor explained to her that she needed a wider seat to accommodate her womanly curves. But the tailor had also said she'd have to wait until she was off probation for more customized bunker gear. She pulled herself up without bending and grabbed the hose by the nozzle.

Jumping back down again, Sandy slung the hose onto her shoulder, dragging it through the parking lot, catching up with the men. When all was said and done, they pulled off about 500 feet of hose. A garden hose, Sandy remembered was about an inch wide in diameter. The fire hoses were two to three times wider and much heavier. The hose dug into her shoulder, but she was determined to continue.

"Flake it out," the Captain ordered.

Billy grabbed some line to show her how to direct the hose into large easy, "S" turns. Wearing dark sunglasses, tall, and handsome in his firefighter gear, he grinned. "Not much time to hang out at the beach!"

She laughed, wiping the sweat off her forehead.

"You're doing just fine." Billy said to encourage her.

"Remember to kick out any kinks in the lines with your boot," their Captain said. "When the hose is full of water, it will be too heavy to lift." The hose line was ready to receive water. "Sandy you're first on the nozzle. Get down on your knees and take hold."

With Billy and another firefighter backing her up, Sandy sprayed water out into the Long Island Sound, and played with the water as it hit the waves. They rotated until it was time to pack hose. Climbing up on the hose bed, she stared out at the Long Island Sound watching the clouds, the bluff of the North shore, and the expansive sky.

"Sandy," yelled Company Two's Captain from below, "Take up the hose!" Hose sections had been decoupled and drained of water, ready for reconnecting and packing. A second firefighter climbed up and reached down for the hose to pass back to Sandy. Packing hose was meticulous and orderly. The hose line had to be folded just right so that it could be easily pulled out during a fire emergency.

The following two Sundays, Company Five's Captain had them practice search and rescue drills. First, they practiced at the firehouse annex wearing masks darkened with a paper towel. Tina was in front, leading the first search and rescue crew. Tables, old barrels, furniture, and built window frames had been arranged to simulate rooms, doors, hallways and stairs.

"Hey! That was fun," Tina said pulling off her mask.

Chris had followed her all around the simulated search and rescue and they both exited successfully, even dragging out a dummy victim together. Sandy found the drill less enjoyable. She felt confined and was unable to see. Kim completed the drill twice.

Their next drill was at the elementary school where Billy and Tina played victims, and Sandy dreamed about how the three girls first decided to join the fire department for high school community service.

"Sandy!" shouted Tina. "Wake up! We've got to get ready for the next firefighting sequence, I mean . . . What was that fire lingo again Kim?"

"Evolution," answered Kim.

Tina tapped Sandy on the shoulder.

"Oh sorry," Sandy blinked. "I was just thinking back on how we got to be firefighters. Kim's ideas eventually work out for the best, right? Like that old boat we had to fix so we could camp out at the bird sanctuary across the harbor." Sandy eyes looked wistful. "And, we did!"

"Dancing too, don't forget the dancing lessons at the library," Tina said romantically twirling around.

"And now firefighting," Kim said with a grin pointing to Tina who looked so foolish twirling awkwardly in her firefighter gear. "Come on, guys let's get going," she happily called to them.

Finishing up the drill, they returned to the firehouse and took off their gear.

Outside, Billy called out to Sandy, "Some of the guys are going down to the beach later. Do you think you and your friends might want join us?" He tried to make it sound as casual as possible.

"Sure, but not before I get in a swim."

By early evening, the wind had shifted behind the bluff. The water calmed. Sandy plunged in, lapping through the water's silky smooth and refreshing coolness. Taking deep breaths of maritime air, she swam out toward the inlet, passing the lifeguard stand. Chris, Steve, Billy and Jim were playing a final round of volleyball as Kim and Tina built a campfire.

"That's not how you build a campfire," said Kim, who had rolled up her jeans and was barefoot. She laughed. Tina ignored her and continued making a small pile of tinder. Tina's nails sparkled bright pink.

"Here, let me show you," Kim said, arranging the dry wood into a sturdy pile.

"Better yet," offered Billy, distracted from playing volleyball, "Let me help you." He used Tina's tinder to light the heavier wood.

Chris collapsed on his beach towel.

Steve grabbed a bag of chips and a soda from the ice chest.

Jim was left holding the volleyball in his hand, and just stared, not knowing where to sit or stand, unaccustomed to hanging out with girls at the beach. "Billy, I thought you had enough of being in charge."

"I can't help myself," he said with a smile. Girls just don't know how to start fires."

"Well, we sure know how to put them out," said Kim smartly.

"Light my fire," Tina crooned as the sun set and the sky filled with color.

Kim finished the fire on her own as Tina glanced up at Chris who caught the look on her face.

He smiled sweetly at her.

Tina blushed from the desired attention.

"Enough playing around," yelled Jim, a bit too loudly. He grabbed the lighter fluid can next to the ice chest and squirted it onto the campfire.

"Hey, we wanted to light it the old fashioned way!" Kim said in disappointment as both she and Billy stood up to get out of the way.

Jim lit a match and threw it at the wood, which ignited immediately.

For a while everyone was quiet, staring at the flames which flared and settled down into a slow burning fire.

"Hey, isn't this supposed to be a beach party?" asked Sandy who had changed into a pair of shorts and a summer blouse. "It's awfully quiet around here." She dropped her beach bag near Billy, spread a towel, and reached into the ice chest for a soda.

"Billy is playing firefighter with your friends," said Chris. He leaned over the fire to light his cigarette. "You better keep an eye on him."

Sandy blushed and looked at the sky, "Great sunset, huh."

Jim muttered, "Sure, like girls would ever make it in a real fire."

Kim brushed the comment off and sneered at Jim.

Tina quietly brushed the sand off her jeans, and busied herself with taking out her towel from her beach bag. Chris moved over to give her some room.

With another interested look, Chris told Tina, "Don't mind him. Want a smoke?"

"No thanks, I don't smoke," she said.

Chris shrugged and turned around to Jim. "Want a smoke?"

Jim took Chris up on the offer. He lit it off the campfire as Chris did and took a long drag. A few seconds later, he had a coughing fit.

They all laughed at him.

Jim angrily grabbed his towel and lighter fluid and took off down the beach to the parking lot, but not before kicking sand in Sandy's face.

"What gives?" Sandy asked blinking.

"I don't know." Billy stared at Jim's vanishing figure before turning his head to watch the distant lights twinkling on the Connecticut shoreline. "Let's talk about something else . . . Why not clue us in on how you ended up at the Sunrise Fire?"

"Sure."

As they sat around the campfire in the darkening evening sky, Sandy, who despite her disinterest in becoming an environmental educator, took on the trappings of one. She began, "Long Island was tinderbox dry which, if you think about it, can mean only one thing — fire! A fiery inferno that would instantly transform one naturalist and one naturalist to be."

Her voice became steady and focused, as she continued, "I was seven and already well on my way to following in the footsteps and traditions of John Muir and Henry David Thoreau, to the more locally known naturalists, Roy Latham, Robert Cushman Murphy, and Dennis Puleston. Right down to the dirt under my fingernails and the sand in my shoes, I was filled with excitement."

"What about the fire?" Steve insisted.

"Shhh . . . " Tina said. "Let Sandy tell the story her way."

As the story slowly enfolded, they were all swept back to the time Sandy first became interested in firefighting.

Chapter 3

Sunrise Fire

"What are we going to do today?" a much younger Sandy asked her mom. Sandy was short for her age, with scraggy blond hair down to her shoulders, a button nose, tiny hands already hardened from not liking to wear gloves, a pair of binoculars around her neck, and her very first field guide in her lap. She flashed happy smiles.

"We shall soon find out," Emma answered. Emma was an older version of her daughter, short and stocky, with a soft smile and unkempt long blond hair. Emma had learned to be a naturalist from a birder friend many years ago.

They sat side by side wearing nature T-shirts, faded blue jeans, and scuffed up hiking boots. Backpacks had been tossed into the back of their shiny new red pickup. Turning onto Whiskey Road, so named because in the late 1700's workers drank their fill and built a very crooked road, Sandy's bright blue eyes lit up for another reason. This road gave passage to the Pine Barrens.

"Mom, Mom! Are we going to collect bayberry and sweet fern leaves? Are we going to find wildflowers? I remember one time we found a tiny, tiny, pink flower." Thinking hard, she pronounced, "trailing arbutus?"

"Very good Sandy! You are doing well to remember the flower's name. But that's a spring wildflower, long gone, along with many of our favorite wildflowers."

"Scrawny, Big Boy, Tiny Tot," giggled Sandy. "I'm naming all the trees on the road, just like you named me. You named me Sandy because the Pine Barrens is so sandy, right Mom?"

"That's right," she said, patting Sandy's head. "Where does the sand come from?" began the lesson.

"I forgot."

"Imagine Long Island covered by a thick blanket of ice and rocks. Now imagine the blanket pushing and grinding forward. Then one day this glacier melted and left behind . . ."

". . . sand!" Her daughter proudly clapped her hands.

"The trees you are naming, pitch pines, grow best in sand, but they don't grow as straight and tall as New England sugar maples. Is that why you have given them funny names, because they grow so crooked with limbs outstretched?"

Sandy nodded.

The shiny new red pickup truck turned sharply. Two shovels in the back of the truck rattled.

"Well then Sandy, we know that the Pine Barrens is a dry sandy forest. What can happen?"

"Fire! I'm not a lady bug, I'm a fire bug!" Sandy giggled in a playful rhyme too young to realize the irony.

Climbing out of the truck, Sandy fitted herself up with her backpack. She grasped her mom's hand tightly as they crossed the road and walked down the Pine Barrens Trail in Rocky Point. Beneath the scattered pine trees were many blueberry bushes.

"What are you thinking about now Sandy?"

"Blueberries! I promise to put more in our picking basket than my mouth!" she giggled.

"I'm afraid the blueberries are long gone."

Sandy looked sad. "But I wanted to pick blueberries."

"That's the way nature is," her mother explained. "Spring, summer, fall and winter, round and round, and here we are in a summer nearing its end and a fall about to begin."

"But I want blueberries now!" Sandy stomped her foot in frustration and crossed her arms across her chest.

"Well, maybe we can still find a few. Do you want to try?"

"Yes!"

Already a strong hiker, Sandy's stocky frame sped away. Knowing the way, it took her no time to find what she was looking for, "I found a blueberry!"

"Eat it!" her mother shouted.

The air was dry and delicate. The plants were well past bearing fruit. Yet Sandy continued searching for blueberries while her mother dropped her pack to study one of last year's fire scars. Squinting in the bright sunlight, Sandy raised her arms. "Mom, I can't find anymore," she said discouraged.

"Sandy, come here. Let me show you how fire helps blueberries grow. Two summers from now, these young stems will grow stronger and be filled with many blueberries. Ready for you to pick! But you must be patient."

Sandy bent down looking closely as her mother measured this year's growth, recording the collected data on a clipboard.

Checking on her daughter, she noticed her pouting, "What's wrong, Sandy?"

"I can't wait that long!" Sandy whined.

"You don't have to," her mother, Emma, explained. "We will look elsewhere. The Pine Barrens has a different look and feel to it from one place to the next for many reasons and the result is what we call a mosaic. And until then there will be beach plums to pick on the beach and cranberries to pick in the bogs."

Emma paused to pull out some juice for Sandy realizing that her lessons were sometimes a little too hard for Sandy to understand. But in time, the words and their meanings repeated over and over in the field as they explored the Pine Barrens would become as familiar to Sandy as everyday words. "All we have to do is keep an eye out for a sunnier spot and we will have found a better place for blueberries."

"Mosaic, mosaic, mosaic" Sandy nodded her head up and down fiercely, determined not to forget.

With the 22 day drought continuing into mid August, many Pine Barrens plants were dying, especially bracken fern so special to Sandy because it grew up from the sand and unfurled bright, green lacy leaves in early spring. Many ponds and bogs had dried up too, leaving black mud to replace the reflective sheen of cool water on a hot summer day. Emma took note of these signs and pointed them out to Sandy. They talked about fire, but only in terms of lessons to be learned. They continued their summer adventures without worry.

A week or so later, on a Monday, a wildland fire broke out in Rocky Point, but Emma was too busy counseling clients to pay much attention. She let it pass without interest. By Thursday, with a free day for more adventure, Emma and Sandy stood on an easterly high point in the Elevated Land, due north of Wildwood Lake. It overlooked the Dwarf Pine Plains: low growing, bushy pitch pines with carpets of festive red berried, bearberry vines underneath.

"Sandy, when you were a baby, I used to bring you up here all the time so that we could look upon the Pine Barrens. I'm afraid the trees have grown up as well." Emma sighed.

"But I can see everything," shouted Sandy who had climbed up a pitch pine. "I can see the ocean!"

"Not everyone is as young and strong as you, to climb trees."

As Sandy scanned the vista, she climbed up even higher, "Mom, I see a fire! There!"

Fire shot up into the sky as the tops of two pitch pines exploded in bright orange flames, a quarter a mile away from them. Seconds later, a large black column of smoke rose above the trees. A strong acrid smell, drifted over to them. The view quickly blackened and Sandy could see no more fire.

"Get down! We must hurry to get out of here," her mother cried out. Quite alarmed, she reached up to grab Sandy's foot.

"But Mom, I want to stay and watch!"

"It's too dangerous," Emma said sharply, "Get down. Now!"

Sandy tumbled into Emma's arms.

Emma quickly placed Sandy on the ground, grabbed her hand, and started heading back to the truck. Still not understanding the severity of the situation, Sandy kept looking back over her shoulder, trying to see the fire.

"Sandy, hurry!" The panic was growing in her mother's voice, "There isn't much time."

They hurried back down to the road and saw several fire engines racing towards the fire. Emma and Sandy drove off in the opposite direction. A police car caught sight of them and made a U-turn to pursue their vehicle. But by the time the police car reached the main road, they had vanished. Years later, the Arson Investigator would hear of a similar red truck near the scene of a brush fire. Turning back to the fire, he pondered, "Who was that firebug?"

For the next several days, Sandy and her mother kept tabs on the fire by watching television.

With nonstop fire talk on the news and the Governor declaring a state of emergency, federal response teams, forest rangers, and firefighters streamed in from all parts of the country to help. Homes and medical care facilities were evacuated to shelters, and relocated again as the fire grew. One doctor would later recall astonished, that he made rounds by car, traveling to any facility that had room to care for his sick patients. There had never been such a response to a Long Island fire!

Sandy's mother felt isolated in their home, so far away from the Pine Barrens. She urgently felt the need to get back out in the field to see what was going on. By the end of the week, she grabbed her clipboard and, with Sandy in tow, made a calculated decision to approach the fire from a safer direction.

"Mom, I can smell the Pine Barrens burning," said Sandy crinkling her nose. The Pine Barrens burned sweet and pungent, dry and scented, with a touch of bayberry, sweet fern and pitch pine. But Emma was too focused on the pursuit to respond. She pulled into Gabreski Airport, southeast of where they had seen the fire start. Wrapping Sandy's blond hair with a rubber band, and doing the same for herself, she said gently to her daughter, "We've stopped here to talk to this brave firefighter."

"But Mom, he doesn't look like a firefighter," Sandy asked, puzzled. "His helmet is yellow."

"He just dresses differently. He's a federal firefighter, from Colorado. See his license plate? You remember. We've seen them on television."

Sandy shyly looked up at the federal firefighter. His green and yellow clothes matched the color of his truck. He was very tall with short cropped black hair. He wasn't smiling.

Walking over to him, Emma asked amiably, "So how's the firefighting going?"

"As well as can be expected," he said. Trained in unified command, he was fresh on assignment, though with twenty years of experience out West. It wasn't too long ago, however, that he was on an engine with a couple of friends fighting wildland fires in Colorado. Today, as the federally assigned Operations Chief, he spent his time figuring out who was in charge: federal firefighters, state forest rangers, or fire chiefs.

Taking her daughter's hand, she said, "We were hoping you could show us a map of the fire."

In response to her request, he scanned the deserted airport grounds half expecting the missing Public Information Officer to appear. Seeing no one, he frowned.

Sandy flashed him a smile, wrinkled her button nose, and looked up at him. "I want to be a firefighter when I grow up!"

The Colorado Firefighter smiled back at the little girl. She reminded him of his daughter. "That's what I said when I was your age and look at me now!" he said laughing and thumping his chest with pride. Then turning to her mother, he said, "You're really not supposed to be at the fire scene, but, heck, no one's listening to me anyhow so I'd just as well talk to you."

Putting down her clipboard on the truck's hood, Emma picked up Sandy so the three could study the map. He pointed to the fire's location and to where the fire departments were organizing, or staging, to fight the fire head on. "You don't stage your resources at the head of the fire," he muttered. "Too dangerous." But what he expected of the fire and what the fire chiefs did were two different matters. He then pointed to the evacuated homes across the street. Standing upright, he explained, "You can see how we're in a woo-ee of course."

"A woo-ee," repeated Sandy, giggling.

"Short for Wildland Urban Interface (WUI). It's where we humans and the wildlands butt up against each other. It increases incident complexity. Our goal is to protect life, property and the environment.

The portable radio strapped on his shirt crackled for attention.

"Excuse me ladies," he said turning his attention to his radio. Pushing the button, he replied "Colonel, go ahead."

"You'll have additional helicopter support from the Army Guard."

"Now, we're getting somewhere. Best news I've heard all morning."

"I'll be on the ground shortly."

Disinterested in their firefighting chatter, her mother said, "Ready to go Sandy?"

"Mom, I want to see the helicopter." Sandy pointed as they both shielded their eyes to stare up into the sky. The helicopter soon whirled in and landed, creating a small dust storm around its chosen landing place. The door opened and an authoritative figure from the U.S. Army Guard approached. The Colonel's eyes and mustache were steel grey. He shook the federal firefighter's hand warmly, "What can we do for you, sir?"

They spoke for a few minutes on coordinating air ground support until the Colorado Firefighter shouted, "Heck, now look at that!" Locally known as stump jumpers, two converted military trucks equipped to carry firefighters, rigged with water tanks, hoses, water pumps, and brush guards, crashed into the woods directly across from them.

Rocking on the heels of his black fire boots, the Colorado Firefighter stood tall, wiping the sweat from his brow with a red handkerchief.

"Colonel, these guys should be working with the engines and doing structural triage: cutting away overhanging branches, breaking up wood piles, opening up evacuated homes to shut off fans and gas lines. I'm sure these local homeowners weren't prepared with a plan to protect themselves and their homes from the threat of a wildland fire as big as this."

The Colorado Firefighter pulled out a water bottle from his truck and drank deeply, before adding, "The fire chiefs tell me their response is orderly. They all go in and all come out. When one stump jumper is out of water, it drops to the back of the line. That's not what I've seen this week. If you ask me, they're just a bunch of cowboys chasing fire — freelancing."

Emma looked official with clip board in hand. She added, "Bulldozing new roads, knocking down trees with their stump jumpers, it's obvious to me that these local firefighters do more damage to the Pine Barrens than the fires ever do."

The Colonel stood by listening, observing.

When Emma and the Colorado Firefighter nodded in agreement they expected the Colonel would agree with them.

But the Colonel wasn't easily characterized by his expression on his face of by his position of authority. With a slight twinkle in his eyes, he said, "One must embrace diversity and allow this diversity to make team decisions or be doomed to failure." The words known to many as Colonelisms were words used to teach lessons about what makes a good leader.

Sandy whispered, "Diversity, diversity, diversity."

Emma smiled. "Sandy, this isn't the same kind of diversity we talk about in the Pine Barrens. The Colonel is speaking about the differences among people. Emma pulled a water bottle from her own pack and gave it to Sandy.

The Colorado Firefighter stared down at the little girl and her mother, considering how strange it was to fight fire on Long Island. He must learn to listen and be patient with the one hundred fire departments working to put out this fire. "Well,

Colonel, I reckon they could start up a wildland fire academy so we can sort this all out."

Feeling part of the adult conversation, Sandy excitedly announced to the Colonel, "I'm Sandy, and I'm going to be a firefighter when I grow up."

"If that's what you want Sandy," her mom said encouragingly. There were many women in the fire service. With confidence in her daughter's abilities, she knew Sandy would be the best and safest firefighter she could be.

"But I'm only a girl." She looked down at her feet disappointed.

"Sandy," the Colonel commanded, "I expect you will continue your studies and do whatever it takes, just like me."

Sandy flashed happy smiles. She befriended the Colonel instantly. "I can be a firefighter, Mom!"

Emma smiled approvingly and curtly thanked the Colonel and the Colorado Firefighter for their time. Then she drove back by way of the Sunrise Highway where the Pine Barrens still glistened green, untouched by fire. The overlook was due north in the Elevated Land. Spotting the staging area, she pulled in between a cluster of fire engines.

Sandy leaned forward. "Look, it's a real firefighter!" She jumped up and down in her seat as the young firefighter with freckles and long red hair walked over to them. Sandy looked straight at him. He wore a black helmet with a Company Five shield. His bunker pants were held up by red suspenders. His sweat soaked, gray colored fire department T-shirt identified him as a firefighter from the North shore coastal community where Sandy lived.

"Excuse me," the firefighter said to them. "The Chief told me to keep this area free of non emergency vehicles. You can park over there," he pointed. Distracted by another spot fire touching down on the south side of the Sunrise Highway, he turned his head. The wind swirled through his hair. It was a hot, parched wind. Turning back, the young firefighter said, "This is my third rotation. "I've never seen such fire."

Sandy slid closer to her mom.

"You mean you may not be able to contain it?" Emma gasped.

He shook his head it. "Pine trees aren't just catching fire; they're exploding in bright orange flames." He warned, "You shouldn't even be here. It's not safe for you and your child. The head of the fire is coming in this direction!"

Several hot ashes landed on the hood of their red pickup. Sandy's eyes widened in fear. Emma backed up the truck and spun around to leave.

Sandy shouted, "Mom, look!"

The smaller of two woodchucks waddled as fast as he could to keep up with his mother. In their haste they would risk crossing a major highway in broad daylight. Not even in the dead of night would they ever imagine this, or dare to, until today. Yet the two woodchucks would eventually make their way to a small family farm and escape the fire. And so would begin the adventures of a young woodchuck, named Parsley, so told in the book entitled, <u>How Parsley Saved The Farm</u>.

"Sandy, roll up your window!" her mother shouted.

"Why do we have to leave now? I want to watch the woodchuck family! Where will they go? Will they be safe? Will the firefighters save their lives too?"

"They'll be just fine, Sandy," her mom said trying to keep her voice calm. "Nature has its ways."

"But they're scared, Mom! Don't leave. Help them!"

Emma sped off.

Sandy turned to watch the woodchucks bravely dart across the highway.

"When I grow up, I'm gonna be a firefighter that saves the animals," she vowed.

Kim stood up and stretched, then doused the campfire with her half finished soda. Disinterested in stories about wildland fires, she said, "We've heard it all before."

Tina stood up and tapped Kim's shoulder, and whispered, "But Billy hasn't."

"Any questions?" Sandy asked of everyone. As she folded her beach towel, she thoughtfully added, "Now grown up, a naturalist to be has become a firefighter." With a smile directed at Billy, she concluded, "And that's how I ended up at the Sunrise Fire."

"Well worth the price of admission," Chris joked. Reaching for the last of the chips, he emptied the bag.

Tina reached down to gather her belongings. "Speaking of which," she added, "Company's Two's fundraiser is coming soon. What a party that will be."

Steve carried the ice chest as the group walked back to their vehicles.

"Tina's got it in her head," Sandy confided to Billy, "that she'll be hanging out — mostly with cute guys."

"I guess Tina's going to be a bit surprised," laughed Billy. "We don't get much time to party, but being Tina, I'm sure she'll find a way."

Chapter 4

Not Just A Bunch Of Cowboys

Fundraisers were regular events, not just about one night, not just about a bunch of cowboys having a party. Friends and families attended firehouse fundraisers. Fundraisers also offered the village several opportunities to show support for their fire department and to get to know their firefighters personally. Company Two's fundraiser was one of several held at the firehouse. Preparations often extended through the whole week prior to the event with final ticket sales, shopping, organizing extra volunteer help, and, in terms of Company Two's fundraiser, a tradition within a tradition that slowed the pace down momentarily.

Several days before the Friday evening fundraiser the Captain, along with the Chef, a retired high school music teacher, firefighter, and engine driver, went clamming. Billy and Jim tagged along. Cruising along the Long Island Sound, it promised to be a warm day with a clearing blue sky. The Captain revved the engine to counter the leaving tide and strong currents of the harbor they entered to the west of where they lived on the North shore.

Billy and Jim took in the sights, sounds, and smells of an expansive salt marsh, known as Little Africa. It lay before them, sheltered from open waters. A solitary wading bird silently stalked fish on an exposed mud flat. The marsh grass stood out bright green against the dark water. They passed by two kayakers paddling along the shoreline.

Finding their way to the Chef's favorite spot, each man took a turn working the clam rakes until they let the boys go at it. Jim's long arms handled the rake as easily as Billy's flexed muscular frame. Several hours later, by late afternoon, they came home with several bags of freshly harvested clams. Shrimp was bought at the fish market.

The following day, Billy showed up eager to help. Spotting Jim on the lawn behind the firehouse, he pounded him on the back in greeting.

"Ow!" yelled Jim, his fairer skin bright red from a day out in the boat.

"Too much sun?" laughed Billy. He walked away.

Jim tackled him.

"Hey! You two!" shouted Company Two's Captain.

The two boys immediately quieted down and joined in as stakes were hammered into the ground, poles positioned, and ropes pulled taut to raise the party tent. When the borrowed church chairs arrived, they unloaded them while Jim spoke about the department's new thermal imaging camera used for detecting fires behind walls.

By Friday afternoon, with an expected crowd of over two hundred fifty people, Sandy stood in the doorway of the firehouse's kitchen with her hands in her back pockets, not knowing what to do. The kitchen was upstairs above the engine bays, set off to the side of the fire department's meeting room.

"You can't beat powdered potatoes," announced the Chef.

Sandy crinkled her nose at the thought of powdered potatoes and canned peas. But she would later be the first to stake her claim in taking home leftovers.

Nearby, the Chef's wife stood. As the Chef eyed the cooling roast beef on the counter, occasionally calling to her for butter or more spice, she knew he would only be satisfied when each prepared dish was cooked to perfection. He was already profusely sweating with a white smock wrapped about his hefty frame, but he barely noticed his own discomfort. Humming in delight, he stirred the simmering commercial sized pots of gravy, peas, and potatoes.

Sandy felt her mother's absence in watching the two of them in the kitchen. "But it wasn't bad all the time," she had wanted to tell her mother. Walking around town, off duty firefighters would drive by and honk their horns. She'd look up and wave. Her mother's long term friends, mostly active environmentalists, seemed cold and distant in comparison.

Despite Sandy's best efforts, she couldn't convince her mom to be a little bit more open-minded.

"Come on in Sandy," said the Chef's wife. "Help me keep the kitchen clean." She handed Sandy a dish towel. "My husband cooks meals at the firehouse, and I cook them at home." She laughed. "It has been that way for thirty years."

Sandy laughed too, and stepped in to help. She wiped down counters, placed dirtied utensils in the sink, and made space for the next tray of seasoned roast beef to come out of the oven. Wearing her father's recent Colorado birthday gift, she washed lettuce and yanked up her sweatshirt sleeves with each passing head of lettuce. It was the largest salad she had ever seen. Dozens of heads of lettuce, boxes full of red and green peppers, and bags of onions and carrots made their way into the kitchen. Salad fixings were sliced and then placed into trays. She felt like she was making food for an army, not for the residents of their community.

Just before the fundraiser began Sandy took a break from kitchen duty. She went outside to husk corn for the steamer. Tina and Kim ran across the street on an errand to the local grocer for last minute supplies. Billy and Jim carried trays of shrimp and red sauce down from the kitchen to the seafood bar.

In no time, the picnic area filled with elected officials, neighbors, and affiliated organizations such as the American Legion, Veterans of Foreign Wars, and The Blue Knights. Sandy was called back to the kitchen. With one last glance, she spotted Billy at the seafood bar serving dishes of raw clams and cooked shrimp. Jim had gone to the walk-in refrigerator to get more clams for the shuckers, a local term for guys who deftly slit open hard clam shells with a thin knife and then cleaned out the clam meat in a second swipe of the knife. Kim handed out cups of red sauce, and Tina was on her way to the salad bar.

The sun set pink with puffy clouds. The pleasant sounds of lively conversation and laughter offset the summer evening's still air. Guests knew what to expect as they busied themselves by forming lines around the seafood bar and the huge salad bar in front of the party tent.

When Rick was next in line, he said to Billy, "Nice job with the clams this year."

Billy's eyes sparkled, and he gave him an extra serving of clams.

Kim scowled at her father's reaction every time he saw Billy. She went off to find Tina.

The 80's cover band, led by a firefighter from Company Three, who was a cook by day and a rocker by night, started in with a lively version of "Girls Just Wanna Have Fun." Tina set her eyes on the band and started dancing in time to the music. Kim came to her side, but was instead mesmerized by people filling bowls and bowls of salad from the salad bar.

"We're short on salad bowls, napkins, and dressing," interrupted Company Two's Captain.

He stood off to the side with a serious look on his face.

"Yes, sir!" they chimed, racing each other up the stairs to the kitchen where a third roast beef had just come out of the oven. Juicy and red, the roast's inner meat would continue to cook as it cooled. A stocky construction worker was rhythmically operating the deli slicer on the first, now cooled, roast beef tray.

"Still moving. That's the way I like it," commented the satisfied Chef as he turned back to stirring pots of gravy, peas, and potatoes. But his quiet and strikingly handsome son, a firefighter for many years, doubtfully commented, "I prefer mine dead," and scooped up a burnt end from the deli slicer's discard tray.

"Me too," smiled Tina as she gazed into the son's handsome eyes dreamily. Even when wearing an auto dealer's T-shirt from where her brother worked as a car mechanic, Tina looked fashionable. She kept her shirt tucked neatly into her tight jeans and she wore a plain silver chain around her neck with a pink, quartz crystal heart dangling from it. Elegantly, she reached in for a scrap of dark meat, totally ignoring the roast beef juice oozing down her wrist.

The Chef's son smiled back.

"Gosh, Tina," cried Kim, "What about the salad bowls, napkins, and dressing?"

"Come on," laughed Sandy, who had just finished loading up a cart with a tray of roast beef smothered in mushroom gravy. "I'll help you."

"Thanks," Kim replied, but she also grabbed the sleeve of Tina's shirt and pulled her along behind.

The evening passed with the salad bar emptying and the last of the clams and shrimp eaten, with third helpings of roast beef, potatoes and peas gobbled down, and with music and dancing filling the evening air. Dessert and hot drinks were served. An exhausted Chef, with a soiled kitchen smock, and Company Two's Captain sat around the coffee table outside of the kitchen going over the money spent and the number of tickets sold, while the three girls and Jim were in the kitchen washing dishes.

Kim's short red hair was topped with soap suds as she scrubbed an empty gravy pot. Tina's T-shirt was stained and no longer tucked neatly into her jeans. Sandy had taken off her sweatshirt, tired of yanking up the sleeves. Jim kept pushing Tina to find more soiled trays to restock the dishwasher. She tried to ignore him, but he kept on pushing her almost to the point of tears. Sandy rescued Tina from Jim's tormenting, and pitched in with the dishwashing.

When most of their paid guests were gone, Billy came up from helping with security. Striking up a conversation with the girls, he teased Sandy, "I see you just about have the kitchen in order."

Jim scowled as he waited impatiently for Billy. It was late. Tomorrow would be spent putting away the tables and disassembling the party tent. With no response, he dropped his dish towel and headed out, still half expecting Billy to follow. But Billy kept his eyes on Sandy.

"Here's your assignment, Billy," Sandy shot back, pretending to be their Captain. "You're assigned to search and rescue. Get your tools, and meet me by the kitchen counter."

"Yes, sir," said Billy playfully. Looking around for tools, he put on a kitchen smock as if it were his bunker gear.

Tina laughed.

Kim handed him a flashlight and a mop.

Sandy couldn't quite keep a serious expression on her face and flashed him a smile.

Billy played into it, deadpan. "Captain, I found wrapped roast beef, a jar of peas, and some mashed potatoes. What shall I do with them sir?"

Tina nudged Sandy and whispered in her ear.

"Ahhhmmm," replied Sandy. "Carry them out of here, and give them to the ambulance crew."

"Yes, sir!" he said, giving Sandy a mock salute.

He reached for his share of leftovers.

On the way out, he continued joking with Sandy. "Keep it up and you'll be all set for your first Structural Fire Academy drill next week."

"Really?" she asked, suddenly anxious. Every interior qualified firefighter had to attend at least one county sponsored drill a year. Sandy knew it would be much more true to life than their drills had been so far. It tested them in real fire situations. Moreover, a paid instructor observed their competence to fight fire, to follow the chain of command in an emergency situation, and critiqued their performance in an after action review.

"Oh, you'll be fine," he reassured.

If it weren't for this trust, she'd feel isolated, alone, and unsure of herself.

Billy and Sandy sat in the back of Engine Two talking quietly on their way to the Structural Fire Academy. They were fully suited up in their firefighting gear, and sat among several other firefighters attending the drill that evening.

"Billy, do you think one of the training drills will be on wildland firefighting?"

"Didn't you know that county's training drills are for structural and vehicle fires?"

"Oh, that's just great," she said, staring out the engine cab window. Missing her evening swim because of firefighter training, she was cross. "If it wasn't for Kim wanting to be a firefighter, there's no way I would've gotten so involved. I could be spending more time at the beach. Thanks a lot, Kim!"

"Yes, thanks a lot, Kim!" he countered with a sly smile. "I wouldn't have had a chance to get to know you."

Sandy stared at a passing farm field before looking back, "I don't mean to complain. Firefighters aren't gonna change so why should I?"

"That's not true," he pointed out to her. "Our fire department, along with several others," he counted them out on his fingers, "participate in Technical Rescue. It's not part of a normal firehouse or a Structural Fire Academy drill. There are even new mutual aid agreements among our departments so that Technical Rescue can respond to emergencies when there is a special need to help save people in difficult places to reach. Firefighters do come up with good ideas once in a while, you know."

He stared into her deep blue eyes and realized Sandy still wasn't convinced. "Maybe the Structural Fire Academy drills will include a brush fire evolution someday too."

Sandy's eyes widened. "Really?"

He shrugged. "Sure, why not?"

Sandy's face relaxed into a smile. "Something to hope for."

Thirty minutes later, they disembarked from the engine to sign in before beginning the drill, known as the Taxpayer. Taxpayer was firefighter lingo for a strip mall. It was a bare bones replica with several metal doors leading into a two story structure coupled with some strategically placed propane burners rigged to emit flame and smoke.

The training staff, clad in well worn bunker gear, gave them their first evolution. "There's fire on the second floor. It's three in the morning."

"Sandy, you watch this evolution," said her Captain standing beside her.

She stood by, watching the first of three evolutions unfold. All of it was familiar, yet, at the same time, unfamiliar too. It wasn't the novelty of a real fire flaring up in the windows either. It had more to do with the sequencing and timing of the event. She was well versed in search and rescue, hose drills, and putting on her air tank and mask, but now she could watch an entire emergency response unfold. The firefighters responded to the scene of the fire in a well coordinated sequence of actions.

The Captain radioed for water. The truck company extended a ladder to the roof. The irons man carried tools to make a forced entry. The can man followed him with a fire extinguisher and tools for a search and rescue. The engine company pulled hose off the engine. And their driver, who was also the engine's pump operator, unfurled a five inch segment of hose and attached it to the fire hydrant. He radioed back to the Captain, "Charging the line."

Water filled the limp hose. Three firefighters from the engine crew held the hose line in front of the main entrance as the truck company forced open the door to do a search and rescue. "We've got bodies in here," Sandy heard over the radio. The simulated bodies were pulled out. Sandy's eyes continued to watch the engine crew on the hose and the ladder company on the roof. The guys from the ladder company cut out a hole in the roof to vent the fire.

It was hard for Sandy to keep up with all the action. It was happening too fast.

"Fire's out."

The evolution ended.

"Get your pack on," her Captain said. "You'll be third man on the hose."

Sandy fumbled with the straps, belt, air tank, and mask. What was common on a Sunday morning drill felt alien to her now. At last, the air pack was firmly fixed to her back, just in time, for the evolution had already begun. Her heart pounded. She reached back to turn on her air and had trouble turning the air tank valve. The Driver's son reached down behind her and turned it open. With the mask over her face, she got into position. In a flash, as the third man on the hose, she was pulled in!

Knowing that she wouldn't be able to see and actually being blinded were worlds apart. Even though she had been drilled in what to expect, it didn't make it any easier. How can I climb up the stairs when I can't see them? Dense smoke filled the strip mall. She held onto the hose with one hand as hard as she could. Instinctively, she reached with her right hand towards the wall as someone shouted, "Right hand lead."

She climbed, kept low, and sucked air.

At the top of the stairs, Sandy lost her sense of direction, "I don't know where I am," she yelled.

Billy, who was second man on the hose, turned back and shouted, "Keep close to me. I need to be able to know where you are. Next time put your flashlight on. I can see you that way."

"O.K.," she shouted back.

"Down on your knees, keep low," the training officer reminded the engine crew. He stood off to the side, in there with them. Sandy remembered that keeping low meant safety, being cooler, and away from any potential flashover — the temperature at which all flammable material would ignite. Meanwhile the hose had lurched forward again and turned a corner.

Sandy hurried to keep up and fell over. Too busy thinking about how to recover, she had no time to panic. Her bunker gear was bothering her again. She strained hard against the heavy, confining men's gear, got up and stumbled forward. When the hose pushed back in her hands, she knew the nozzle was open. She held on tightly, and leaned forward into Billy who did the same to the firefighter on the nozzle.

Metallic sounds of water being sprayed onto the simulated fire echoed in Sandy's head. Without success, she tried to slow her breathing and not waste air. What happens if I run out of air? Water flowed back on the floor towards her knees and boots. Suddenly the air cleared. The ladder truck must have vented the roof, Sandy realized.

"You O.K.?" she heard the training officer ask.

She nodded.

"Good. Turn around and take the hose out with you. The fire's out."

She pulled off her mask and dropped her pack. The sky had darkened from twilight to night. She went to stand with the men listening to a review of their performance.

Billy handed her a sports drink.

Sandy downed it, not realizing how thirsty she had become.

"Billy, do you want to be the irons man for this evolution," Rick asked.

"Sure, Captain," Billy said confidently.

This would be Billy's third evolution! Sandy was amazed by his stamina.

"Just need to change my air bottle. This one's nearly out of air." After exchanging tanks, he grabbed the irons, an axe and a leveraging bar.

"Fire on the first floor," Billy heard the instructor say as he took quick strides towards the point of entry. Rick took hold of the bar and wedged it in the doorway near the lock. In the stark light of Company Four's electrical lights, Billy took easy swings. He whacked the bar with the head of the axe until the lock broke.

Rick held the door cautiously closed with the bar. "The fire might be right behind the door. Get in position, down on your knees," he instructed. Billy nodded. Rick then signaled for the can man, the Driver's son, to stand by. Fresh firefighters were on the hose, in position to throw water if needed. No flames were seen at the entrance. Billy scrambled in with the driver's son, and Rick as officer. Sandy waited as they pulled out a victim and as the engine crew went in with the hose. A second hose line crew went around to the back of the building. Sandy joined in to help feed them hose.

With the fire out and their final performance review over, the firefighters packed hose and left for the firehouse. In the engine's cab, Billy sat talking to an older firefighter about firefighting in the FDNY.

It was nearly ten by the time Sandy finished up at the firehouse and made her way home. Exhausted yet energized from the day's events, she entered her house.

"Hi, Mom," Sandy called out excitedly, giving her a hug. "I can't wait to take the firefighter classes. It was great fun tonight," she babbled on enthusiastically.

"Why don't you start with a shower?" Emma offered gently pulling away from the smell of soot and sweat emanating from her daughter. "Then we can talk."

After she scrubbed herself clean, changed and put her dirty clothes in the wash, Sandy went into the kitchen where her mother was just placing a batch of corn muffins in the oven.

"Do you want some dinner?"

"Nah, we just had some pizza at the firehouse."

"Now, tell me how did your drill go?"

They spoke for a while as Sandy helped her mom clean up. The two looked even more alike as Sandy had grown up with mannerisms very similar to her mother's.

"So the drill went as you expected. That's great."

"Well, not exactly."

The oven timer filled the kitchen with a mechanical, "click, click, click," for several minutes before Sandy reluctantly admitted, "There's a lot more training in structural firefighting than I expected, but, on a happier note," she concluded, "Billy thinks they'll have wildland fire drills at the Structural Fire Academy someday."

Emma said nothing to either discourage or encourage her daughter. Having spent the last five years trying to accomplish that very same task, Emma had become an environmental advocate. Exchanging leather boots for slip on shoes, worn blue jeans for dress slacks, and a pickup truck for a sedan, her time was now spent attending meetings, making phone calls, and finding a lost committee chair who would lead the charge in organizing wildland fire drills at the Structural Fire Academy.

But once the lost committee chair was found and oriented, he ignored Emma, never acknowledging her for what she knew and how she had helped. The politics of fire in the Pine Barrens was harsh. Emma didn't want to discourage Sandy for thinking idealistic thoughts, but at the same time found it hard to be her bright and cheery mother.

The oven timer rang, and broke the silence.

Emma's response was dull and automatic. She took the freshly baked sweet corn muffins out of the oven and placed them on a rack without pleasure. Sandy sensed something was wrong, and gave her mother a questioning glance. Her mother looked away. Sandy pulled two of the muffins out with a fork, smearing them with butter, hoping the muffins would cheer her mother up. Emma poured two glasses of cold milk. They silently ate the piping hot, sweet muffins.

"It's late, Sandy. You should be off to bed."

"Good night, Mom," Sandy replied, obliged to wrap her arms around her mother's neck. Sandy went upstairs thinking, "Maybe she thinks I will loose interest." She quickly changed and went to bed, thinking, "I must try harder."

Emma returned to her office, a sun porch off to the side of their living room. She threw down her pen in anger. Her daughter's training as a naturalist and then as a conservationist, and now as a firefighter should go no further on Long Island.

She turned off the light and went to bed. Tossing in her sleep, Emma began making plans for Sandy to continue her education and training out West. "At all costs, Sandy mustn't become involved in the politics of fire in the Pine Barrens," she vowed to herself.

Chapter 5

I'm In Charge

As much as Emma tried to keep her daughter away from the politics of fire in the Pine Barrens, Sandy was like a moth attracted to a flame. But the more Emma spoke of becoming a Western firefighter to her, the more Sandy became determined to do the opposite. Breaking free, Sandy drove "out east," a local term describing any point east of where one lived on Long Island, to find peace and tranquility in the open stretches of the Pine Barrens. It was a crisp, clear November day. She was off from school, with some free time on her hands.

Turning onto Whiskey Road, she saw pitch pines and breathed in the sweet dry scent of the coastal forest. Then to the Peconic Ponds, she thought about threatened tiger salamanders getting ready to mate and breed in late February, early March. A slender amphibian with short legs, bright orange markings, and a long tail, Sandy fancied the tiger salamander as being the most exotic animal in the Pine Barrens. Near the Peconic

River, she imagined how things would be when bird's foot violet bloomed blue along roadside edges again and warmer winds would blow. Beyond the Elevated Land to Gabreski Airport, she thought about the Colonel and how she first met him.

Turning back on Sunrise Highway, Sandy took note of the young pitch pines and scrub oaks growing into the former burn site. Along the Carmans River, near the wildlife refuge, she wanted to see what birds were around this time of year. But it was getting late. She headed to the Structural Fire Academy instead and parked. All around her stood silent pitch pines, gentle figures, each of them sharing with her a sense of place and purpose, which made her drives out east to the Structural Fire Academy special.

With pen and notebook in hand, Sandy walked directly to the Structural Fire Academy's main entrance. Opposite the entrance was the county's official headquarters for emergency response to both manmade and natural disasters. In the back of the academy was the Taxpayer where she had her first simulated fire drill with Billy. Below the academy was the Maze, a series of tunnels and crawl spaces designed to test a firefighter's ability for search and rescue under blackout conditions. It had a reputation for weaning out the faint of heart. She wasn't planning on being one.

The classroom contained a mix of students, and a tough, seasoned FDNY firefighter. He made it clear to them that firefighting was serious business. They were all professionals, volunteers included. Sandy took a seat in the third row.

"If you don't wear your gloves, bad things can happen," he instructed. Reaching for a brand new pair of firefighter gloves on a table, the instructor shook his head, "What if you get your hands burned, then what will you do?" He tossed the gloves aside and pressed, "What do you use your hands for?"

Letting the words sink in and their imaginations to mull it over, he finally confirmed their worst suspicions, "Everything. That means having someone else help you do things you wouldn't even want your mother doing for you anymore. So if you start taking off your gloves to fit your mask or whatever you're doing, you're going to get into a bad habit."

He pulled out his worn pair of gloves from his brief case and slipped them on. "Learn to work your hands with your gloves on. You don't want to get fire on them." Taking off his firefighting gloves fondly, he cautioned, "As for your bunker gear, zip up your jacket, snaps, collars, and all. Be prepared. You don't want burning embers down your back. I've seen it happen. I don't want to see any of you getting second degree burns by being casual about your personal protective gear."

He had hooked them in; the rest of the hour and a half session went smoothly.

Sandy got her book stamped and drove home.

During math class, Kim sat thinking. Her *best idea ever* wasn't quite working out the way she expected. No matter how successful she had become at being a Junior Firefighter, her father rejected her. Billy could do no wrong! But she couldn't blame them for everything? Her hesitation during a carbon monoxide monitoring drill was glaringly obvious, at least to Jim. "Now, that was real stupid!"

Staring at the back of Tina's head, Kim caught herself thinking about how nice Tina's hair looked and how hers was like a guys cut, cropped short and never combed. "What am I thinking about that for?" She must talk to Sandy about this. Tina would probably want to take her shopping! Kim laughed at the thought and it made her feel better. But Sandy had her own issues. And Sandy didn't think much about her kind of firefighting.

Home from school, Kim ran into her house and headed upstairs into the safe haven and comfort of her own room. It was a converted attic, more like an extension of the firehouse than a girl's bedroom. There were fire frequencies and alarm codes posted on bulletin boards, and newspaper clippings taped to the wall. Next to her window, there was a poster size map of the county with red pushpins pressed firmly into a dozen or so recent fire locations. A scanner sat on the corner book shelf. Each of these items helped her fill in the details of the most recent working fires of interest to her.

Her plain bed was pushed off to the corner.

A workbench and cork boards held an assortment of electronic equipment, wires, and cables.

Kim closed the door and reached up to turn on her fire scanner. Tossing her coat and daypack onto her bed, she rummaged through the box of spare electronic parts on her workbench, including a programmable gas monitor. Picking it up, she roamed her room, checking for imaginary gas leaks. Reassured that she knew how to use it, she put it aside and found a pager clip. She attached it to a recently purchased pager she had bid for online. With help from a desktop computer, she reprogrammed it to the frequencies she needed to monitor local county fire alarms.

The fire scanner crackled.

She paused to readjust the antenna she rigged: a wire up through the corner of her room's window to the roof. Scanners could work through many more frequencies than pagers, but she found their reception, the ones she could afford, weren't nearly as good. In her closet, looking for an antenna booster, she pulled out a box full of old parts and found two figurine dolls, a woman and a man, instead.

"Hey, I remember you," she laughed, taking hold of the woman figurine. "We climbed up in engine's hose bed when my father wasn't looking, but as for you," she pointed to the man of the house, "I told you to stay home and cook dinner."

Kim's normally stubborn face turned soft as she also remembered the day her father had called her down off the engine to stay put in the firefighter lounge. While he responded to a fire alarm, she listened to the firehouse scanner and heard her father get in trouble while ventilating the roof. She sat alone, bravely not moving until he returned and she knew he was safe.

Kim wiped a fearful tear from her face. "We're older now. Getting hurt is part of the job." She dropped the doll back into the box and pushed it deeper into her closet before closing the door.

A sequence of tones, very much like a fire alarm, called for her attention. She pulled out her cell phone. It was Tina.

Returning to the Structural Fire Academy for another lesson on firefighting, Sandy listened to a town fire marshal wearing a white shirt adorned with several silver badges.

"What if a gas grill catches fire? What do you have to be careful about?" He reminded them, "Boiling Liquid Expanding Vapor Explosion — B.L.E.V.E." Again, he questioned both Sandy and Jim, and the rest of the students attending the Structural Fire Academy class.

Blank stares weren't the answers he expected.

He turned on the slide projector and pointed with a laser pen, "Heat will create boiling liquid within the pressurized propane tank. The liquid becomes an expanding vapor that has the potential to explode. So what do you do for fire control? He changed the slide. An animated cartoon of the word B.L.E.V.E. showed a propane tank exploding, with two firefighters blown away. If you're not prepared for it, you'll be part of it."

Jim raised his hand and answered, "Keep the tank cool, sir. Hose it down, until you can get to it and safely shut off the gas valve that's feeding the fire."

"Correct." He changed the slide. It pictured several crouched firefighters hosing down the tank. "Change nozzles and use a fog stream instead of a straight stream. Fog nozzles broadcast wider streams and also draw cool air into the fire, pushing heat away as well as cooling the tank more effectively than straight stream nozzles."

The next slide pictured a hose line crew in a kitchen with flames extending up into the cabinets. "What should you be doing to control the fire in this situation?"

Jim answered again, swirling an imaginary hose, "Straight stream at the ceiling to cool down the gas vapors, and direct attack on what's burning."

"Correct." The instructor pointed to one of the probationary firefighters sitting in the back of the class. "You. Tell me what we're assuming?"

Startled, he sat up straight in his chair and squirmed, "Ventilation?"

"Correct," said the instructor, "You want the smoke and heat to be lifted out of the building while you're on the attack line. There'd better be a truck company positioned outside to vent the roof and windows. "

Sandy couldn't imagine herself going up on the roof. She wanted to be a firefighter with her feet kept squarely on the ground or so she thought until the next slide pictured two firefighters creeping down into the basement.

"Now what about basement fires?" The instructor asked. "You've got only one escape route and the floor above you may collapse. It's hot. The stairs you're on act like a chimney. The fire's aiming for your face."

The class was quiet.

"Today's lesson is about controlling the fire," repeated the instructor, reinforcing the purpose of their lesson, "not having the fire control you."

Jim waved his hand again, but the instructor deferred to Sandy.

Sandy wasn't so sure she was suited for basement fires either. She guessed, "Ventilate by cutting a hole in the floor above the basement?"

"Correct. And get down to the level of the fire. Get off the stairs."

After a few more examples, he reviewed several watch out conditions. "When a building is about to collapse there are sounds like creaking, straining, etc. There are certain structures that collapse fast and easily due to their construction, most commonly warehouses. They have truss features, beams and bars, upon which the whole roof depends. A sign that a roof is going to go is the spongy feel underfoot, very nerve-racking. I've fallen through a roof, but managed to catch myself before I went all the way through."

Sandy blinked.

Jim whistled.

The instructor continued, "Don't be caught in a situation where the fire is behind you. You want to face the fire or have it be to your left or right, never below you. Also watch out for weak stairs or floors, suspended loads like air conditioning units, hazardous materials that may spill, electrical hazards, and signs of exhaustion from team members."

Pointing to a quiet student in the front row, he said, "What's a backdraft?"

"When oxygen is introduced to a fire that has consumed most of its oxygen and is waiting for more."

Sandy thought about what she had learned in her chemistry class. Intent on adding her thoughts, she raised her hand and said, "The introduced oxygen will support a chemical reaction, oxidation, and reignite the place."

"Correct," said the instructor. "That's why we ventilate over the fire. Heat will rise and escape, cooling everything down without introducing oxygen. The most obvious sign that a backdraft is about to happen is a puffing black smoke coming out of the house. Remember that."

Again, the instructor pointed to the back of the class. "What's a flashover?"

An older student said, "Oxygen is present. Superheated particles and gases in a fire become so hot they explode."

It's not fun," the instructor responded. "Watch out for an eerie silence, extreme heat, and an enclosed area that has not been ventilated."

Finally, the instructor spoke about controlling wildland fires. Sandy looked forward to a lengthy discussion, but there was only a brief mention of terminology. Disappointed, she held out her attendance sheet to be stamped, drove home, and told her mother she had to study for an exam. She called Kim and then Tina, but their cell phones were busy.

"What's doing?" Tina asked over her cell phone.

"Nothing much," Kim answered.

Excitedly Tina said, "Did you know Sandy almost made it to a brush fire!" Waiting for a response, Tina imagined Kim sitting on her bed, disinterested, staring at one of her news clippings showing a recent house fire. Tina shrugged. "The brush fire was actually a rekindle of the first fire. Sandy didn't see much. She just said her hands got cold even with gloves on. We both thought it was too cold for a brush fire. It's been in the teens all week long! But Sandy's mother said that doesn't matter. It's been dry and . . . "

"Want to know about the boat fire last week?" Kim interrupted.

"Oh . . . O.K." She had heard about it from Sandy but was willing to hear it again.

Kim's voice shot up an octave. "I listened to the whole thing! It started as a car fire alarm, turned out to be nothing.

Ten minutes later, the alarm sounds off, again, this time for a boat fire. Within minutes, three boats at the marina were on fire. It was around five in the afternoon, but it's dark outside this time of year. Sandy got there at the end to pack hose!"

Tina laughed. "We're real good at that, aren't we?" In a more serious tone, she asked, "So why all the fires, Kim? Do you think there's an arsonist living here?"

"Don't know. We may have an arsonist living nearby. That's what I'm hearing."

"Does that happen often?" asked Tina anxiously fingering her necklace.

"It runs in cycles. They're always out there — somewhere," offered Kim mysteriously.

The scanner went off with an alarm. Tina waited as she listened to Kim talking and taking notes. When the alarm went off for the second time, it was nearly midnight. Tina finally said, "G'night."

The next morning, Kim made her grand entrance into the kitchen, disheveled and yawning. She had stayed up to listen to several more fire calls, taking notes about which engines responded, and what were the causes of the alarms. Collecting all her notes in hand, she then submitted an article to an online firefighter newspaper, and collapsed on top of her bed, fast asleep with the fire scanner on.

This prompted her brother to complain, "Can't you lower that scanner? I can't sleep."

Kim helped herself to some breakfast and ignored him.

"I think you should listen to your brother," her mom said, pointing to her son and to her daughter.

Taking a seat at the kitchen table, she said, "Sorry, I'll try to rig up something."

Her mom nodded approval.

"But that's what you said a hundred million times before," her brother complained.

Her father teased, "Why don't you just watch some reality TV? It would be a whole lot quieter around here." He laughed.

Kim dropped her spoon loudly on her plate in frustration.

Rick's expressive eyes dimmed, "You're my daughter and you're only a Junior Firefighter because your mother said you needed community service credits to graduate high school. I would think that you two would've come up with something more appropriate for a young woman. Firefighting is serious business."

Kim automatically responded, "I'm tired of hearing you say you respect my life decisions, but then you won't support me being a firefighter."

Their fiery eyes locked as Kim's mother went to make some more toast. She sighed at the prospect of facing yet another meal filled with flared tempers and rising voices.

"This isn't a game," her father continued. "Staying up all night listening to fire calls is not going to make you a firefighter. You've got to drag hose and carry your weight of tools. If you can't, no one will want to partner up with you when it comes to a working fire."

Kim ignored the suggestion that only men were capable of firefighting. In response, she said, "I can be just as good as your Billy!" She protested.

Her father gave her a doubtful glance, reaching for his cup of coffee. Taking a long satisfying drink, he put down his empty cup and impatiently groaned, "Ask your mother."

Her mother expressed concern for her daughter's safety. Grasping her daughter's hand, she added, "There's no need to put in more hours. You've already done the community a great service."

Kim's eyes flashed in anger. She wouldn't let either of them get under her skin. She refused to doubt herself. Abruptly she stood up, pulling her hand away. Accidentally, the table rocked and her brother's half emptied glass of juice tipped over.

"Sorry," Kim muttered under her breath.

"See? You just keep messing things up," said her father who took one last bite of toast, "at the firehouse, and now here." Retrieving his coat, he kissed his wife goodbye and tapped his son fondly on the head. He closed the door behind him with finality.

Kim stared at the tipped over glass, feeling her confidence vanish as she stared at the juice running down the table to drip on the floor.

Her mom jumped up to get a sponge. "Kim, before you leave for school, help me with the dishes."

Biting her lip, Kim cleaned up.

Her little brother caught the school bus.

She preferred to walk, and fretted all day. Why doesn't he just leave me alone? Why is he always the one in charge? On her way home from school, she cast off her self doubts for good by making plans.

All she had to do was wait for the right moment.

With her mother in her office, and Sandy done with cleaning up after an early dinner, Sandy decisively called Kim. As she waited for Kim, she thought about what Tina had told her. According to Tina, Kim was up to something big. Tina also warned Sandy that Kim would be jealous about not being the first one of the three to attend the Structural Fire Academy. But Sandy wanted to talk about her disappointment with the firefighting classes.

Kim's conversation jumped from topic to topic, from one minute to the next, whether it was about listening to her scanner, rummaging through her workbench, or fussing with her computer.

Sandy heard her pacing and imagined her workbench a mess and her bed unmade. She held her breath and listened, waiting for the right moment to broach the subject.

"Sandy, how's you classes at the academy? I need to know!" Kim paused to listen to Sandy. "What? Oh! Forget about learning about wildland fires!"

Used to being snubbed by her Captain, but not by her friend, Kim, it stung. Without thinking, Sandy said, "You know, I've got the textbook, <u>Essentials of Firefighting</u>. And I just had a class on forcible entry. It's all about breaking and entering." She voiced the words, "so there," to herself.

"I know what it's about, and so should you."

"Well, I didn't know that during an emergency, firefighters could legally break into your house. I never thought about it."

Despite her annoyance at not being the first of the three to attend firefighting classes, Kim couldn't contain herself, "Cool tools, huh?"

For a moment they talked about the class in detail. Sandy recalled what the instructor had said about firefighter safety and brazenly imitated one of the instructors, "You're gonna get hurt. It's part of the job but minimize it."

"Of course, excellent."

Getting along much better, Sandy let it slip out again, "I'm still hoping we talk some more about wildland fire though."

"Oh forget about it, Sandy. That class on breaking and entering is best. What's the class tonight?"

"Ventilation."

"Oh, I gotta go to that!

Sandy voiced hesitation, "You can't go."

"What! Not even to one class! Come on, give me a break! I'll sit in the back of the room," she added as she ran her fingers through her short cropped red hair with her cell phone glued to her ear.

"Sorry Kim. They're only open to probationary firefighters. You know that. And besides, I'd never hear the end of it if Tina heard I helped you sneak into class."

Kim protested.

"Nope. You can be as stubborn as you want, but it's not going to change anything. Look. I gotta go."

"Well, then," Kim said in a huff. "No one can't stop me from studying firefighting on my own."

"Bye," Sandy emphasized the word.

"Bye," Kim shot back, pocketing her cell phone, returning to her desk smiling. She went online to order the <u>Essentials of Fire Fighting</u>, using the online account her mother had helped set up. "There, I did it, and plan to do more than just be a dumb old Junior Firefighter." She'd show her Captain a thing or two. At dinner that night, Kim kept her cool, inwardly defiant.

No opportunity would come to her until a late January thaw set in. Temperatures climbed above freezing and to Long Islanders, it felt like a heat wave. Kim slept with her window opened, welcoming in the milder winter temperatures, sleeping peacefully.

Her dad's pager woke her.

She jumped out of bed, plugged her ears into her scanner and listened. The report was of a possible working fire just around the corner from her house. Kim was ready.

Her dad was already out at the scene by the time she finished dressing. As she silently crept down the stairs, she smiled at her rationalization; it made sense to her to show up at the fire scene unannounced, just to watch. When she reached the back door, she held the doorknob until the door was completely closed. She tried to be quiet because she didn't want to wake her mother, and then ran down the street into a blanket of fog.

Gloomy street lights partially lit her way. She turned the corner. Her red hair glistened from the mist and then the flicker of red flames.

"Wow! I've never seen a working 13-35 up this close."

An eerie orange glow shone through the upstairs window; the truck company was already setting up a ground ladder to reach the roof for venting. Fire police were already setting up additional lighting and directing what little traffic passed by. Engine Three was already flaking out fire hose. Billy was already at the door swinging an axe head onto the Halligan, an iron bar with hooks to wedge open and break into a locked door.

Kim ducked behind a neighbor's bush so she wouldn't be seen.

"Get down," Rick reminded Billy. "Open the door slowly."

With the truck company venting the roof with a power saw, the engine driver charged the hose line.

"We've got somebody in here!" radioed Rick after Billy and he began search and rescue.

Moments later, they assisted a stunned man out of the house to a nearby ambulance.

With the fire adequately vented, black smoke billowed out from the roof. The attack line was already in the house.

A second search and rescue crew was ordered in to continue searching.

Discarded used air tanks littered the lawn.

Daringly, Kim crept closer, lurking across the street, in the shadows.

Two more engines pulled up, mutual aid calls from nearby firehouses. Sandy arrived in Engine Two, glancing about, donning an air pack, and grabbing a pike pole to help with mop up. Mop up was the tearing into walls and ceiling tiles to check for fire extension.

"I bet Sandy probably saw me," Kim considered. Yet Kim stayed to study every detail of the emergency response and was ready to jump out and help if she had to. So absorbed in the fire scene, she didn't care who saw her now.

Chapter 6

Tug Of War

Walking into the early spring fire prevention class, Billy was aware of every girl in the room noticing his good looks. To everyone in the class, he appeared to be at ease. He took a seat, smiled back and lightly chatted. But inside, his stomach churned. Billy didn't know what to do. He had spotted Kim at a working house fire, again, and was amazed. His mind struggled with wanting to be her friend and with the pressing need to correct the situation before anyone got hurt. Meanwhile, with his Structural Fire Academy classes completed, his final exam passed, and his Firefighter Hands-on training underway, Rick kept dropping hints.

Rick's plan was for Billy to learn to drive the engine and, once that was done, it would be a short hop to becoming an officer. Billy hated the thought of becoming an officer. He was frustrated with his own good looks and the assumptions people made about him. They assumed he was a born leader who would make sound decisions, take charge and give directions. They also assumed he was their friend, and would not rat out on any of them.

The classroom continued to fill up with students.

Tina entered the classroom in style, with a fashionable sales rack special: flared skirt and a fluffy blouse. She pranced around the classroom flirting happily. The girls plainly admired her, except for Kim and Sandy who giggled at the silliness.

"Hey Tina," said the Chris, eyeing her with interest.

"Hey Tina," said Steve, banging his desk for added sound effects.

"Hey Tina," said Billy teasingly, making gentle fun of her with a sly smile.

Blushing, Tina stared at him. Billy wore a loosely fit shirt with his sleeves rolled up to reveal his muscular arms.

Jim burst into the classroom. Barely in control of his lanky legs, he knocked Billy against the wall. "Sorry, I'm late. I had an important meeting with my uncle. Too, bad you two don't get along."

Billy got up and took another seat, annoyed at being reminded of Jim's uncle, your buddy and best friend until you offered him advice. The man cracked jokes behind your back. "Big man? He thinks he's the coach, eh?" It wasn't too long before the rest of the team snickered each time Billy showed up at baseball practice. Eventually, Billy quit the team thinking he wasn't good at baseball.

"Hey Billy, I said I was sorry," Jim reached over to playfully punch him in the shoulder. Billy ignored him.

The Fire Police officer entered their classroom, and waved his hands to settle down the students. He cleared his throat. This was the same old fire prevention course modified just yesterday in haste for young adults. Would the subject still be as interesting? Did they remember anything? As he took a deep breath, he scanned the classroom. Several of the students looked familiar to him.

"Hi, my name is Mr. Jerard. You've probably had many other instructors this year, as well as materials to educate you on the dangers of falsely reporting a criminal incident or fire emergency, but I am here today to get you educated in fire prevention." He pulled out some notes from his freshly pressed uniform's white shirt pocket. "Today, you're in high school." He glanced back down at his notes nervously. "Ahmm. We're going to start with fire hazards. A fire hazard is anything that encourages a fire to start or increase." He looked up.

Respectfully, the students politely listened.

He cleared his throat, "Let's see. To me a fire hazard is a fire waiting to happen and is indicated by poorly maintained electrical appliances, surge protection, and overloaded outlets."

By this point, a few in the back began to yawn.

"Ahhh, hmmm," he casually offered, stuffing his notes into his pants pocket. "It was early one morning. We were short on crew and called in a signal 24, for mutual aid." He pulled out some of his props, from behind the desk, a radio and his helmet, sooty and worn, with a bright white shield.

The white shield read, "Chief."

Tina blurted out, "Gosh, a Chief? He must have been really good-looking back then."

"Tina, shut up!" cried out the student that had just yawned.

"What happened next, Chief? asked several students earnestly.

"Ex-Chief, please." He continued, "Turned out to be a 13-35, a working house fire, caused by lightning. Lightning hit the wires, ran through the lines and blew out a television set. The guys ripped down the walls to chase the fire. By then the fire had run through the walls and up into the attic." Walking over to Kim, he directly asked, "What fire hazards are common to an attic?"

Kim grinned. Mr. Jerard was a close family friend. "Lots of stuff. Boxes, books, paper."

"And why does that make it difficult for a firefighter, Billy?" asked the instructor.

"It's hard for the search and rescue crew to find the fire and any victims, and there's more fuel around. A fire can more easily spread that way."

"Very good," said Mr. Jerard. "Don't forget there are other fire hazards in the house. For example, cooking food and getting distracted."

"Like San-dy," Kim teased, drawing out her name for dramatic effect.

The class laughed. Sandy had a reputation for being distracted, often staring out windows for no apparent reason.

The instructor cleared his throat. "And what about the need for proper storage of gasoline?"

He pointed to a young man in the back of the class.

"The fumes can build up, and then explode if there's a spark."

"And the spark can come from?" He motioned encouragement with his hands.

Tina answered, "Sparks from an old vacuum cleaner?"

"Leave it to Tina to come up with that one," Jim remarked to Billy with a hefty laugh.

"You shouldn't be treating her that way," Billy muttered, but his words fell on deaf ears.

Holding the classroom's attention Jim added, "Better leave her out of power tool safety inspections." He cracked up.

Steve snorted.

Billy put his head in his hands and shook his head.

"Keeping tools regularly inspected is a way to eliminate fire hazards, very good," the Ex-Chief said. He stepped forward to make a concluding remark, "Remember, fires still happen. So keep fire extinguishers on hand, properly charged. If there is a fire *and* only if there's a real fire," he cautioned, "call 9-1-1. Get everyone out. Keep low and don't be a hero."

Reaching for his notes again, his tone changed, "Ahmm, now we shall talk about the fire safety surveys."

The students sank back into their chairs.

Perplexed about what to do, the Ex-Chief hesitated just for a moment before tossing his notes in the garbage can. He turned to the students and said, "Everyone stand up, take your notebooks, and follow me!"

Out in the hallway, he said, "We're going to do it the real way. Take a survey of the school property — that's what we'll do. After all, the school is your house during the day."

Getting occasional odd looks from teachers along the way, they hurried to keep up with him. The Ex-Chief pointed to fire hazards or imaginary ones if none were physically present. The students gathered around him closely when he did. In the cafeteria, they inspected electrical cords. In the chemistry lab, they made sure all chemical bottles were properly secured and labeled. The teacher stood with them and helped identify the chemicals. In the basement, the heating system's annual service records were checked as well as the basement's cleanliness.

Back in the hallway, Mr. Jerard pointed out the fire alarm boxes, "There'll be no monkey business with the fire alarms. Leave them be until the day you really need them. False alarms breed complacency. Think about that, too, before causing any mischief!"

"Right. Sure. Yes, sir," were their collective responses.

Outside, the Ex-Chief brought them to the corner street. Stopping at the nearest fire hydrant, he instructed, "We're going to walk around the school property to locate each fire hydrant. On our way, we will also note additional fire hazards."

Jim moved to the front and cut Tina off.

"Hey!" Tina cried out.

"Sor-ry, Tina," he said in an exaggerated apology.

His classmates laughed.

Tina turned away and looked upset.

Billy pulled Jim aside. "Jim, don't you think Tina deserves some respect now that she's on probation, like you?"

"What are you talking about?"

Billy took a long breath and explained, "Besides bumping into her just now, remember last Sunday's drill for example."

"Oh yeah," Jim laughed. "Tina and her shiny pink nail polish." Mimicking, he put on imaginary gloves and reached for a wrench with his long arms to remove the fire hydrant cap in a girly girl manner. Impatiently, Jim threw his arms up and said, "There'd be an inferno by the time she got water to the fire."

"From what I remember," Billy countered, "She did open the fire hydrant to let the water run clear. She just lost her grip."

"So, I helped her close the hydrant."

"More like you ripped the wrench right out of her hands," Billy protested, recalling Jim's bark, "Here, I'll do it," and Tina's sagging shoulders as Jim finished their assignment.

"What gives, Billy? The drill's over! What difference does it make? Come on, we've got to catch up with the class." He grabbed Billy's shoulder to push him along.

Billy pulled back.

Jim shrugged and walked off without him, pushing into the crowd of students to stand beside the instructor. Billy followed more slowly, lost in thought. There had been an incident where a firefighter got so ticked off at his buddy that he dropped a charged hose line. The unrestrained hose threw his buddy against the wall. What if Jim's attitude carried over to a real working fire, someone got hurt, and the fire situation worsened?

"What about wildland fires?" Sandy said and raised her hand. "Wouldn't that be an additional fire hazard?"

The instructor paused, with a puzzled look on his face, "I've never thought of that one. Good question," he said. "But I expect that is a more common concern for firefighters out West." The instructor checked his watch and waved the students on, "Let's get back to completing our survey."

Kim stood still for a moment, laughing.

Sandy gave her a sharp glance. "All this talk about house fires and how to prevent them is pointless if the trees catch on fire."

"It was a fair question," Billy said drawn in.

"I can't see why Sandy makes such a fuss," Kim lashed out. "If she wants to fight wildland fires so badly, she should move out West."

"You really want your best friend to move out West?" asked a startled Billy.

Kim's freckles stood out even more. Relentlessly she argued, "I'm just trying to make a point."

"So what's your point?" Sandy pressed, now face to face with Kim.

Kim ignored Sandy and looked at Billy. "She's volunteering in our department. That means she has to fight fires the way we fight them. That means structural fires and brush fires, not wildland fires like they do out West."

Tina had walked back to them when she realized they had not been following the instructor. Not happy seeing her two friends argue, she reached out for the two of them.

Sandy brushed her off. Wanting time alone, she walked off to take a lap around the high school track.

Billy went after her.

Kim went to follow too, but Tina held her back, saying, "Let's go. The class is on the other side of the field already. We'll catch up with them when we survey the track."

Feeling her absence, Kim called out, "Sandy, I'll see you then, right?"

Tina pulled her away, "Come on, let them be."

"Sandy," Billy called out, catching up to her. "Sandy, can I talk to you?"

"All right, all right," Sandy broke her silence. "I'm not mad at you! I just couldn't take *her* attitude anymore. She's always complaining about her father being so set in his ways. You'd think she'd be a little more sensitive to my interests, but she's acting more and more like her father!"

"Something's really bothering her to make her act that way." Persisting, Billy stared into her eyes, whispering, "Did you know Kim's been sneaking to working house fires?

"Yeah, so what?"

He shook his head. "Freelancing is dumb and dangerous. Why does she do it?"

Sandy gasped, "She isn't supposed to — is she?!"

"No." He raised his hand emphatically. "Besides being dangerous, she could get into big trouble, showing up on her own like that. She should know better. After all, she is Rick's daughter." His voice trailed off, feeling obligated to set the matter straight, but not knowing how. The maritime breeze off the harbor blew gently as the two walked side by side and lapped the track. Despite the cool North Shore breeze, it was a warm afternoon.

"I wouldn't put it past her to freelance," Sandy confided. "She's that frustrated over her dad not supporting her life decisions. Her dad treats her like she's still a little girl. Little girls never grow up to be firefighters. Kim takes things into her own hands. That's how we got to be firefighters. She found a work around her father."

Billy eyes widened. "So that's why Kim's been acting so hotheaded. Rick has been shutting her out of his world."

"Why the surprise? Didn't Kim's dad ever mention that to you?"

"No. We spend our time talking about the fire service and firefighting, not about our personal lives outside of the firehouse." He paused.

Sandy picked up a pine cone. Tired of talking about Kim, she asked, "Want to go with me and my mom on a fire training drill with a real Colonel in the U.S. Army Guard? I mean I know it's a wildland fire drill, but would you be interested anyway?"

"Is this a date?" he teased.

Sandy couldn't help blushing. She hoped he wouldn't notice.

"Sure, I'd like to go," he said. Sandy was easy to talk to, so unlike the other girls whose interest focused only on his good looks. He dared to ask, "Do you think I could talk to the Colonel about why it's so hard to be a good leader?"

In a light hearted, authoritative tone, Sandy imitated the Colonel, "One must embrace diversity and allow this diversity to make team decisions, or be doomed to failure." Sandy shrugged. "My mom and I call them 'Colonelisms.' Sometimes they are hard to figure. But now I think I understand what he means. I just wish Kim would accept me the way I am, and get passed it."

Relieved by Sandy not making a big deal of his dark secret, he picked up the pace. Her short legs couldn't keep up with his and she ran after him. "Hey! Slow down!" Reaching him, she gave him a friendly push.

Billy laughed, and then got serious, "Diversity's a good thing? It's more like competing interests. Isn't it up to the Colonel, not the team, to make the decisions?"

"Maybe. I dunno," Sandy said. "Better ask the Colonel, not me. He'll be O.K. about it."

The students finished the survey of the field. Billy and Sandy rejoined the group. They returned to the classroom and took their seats.

Mr. Jerard put his hand to his chin. He realized that high school students needed to know certain things. He talked about cars, reminding the students, "Don't drive cars with catalytic converters onto heavy grass or park them over dried leaves. It'll start a fire. Be careful wiring your car. You need to know what you are doing." With a glance around the classroom, he added, "When you go off to college, don't use cheap extension cords to plug in toaster ovens and other appliances that generate heat."

Rummaging in his duffle bag of props, behind the teacher's desk, he pulled out a cheap electrical cord destroyed by fire and another more reliable one. He handed them to the class for a closer look. "And a final reminder!" He cleared his throat.

Sitting on a student's desk, he pointed his finger at them. "If you're in the middle of a real working fire, call 9-1-1. Even if it's a small fire, don't even think about it. Two men were working on the roof the other day, and they called their boss instead of 9-1-1. By the time we got to the fire, the roof was involved. So make that call."

Relieved, he excused the class.

They applauded.

Raising his hands to quiet them down, he said, "Thank you. If you have any more questions or if you're interested in becoming a firefighter, talk to . . ," he pointed to the firefighters attending the class, and motioned for them to stand up.

There was another round of applause.

The last ones to stand up were Billy, Jim, Sandy, Tina, and Kim. Smiling at the crowd, they stared disconcertedly at each other. Tina was hurt by Jim's badgering. Kim and Sandy weren't paying any attention to each other. Billy was staring at Kim not knowing what to do or say about her freelancing. Jim was staring oddly at Billy and Sandy.

The class quieted down in anticipation of one of them speaking.

Fire pagers went off. "Cross street of Sunset View and Bluff Road. Signal 12. Time 15:30."

Tina jumped at the sound of the pager clipped to her skirt. This was her first fire alarm as a probationary firefighter! She had hoped to somehow find a way out of her community service by now. But she was loyal to her friends. Not wanting to let her friends down, she became a probationary firefighter after she turned eighteen. "What am I doing? I really have to respond to alarms," she kept thinking dazed.

"A brush fire!" Sandy cried out. "Wow! This is it!"

Jim rushed out.

Billy caught a glimpse of Tina collecting her books and yelled, "Come on, Tina. Forget about that stuff! Let's go!"

Out of the high school doors and off to the firehouse they sped. Kim was well on her way out the classroom door when the Fire Police instructor grabbed her arm, "You're still a Junior, aren't you? Juniors don't respond to fire alarms. Watch yourself," he warned before he left the room.

Down at the firehouse, Sandy reached for her gear as her mind went into overdrive. She imagined flames twenty feet over her head. It could get very windy on the bluff, too! She grabbed her helmet from the rack over her head. Billy and Jim were gone. The Brush Truck had long since left. Frantically, Sandy looked around for Tina, but she was nowhere in sight. She jumped onto the next engine and was off.

Tree plantings at the 9/11 Memorial

PART B

PROTECTING THE FOREST

Chapter 7

Every Day Is Earth Day

It was five years after the Sunrise Fire, and Sandy was 12 years old. Being groomed to be a naturalist at an early age, her room looked more like a nature center than a girl's bedroom. On Sandy's night table were interesting finds: deer bones, a box turtle shell, scattered wild lupine seeds and a pitch pine cone. An aquarium bubbled with fish collected from the Long Island Sound. Parsley, a stuffed woodchuck wearing a Long Island Ducks baseball cap, sat on the chair beside the bed. Stacks of field guides filled book shelves.

"Sandy, wake up! It's Earth Day!" Emma called, knocking on the bedroom door. Emma looked quite refreshed and exuberant. In the same five years since the Sunrise Fire, Emma had transformed herself from a naturalist into a conservationist. It complemented her well. Dressing the part, wearing leather boots and a dark wool sweater, she peered in to her young daughter's bedroom.

Tacked to Sandy's bedroom walls were pictures of the Pine Barrens and Long Island beach scenes. A Smokey Bear poster read, "Remember Our Friends in the Forest." With his shovel grasped firmly in his hand, Sandy imagined the cartoon character joining them on tree planting days.

"But Mom," Sandy yawned, "every day is Earth Day. That's what you tell me, right?" She buried her head back in her pillow.

"It's also a day scheduled for planting, Sandy! Breakfast will be ready in five minutes."

Sandy rolled over and opened her eyes to watch another chickadee fly to the bird feeder.

"Sandy, I'm surprised you didn't hear the birds calling this morning."

"Of course I did, Mom. I heard the woodpeckers and cardinals calling, but I wasn't ready to wake up yet."

Emma opened a window to let in some spring air, and said, "I'll be downstairs."

"OK, Mom!" Sandy took the hint and tossed off her Native American blanket, purchased at the annual Shinnecock Nation's Pow Wow, a festival with dancing, feasting, and trading. Sandy dressed quickly, lacing up work boots, putting on a T-shirt, a red plaid, woolen shirt, and slinging her day pack over her shoulder.

She went downstairs for breakfast.

Ever since Sandy was a little girl, she could remember planting days. Spooning some raisins and brown sugar into her oatmeal, she thought about the adventures she shared with other naturalists to be. A blind girl taught her several new birdcalls. A meticulous gardener with pigtails told her how to buy the best ham hocks on Long Island for collard green soup. The kids with "spice in their pants," the nickname their teacher had given them due to their behavior, made a video of their planting day. Even the "bright kids," putting in community service time to cover all the bases, eventually got excited about their adventure in the Pine Barrens.

"Mom, it's the 9/11 Planters today, right?" 9/11 was short for September 11, 2001, the day the United States was attacked by those who held the belief that violence was the only effective solution. Several planes were hijacked and purposely crashed into New York's Twin Towers and other designated targets. On that day, Sandy's mom shut off the television and busied Sandy with making plans to plant thousands of trees in memory of the lives lost.

"Yes, hon. We're planting at the 9/11 Memorial," Emma answered as she finished her cup of coffee. Plopping the mug down on the table, she added, "Come on Sandy, time to go!"

Sandy quickly washed her dishes and stashed a water bottle and a prepared sandwich into her day pack. Slamming the front door behind her, she hopped into the idling red pickup truck. Fifteen minutes later, they stood in the state forest parking lot, a short walk from the 9/11 Memorial. With help from her mom, Sandy unloaded shovels and gallon buckets full of tightly packed and watered pitch pine tree seedlings. They planned to plant five hundred today, which would add to the thousands already planted.

In no time, all of the 9/11 Planters arrived and piled out of their van: a half dozen girls and boys accompanied by a social worker, an intern, and a mother. Sandy knew they were here to learn about more productive alternatives to violence. That was the reason why the social worker had first contacted her mom. By participating in community projects that would help restore the Earth, they would become part of something positive as well as hone their coping skills.

After dispersing planting equipment, Sandy took the lead. She knew the way by heart and directed them easily. Her mother and the social worker followed up the rear. Squeezing between young pitch pine stands, they walked single file between two hillsides burned out by the Sunrise Fire. Most of the dead pitch pine trees had long since fallen, and now the Pine Barrens began to show signs of transformation into another pattern of growth and beauty. "Fire is nature's way," she said, silently affirming her mom's words, and excitedly thinking, "It's not a question of if, but when the next wildland fire will strike!"

Sandy stopped to wait for the rest of the group to catch up, and to give a little talk, the way her mom had taught her to tell the story of the Pine Barrens. She began, "We are in a special forest. It's not like those dark forests up north. It's a forest of the coast. That means, it's sandy like the beach and trees don't grow tall. That's why I like it. My name is Sandy and I am small, too!"

The group laughed with her, and as the trickle of laughter got out of hand, they distracted each other by yelling back and forth and shouting.

"Better calm down and pay attention to me!" Sandy raised her hands in a calming motion. "There's going to be a test afterwards. Nah, just kidding."

When they quieted down she continued, "The Pine Barrens also protects our drinking water. Sandy soils allow water to drain quickly into what's called an aquifer. This is where our drinking water is stored. By protecting the Pine Barrens as a nature reserve, we also protect our drinking water," she emphasized.

Sandy glanced at her mom who nodded, and with an excitement hard to contain, she added, "And the Pine Barrens can get real dry, dry enough for wildland fires!" She paused to show them the evidence that she had found: a black scorch mark on a tree, the tall dead pines above their heads, and the lush new growth of the young pitch pine trees below. "Fires aren't bad, and neither is drought, rain, or snow. All of these help make the Pine Barrens special!"

A boy with outdoor savvy told Sandy, "I spend hours and hours in the woods. I like nature."

"What's it to us?" said a heavyset boy, holding a shovel, looking disinterested, as he was hot, sweaty, and tired already.

Still making eye contact with Sandy, the boy with outdoor savvy said, "My dad and I go hunting. He takes me all over the Pine Barrens. We go fishing, too. I love doing it all and that's why I'm out here planting. Hey! Do ya think we're going to see any snakes?"

The mother standing beside him, said, "Snakes! How far are we going? Why don't we plant trees closer to the road?"

Sandy laughed. "Oh, there's no poisonous snakes on Long Island. Anyway, you need to be more concerned about ticks. Ticks aren't tiny insects, they're really arachnids, like spiders and mites. Everybody check your pants for ticks. Matter of fact, here's one crawling on my jeans now."

She pulled out some tape and slapped it on the tick, attaching the tape to a piece of white paper. She showed the tick to the group, saying, "Some ticks carry disease. It's important when you go home to check yourself. If a tick attaches, pull it off carefully so that you will also remove the head. Keep an eye on the tick bite. If you get a rash or a fever, call your doctor right away. And put your clothes in the wash so the ticks don't crawl into your house!" She hoped they would mind the lesson.

"There's a snake," shouted the boy with outdoor savvy, pointing in its direction.

"Wow," said Sandy. "That's a black racer!"

He took off to chase it followed by two other boys and a girl with pigtails. Sandy remembered her from last year.

"Hey," Sandy admonished. "Don't chase the black racer. They might not be poisonous, but they do bite!"

The social worker shouted, "Get back on the trail boys and girls. Let's keep on moving."

Walking along the trail, Sandy tapped her mom's shoulder and spoke loudly, hoping to draw in the interests of the students. "There's a lot more downed dead trees," she said anxiously. "Does this mean that the Fire Danger is now HIGH in the Pine Barrens?"

"Let's see," she smiled, wrapping a rubber band around her long hair. Attending to the group at their next accustomed stop along the trail, she spoke up. "Has anyone ever seen a Smokey Bear sign?"

One boy raised his hand.

"Very good. In the United States, Smokey Bear signs predict LOW, MODERATE, HIGH, VERY HIGH, and EXTREME fire conditions. By knowing what to expect, firefighters can be more careful. Forest friendly firefighters can be trained to apply minimum impact suppression techniques on days when the Fire Danger is LOW to MODERATE."

Sandy grabbed some pine needles from the forest floor in anticipation.

Her mother continued, "Now, we're going to show you how to be as smart as Smokey, but first you have to understand forestry terminology."

Sandy handed out pine needles to each of the students and encouraged others to do the same, and said, "Dead pine needles are one hour fuels which means that it only takes one hour for them to dry or one hour to get wet. They reflect changes in the weather." She then picked up a branch and pointed to a log to show the differences between ten hour and hundred hour fuels. "Ten hour fuels take ten hours and hundred hour fuels take about four days to reflect weather changes."

Emma plucked some pine needles from a young pitch pine to pass around. "But live fuels, especially the oak trees when they leaf out, decrease Fire Danger. The more live fuels, the moister the forest is as a whole. That's why spring fires are fast burning; there are no live fuels to slow them down. And why summer fires can be slow burning and very intense, depending on drought conditions."

Sandy then broke off a chunk of wood from a rotting log and handed it to the girl next to her. "Feel how damp it is. This hundred hour fuel will take about four days to reflect weather conditions. That means we need about four days without rain before it dries out."

The girls felt its dampness and passed it around. The heavyset boy threw it at the boy next to him. With an offensive gesture, the boy next to him angrily said, "Your mother."

"Who you looking at?" said the heavyset boy to Tony who wore baggy jeans and an oversized, orange basketball T-shirt.

Tony shot back, "Fatso matso."

Before the incident threatened to flare up, the social worker sharply said, "O.K. that's enough. That wasn't a polite thing to say, Tony. And to the heavyset boy, she explained, "Sometimes people say stupid things. You have to be the wiser."

The heavyset boy dropped his hands, looked at the sandy ground below, and shrugged, "Sorry."

"My daughter wants to know if Fire Danger is HIGH today. She even looks a bit anxious, doesn't she?" Sandy played her part, as her mother continued, "It's important to understand that the information posted on the Smokey Bear signs is a prediction. It isn't an exact science. And sometimes . . ."

Emma's face darkened as if by a passing cloud.

Sandy picked up her mother's anxiety and knew it wasn't feigned.

Her mother took a deep breath and said, "There are differences of opinion."

"You mean they fight?" asked one of the quiet girls. This got a round of nods and cracks from the group.

"You see even adults have trouble working together," confided the social worker to her students.

"But why do they fight?" the girl asked again.

"I'll try to explain," continued Sandy's mother. "None of you may remember, but one summer the experts got to thinking that fire conditions were as bad as 1995, and so they closed the parks."

"I remember that," said the young girl with the pigtails. I saw them posting signs."

"I remember, too," offered Sandy, "I asked my mom, 'How can there be a fire when the clothes on the line don't dry.' It was so hot and sticky. We had to dry the clothes in the dryer."

"It made no sense to me either," said her mom, "Maybe they were right, and maybe they were wrong, but it got me so curious that I began studying Fire Danger on my own. And you know what I learned? I learned that the Pine Barrens isn't much like forests out West. We're different."

"We're bad," said the boy with outdoor savvy, slapping hands with Tony.

"No, we're not bad," Emma corrected, "But we are different. We live in a coastal forest, as Sandy said, where sand keeps the forest dry, but our maritime climate keeps it humid. This makes Fire Danger calculations difficult and different from out West. On Long Island, we give it our best guess until someone can come up with a better way to figure it out."

"Mom," Sandy asked resting a foot on a fallen log, "So what do you think the Fire Danger is today?"

"I want the 9/11 Planters to answer that instead. Let me give you some clues. Think about heavy fuel loads such as these around us, as Sandy pointed out, and how the weather affects them. So, on a day like today, you've learned that the hundred hour fuels feel damp, right?"

They nodded.

"Is it windy?"

"Not really," answered the girl with pigtails.

"Has it rained recently?"

"Yesterday," said Tony.

"Does it feel very dry today?"

"I'm sweating, so it can't be," gasped a heavyset girl standing next to a skinny girl who wore an extra small sized tan flowered shirt and jacket. She was about to crack a joke, but caught the eye of the social worker and decided the better of it.

Sandy's mother waited until she could see each one of them thinking. "Make your best guess," she prompted.

Tony offered, "No Fire Danger, no way.

"Which means, it is LOW," Emma clarified.

They walked on silently, turning onto an old road that led to the planting site. After several years of planting, the planting site was filling in with young pitch pines. The 9/11 Planters, having carried buckets full of baby pitch pines, shovels and a cooler full of cold drinks and ice, all collapsed at the crest of the 9/11 Memorial.

Sandy wrinkled her brow. "Come on. We just got here. Get some drinks and I will show you where to plant!" As she waited she asked her mom, "Why don't young pine trees just seed in on their own?"

"The State Forester and I aren't sure, but I think it has something to do with the soil."

"You mean the sand?"

"That's just one component of Pine Barrens soil. There are microorganisms, fungi, and plant food in it as well. That's what makes it alive. I think the soil in this old sand pit has lost its life. We're hoping that the trees we plant will help bring back life more quickly."

Sandy looked at the planted pitch pines from several years ago. Some had done well. They stood three to four feet tall. A few even had pine cones. "Mom, the forest is growing back!"

Her mom nodded in satisfaction.

"O.K. guys. Let's go." Sandy called.

She led them into the 9/11 Memorial, bending over to inspect the young pitch pines planted last year. Several of them had lost their needles and looked dead. But on closer inspection, she noticed that a bright green shoot grew next to what she thought was a dead stem.

The group gathered around to look.

Sandy then walked them over to an area in need of planting. She held her favorite work tool, a long yellow handled shovel that reached up to her chin. Handling it lightly, she dug a hole. Unbundling the tree seedlings, each no more than a foot tall with exposed roots, she showed them how to plant one deep into the earth. "Pack the soil firmly and make sure the young pine stem stands straight and tall."

Pointing to the buckets full of young pitch pines, she suggested, "You can use the water in the emptied buckets to water some of the baby trees, but we will have to rely on Mother Nature to do the rest."

The group dispersed.

Several dug holes.

Others grabbed buckets and planted tree seedlings.

Sandy tossed off her red plaid, woolen shirt and paused to get some water to drink from her pack. Then she went around pouring bucket water from one of the emptied buckets onto the newly planted one foot tall pitch pines.

Meanwhile, Emma took out her notebook and a tape measure to collect data about last year's tree seedlings and their growth. After completing her measurements, she called to Sandy, "I need help up here brushing over the old road so the dirt bikers can't get in!"

"Why bother?" said the heavyset boy as he topped the crest of the 9/11 Memorial. He pulled out a drink from the cooler.

"We brush over the road to hide it from dirt bikers. In just a few minutes, they could easily rip apart all that we've accomplished." Emma demonstrated how to protect their plantings. "There's not enough law enforcement to catch them, so we must help out."

Once they got the hang of it, the boys crashed through the woods, dragging fallen logs to throw on the old road. As they searched the forest floor for bigger logs, the boy with outdoor savvy said, "I found a bird's nest!"

They all went to take a look. In a dead tree, they clearly heard baby birds chirping loudly.

"Come on guys," Emma gently reminded, "Let's get back to work!"

Below, in the 9/11 Memorial the girl with the pigtails asked, "Any more?"

"I don't think so," said the social worker.

"Here's a few more." The intern pointed to a bucket filled with a dozen tree seedlings in need of planting.

"We can finish here," said the social worker to Sandy.

Sandy took a moment to walk up to the far side of their 9/11 Memorial. It was one of her favorite secret places in the Pine Barrens. It looked down upon a grassy opening where a solitary pitch pine stood. After the Sunrise Fire, everything on the far hillside had been burnt completely to the ground. Today, it had grown back with bearberry, an evergreen vine with shiny red berries, and low growing sedges, similar to grass. In her secret place of sedge and sunlight, stillness and peace, she listened to nature's sounds. Friendly birds flitted from one pine cone to another, eating seeds, calling out, "Chick-a-dee-dee-dee."

She caught sight of a flock of wild turkeys nibbling at acorns in the underbrush and a red tailed hawk circling overhead. The grassy sedge was still brown beneath her feet. The tall and solitary pitch pine kept her company. She daydreamed, resting her back on the trail with her hand behind her head. She had forgotten how much she enjoyed just being in the Pine Barrens with her mom.

"Sandy, where are you?" Then a chorus of "Sandy, Sandy, Sandy" calls repeated louder and louder.

Sandy jumped up. "Here I am! I'll be right there." She took a shortcut back to them. Out of breath from running, she cried, "Mom, it's time to go already?"

"Not just yet," her mother said. "Tony wants to take a picture. Come sit down on this log with us."

"But where is he?" she asked after joining up with them.

"Up here, in the tree," he shouted.

"Trees!" Tony called, as the group laughed and smiled for their picture.

With their picture taken, the boys and girls ran ahead.

Saying their farewells to the 9/11 Planters, Emma and Sandy lingered. They spoke about the next impacted site in need of planting, and about one that they heard about from a local hiker. "Firefighters should be the first ones to tell us," Emma admonished. "Now it will be so much harder for the plantings to take because the bulldozed fire line has been exposed to the sun and the soil may be without life."

"I'll help. I will call them and explain why they need to tell us right away. Just like you've taught me."

Reaching for her daughter's hand, she emphatically said, "You must continue your studies as a naturalist and gain more experience teaching at a nature center, and not get wrapped up in the politics of fire in the Pine Barrens. This is what I must do, but not you."

Sandy silently thought, "Why can't I? I know many things now!" But as time passed, Emma kept her word. She kept steering Sandy in another direction, insisting Sandy use her talents as a naturalist and become an environmental educator and not an environmental advocate. Sandy resisted.

Still not knowing what she should to do with her life, Sandy spent many hours at the beach daydreaming, until one day her friend came up to her and said, "We're gonna join the fire department for high school community service."

Shortly thereafter, Sandy responded to her first brush fire as a probationary firefighter, geared up with not just her firefighter gear but with the lessons of a naturalist and a conservationist close to her heart.

Chapter 8

Brush Fire!

With Tina nowhere in sight, Sandy jumped onto the next engine out of the firehouse. Excitedly, she glanced about. Firefighters sat expressionless and radio communications were hard to make out. The engine siren blared once and twice through the village, and then repeatedly as the engine raced up the hill to the bluff's main road. At the fire scene, they were ordered out of the cab and told to follow the hose line along a footpath. Sandy being short in stature, soon fell behind.

Tugging on her firefighter gear, she scanned the forest around her until she spotted the fire. It wasn't at all what she imagined. Why should anyone put out such a small fire, she thought. She ran over to the Brush Truck and grabbed a hand tool. The plants were so similar to those in the Pine Barrens that it was easy to imagine being there. Raking the foot path clear of dead leaves, needles and twigs, she waited for a slight push of wind to carry the fire closer to her.

When the flames reached the fire line she created, they went out completely. Sandy leaned on the rake with satisfaction and grinned happily. The fire had worked its way towards her, and then just went out on its own! She had read about this type of forestry conservation, known as wildland fire use.

"Sandy what are you doing?" demanded the Assistant Chief who had fitted the three girls up with bunker gear nearly a year ago. To him, it looked as if she was having a little too much fun with fire. "Pull more hose to the fire."

Sandy had enough sense to realize that she was there to put the fire out. She obeyed his direct order, quickly put the rake back into the Brush Truck, and ran up the trail to drag the fire hose as hard and as fast as she could. The bluff was not an easy place to fight fires. She had to drag hose, duck under branches, and scramble down a steep hillside well off any foot paths. She felt the load of her gear bearing down on her. Even if better fitted, it was like wearing a spacesuit on a planet with high gravity. She felt heavy and constrained, while trying not to stumble over fallen logs and tangled roots.

"Billy," shouted Company Five's Captain in a clear and direct voice, "You and Jim, ready on the nozzle?"

Without the ambiguities of social scene expectations or leadership quandaries, the two easily responded, anticipating each other's move. They knew what to do before ordered.

"Yes, sir!" they answered.

Billy felt Jim lean into him in anticipation of the line being charged. Jim's adolescent gawkiness was gone. Billy's self-consciousness was replaced by a confident grip of the nozzle. Seconds later, water charged the line, hissing as it hit taller flames in a hot pocket of fuel. Billy moved slow and easy so Jim could steady the hose behind him. Another hose line crew worked the other side of the fire, out of sight.

"Sandy! What Company are you with?" shouted Company Five's Captain. Thinking enough hose had been pulled to reach the fire, Sandy had long since dropped her hose and was standing aimlessly by herself.

"I don't know. I just jumped on an engine." When responding to emergencies, firefighters could respond in either of the fire engines.

There was no time to consider her anything but a responding firefighter on probation thought Rick. "Stay with us then. Keep pulling line down to Billy and Jim." He pointed.

As she strained to pull the hose towards them, she kept thinking about how easy it would be to move around in Western wildland firefighting gear. Her gear was constructed to withstand structural house fire conditions. Western firefighters wore different gear when fighting wildland fires, lightweight, flame resistant, yellow and green shirts and pants. Why couldn't they do the same in her firehouse?

In no time, Billy and Jim went out of sight again.

"Keep feeding them line, Sandy. Good."

Company Five's Captain didn't let up on her, and she kept moving. She felt roped in with no time to wonder about forestry conservation. Being part of his meticulous efforts to keep the fire under control and the fire crews together, she listened and made more eye contact with him. She appreciated his experience.

"Fire over there," someone shouted and pointed to a flare up.

"More hose," Jim shouted.

Sandy instantly pulled several loops of hose.

Company Five's Captain, ordered, "Sandy that's enough hose. Take one of these shovels and dig out any smokes you see." Sandy looked puzzled, so he explained, "See that wisp of white smoke in the leaf litter there, under a fallen log? It means that the ground is still hot and the fire could rekindle if enough wind hit it or if it dried out any more."

She nodded. The work wasn't as easy as she thought it would be. The shovel hit against roots. She was getting hot and tired, but she wasn't the type to give up. She'd rather collapse in her tracks first than to let the guys think she was a wimp. To really make sure the fire was dead out, she took off a glove and, with the back of her hand, felt the ground and the fuels to see if they were cool to the touch. If not, she'd call for more water to douse the hot spot.

When the last of the flames were hit by water and no more smokes were to be seen, the Chief called the fire out by radio. The water pressure dropped. Hose lines were decoupled and emptied. Sandy and several firefighters pulled hose back up the bluff to the engines. At this point, she realized it would soon be time to pack hose. She readied herself.

Jim took off his bunker jacket, tossed it aside, and went to get a cold drink from the ice chest in the Fire Police Van. He stood off to the side with an angry scowl, taken aback by Billy's engagement with Sandy.

"Sandy, You did real well. You should take off your jacket. You don't want to get overheated."

She looked around to see that everyone had already removed their bunker jacket. She did the same. Her T-shirt was dripping with sweat.

"Here, have a drink," Billy handed her a water bottle.

"Thanks, I'm really thirsty!"

"You O.K.?" He sounded concerned.

Jim rolled his eyes as he tossed his empty drink back into the ice chest.

"Sure am! This was great!" Sandy exclaimed as they climbed onto the engine bay. For a while, they concentrated on packing hose. When finished, they hopped off and Sandy spoke up, "Billy, do you remember the water bucket training drill? It's the day after tomorrow, first thing in the morning." She bit her lip anxiously, waiting.

To her surprise, he nodded. "I've got my permission slip filled out and signed."

Sandy flashed a happy smile and gave him more detailed directions.

On the ride back to the firehouse, with bunker jackets piled high in the back of the cab, Sandy squeezed in. Two firefighters talked about the recent rash of brush fires. Sandy thought about asking permission to respond to a brush fire in wildland firefighting gear instead.

Back at the firehouse, Sandy approached her Captain.

Clearly uncomfortable with her persistent wildland fire interest, he commented, "It's not the way we do things here."

"But everyone takes off their bunker jacket at the fire scene anyway."

He just shook his head. "You'll have to put in a request to the village's Fire District. It's unusual for us to get so many brush fires. We don't have wildland fires like they do . . . "

" . . out West," she interrupted, frustrated as he never appreciated Long Island's wildland fires. He and everyone else kept on calling them brush fires as if they didn't count. She stared at him angrily with her arms by her side and her hands tightly clenched.

Tina, who been waiting standby at the firehouse, signed for her point. Firefighters, including probationary firefighters, had to sign in to maintain a certain number of points to be considered active firefighters. She grabbed Sandy by the arm, "Come on, leave it alone."

Sandy's Captain looked relieved when the two left the firehouse. Out in the parking lot by Sandy's pickup truck, Tina offered, "Did you get in on the action? Was it as exciting as you hoped it to be?"

"Yeah," Sandy said feeling better. "It was great! And I finally got to see fire . . . You know," she pounded the hood of her red truck for added emphasis, "I've got an idea!"

"You're up to something no good. I can tell." Tina wagged a finger at Sandy, raising her eyebrows. "You sound like you've got one of Kim's ideas, which lately means trouble."

"Hey, never mind about Kim." Sandy wagged her own finger at Tina. "How come you didn't make the engine?"

"Oh," she said fingering the pink heart on her necklace looking guilty, "I had to go, you know to the bathroom. By the time I was finished the engine had gone." She stopped fingering her necklace and put a hand on her hip. "Hey! Don't change the subject! What were you thinking?"

"About my mom's Fire Awareness Reports for wildland fires. It's a field report useful to anyone interested in Long Island's wildland fires. But she can't get firefighters to use it. Well, we're firefighters now and I just happen to have a blank Fire Awareness Report in my truck, behind the seat. We can test it out by going back to the fire."

"Do you think we should? I mean it's private property. We'd be trespassing now that the fire's out."

"Well, I don't see anything wrong with that," Sandy quipped because to her, it seemed logical. "We can say we are just investigating the fire."

Tina's eyes squinted and looked doubtful. This sounded like freelancing, but she hopped into Sandy's truck, saying, "Fine. Just promise you'll drop me off later back at my house."

Sandy drove them back to the fire scene and parked where the fire engines had been a few moments ago. She handed Tina the clipboard with the Fire Awareness Report. They scrambled through brush, up and down the steep bluff. Sandy was on a mission to walk the fire's perimeter. At breaks in the bluff's forest canopy, a harbor view suddenly opened up below them. The village looked small from high above. The sheltered cove kept the water calm. Several boats cruised out of the harbor. Any wind had since died down.

As they made their way around the fire's perimeter, Tina's blouse blackened with soot and ash. "It's a good thing I was planning to throw this old blouse out," said Tina.

Sandy was too intent on trying to figure out if the fire scar was a circle or a square to get an estimate of its area. Finally, she decided it was square, and started pacing off its length and width.

"Sandy, look how small the ferry looks from up here."

"Tina, pay attention. Can you write down that it's about 80 by 100 feet? Or 8,000 square feet, less than a quarter acre meaning it's classified as a spot fire."

Tina stared down at the clipboard filling out the report. She wrote down spot fire, and guessed that the resources used must mean how many engines and brush trucks there were. "Sandy, what about rate of spread and flame length? And what does severity mean?"

"Write down creeping and few inches to half a foot. Severity means how bad it was."

"I'll write down awful, then."

Sandy laughed, "It was a light burn. Just the top layer of leaves."

Tina didn't mind helping Sandy. It didn't seem as if they were doing anything wrong, even if they were technically trespassing. She calmly continued to fill out the form with Sandy's help.

"Tina, Mom said the Fire Danger was LOW today. That makes sense because the fire was easily contained. Write that down too."

"O.K. What about fire line rehab?"

"None needed! We were forest friendly!"

"Remarks?" Tina asked.

"What do you think Tina?"

"Nobody got hurt. No houses got burned. And no fire line rehab needed. We aced it!"

Both pagers sounded off, "Signal 13, Automatic alarm."

"Sandy!" Tina's heart skipped a beat in anticipation to responding to a real fire. The last time she had kicked off her sneakers, put on her gear, grabbed her helmet and jumped onto the first responding vehicle, it was on the ladder truck. At the fire scene, the more experienced firefighters dashed out, leaving her to fumble with her pack and stumble awkwardly after them. When she reached them, one of the firefighters half kidded, half

FIRE AWARENESS REPORT

Date: _4/19/06_ Report by: _Sandy Lewis_

Fire Danger: _Low_

Fire Location: _The Bluffs_

On Site: Fuels, Topography, Weather - Fire Behavior

Fuel Type _bushes & trees_ Live Fuels: _none_

Topography: _steep_ Temp: _warm_ Humidity: _sort of dry_

Wind Direction/Speed: _wind died down_ Severity: _light burn_

Rate of Spread: _creeping_ Flame Lengths: _few inches to half a foot_

On Site: Response

Size Class of Fire: _spot fire_

Resources: _2 engines, 1 brush truck, and fire police van_

Fire Line Rehab Needs: _none needed_

scorned, as he knew it had been a false alarm, "Where are your tools?" Tina stared at him blankly.

"Let's go!" Sandy responded. Sandy grabbed the clipboard from Tina who hung back uncertain, her heart racing. "Come on Tina. We can make it, if we hurry."

By the time they got to the firehouse, the engine was rolling back into the bay. The alarm had been a false alarm. The hospital staff had been overhauling the electrical system and triggered the fire alarm by mistake. Tina was very relieved when she signed for her point.

Sandy went back to her truck to retrieve the Fire Awareness Report and handed it over proudly to her Captain. "Here. It's a report about the brush fire, a Fire Awareness Report."

Reluctantly, her Captain reached for the report to take a look. The Chief stood beside him.

"You were at the fire scene?" interrupted the Chief. He had heard unconfirmed rumors of Kim showing up at fire scenes unannounced, and now it seemed it was Sandy's turn.

"After the fire, though," she answered calmly.

"On whose authority?!" He knew the answer, only taunting her to make his point.

"No one's," Sandy's said defensively. Her voice didn't carry as well as his. "I just thought it would be a good idea."

"You're not to be at the fire scene unless you're on an engine!" Louder and more threatening, he warned, "Don't let me catch you freelancing again!"

Sandy's face reddened. She felt trapped. It appeared as if she was freelancing because the Fire Awareness Report had no meaning to either her Captain or the Chief. "O.K.," she said to end it before she would burst into tears. Billy and Jim returned from the alarm, geared up, amiably chatting about a recent working fire on the South shore.

"I'm out of here," cried Sandy. With her keys balled up in her fist, she angrily left the firehouse as a startled Billy looked up with a concerned expression on his face.

Jim balked. "You're with me, not her, forget her for a minute, will ya?!" Billy turned back to Jim thinking he was right. The two walked into the firehouse lounge, planning to order some pizza and watch a football game. Tina was left to fend for herself.

When Sandy caught Billy's eye the next day at school, he wasn't sure what to expect.

"Billy! The water bucket drill's tomorrow morning! The Colonel will be there. You're still going, right?" asked Sandy.

Relieved, he nodded.

Chapter 9

The Colonel

Billy never realized until now how much he was looking forward to meeting the Colonel. It was as if he was meeting a movie star. The Colonel was the real deal, a military man from the U.S. Army Guard. "The Colonel," he voiced the words out loud as he drove to the rendezvous point, down a bumpy road near Wildwood Lake. "What should I say when I do meet him? Will I be as taken with him as Sandy said I'd be? The Colonel," he said again with added emphasis. "That's what everybody calls him."

The rendezvous point was a sunny open field dotted with little bluestem grass and blueberry. Close to the Atlantic Ocean and Flanders Bay, the South shore air felt chilly and damp. Otherwise, it promised to be bright and sunny day. He climbed out of his truck in anticipation of meeting the Colonel. Sandy was driving out with her mom. For the moment, Billy was on his own.

Scanning the assembling crowd of police officers, firefighters, emergency medical technicians, military personnel, forest rangers and park officials, Billy spotted him. The Colonel walked swiftly. His confidence and authority contrasted sharply against his plain army fatigues, flight vest, steel gray hair and steady eyes. People gathered around him.

Billy walked over, hesitant to introduce himself, content just to listen.

"Well, hello, Colonel, how ya doing?" asked a park police officer with an easygoing smile.

With an equally warm smile of recognition, the Colonel greeted the officer, firmly grasping his hand, "Glad you could make it, Sergeant."

"My, my, Colonel. Don't we have just a perfect day for flying? I spotted a red tailed hawk circling overhead who apparently thinks so too," the Sergeant offered chuckling. "Seriously," he said moving closer. "My boys are all excited about the next car lift. They've been patrolling all over the Pine Barrens, poking around, and hoping to find an abandoned car so we can lift it out by helicopter. And would you believe it Colonel, they just found two more!"

The Colonel listened intently without comment.

"Sling loading is all they want to do now. You guys get to train helicopter pilots. We get to clean up the Pine Barrens by airlifting abandoned cars."

Listening was a gesture of respect for the people he worked with. It built trust. The Colonel took out a notepad and wrote down each abandoned vehicle's location and who had the pleasure of reporting it.

Several more uniformed and non uniformed drill attendees gravitated towards the Colonel. One was a state law enforcement officer who whispered to Billy, "The Colonel is a quality man," and smiled. Billy nodded as he continued to find it easy to join in and even to take a look at the set of photographs being passed around. One picture showed a junked car, completely rusted out. Billy overheard them talking about it being stolen for a joy ride and left abandoned for years, an eyesore they called it. There was no way of pulling it out as the forest had grown up around it.

Steel chains placed under and around the car were secured together with a large hook. The helicopter dropped a hooked line next. Another series of pictures illustrated the airlift. With the two hooks attached, the helicopter lifted the car. Transported across the sky, the abandoned car was then lowered onto a flatbed truck and carted off for recycling. The last picture showed the forest view again without the eyesore.

"Thank you for the pictures," the Colonel said to Photographer. He shook the man's hand warmly, and said, "How's that hiking bridge holding out?"

"Doing fine, once you air dropped the new lumber for it. We really appreciate your help, sir." He nodded his head slightly in acknowledgment.

"Just keep coming up with project ideas and we'll be glad to help out. We live here too." For the Colonel, these were significant opportunities for the U.S. Army Guard to help the community. Out West, they would've used a trained firefighter to be the helicopter manager for the water bucket training drill. On Long Island, it was not the case. Out of necessity the Colonel coordinated the effort.

"All the same, sir. You make us all feel part of the team. I'm still amazed by your last call from the field. I put it on the speakerphone and the whole office felt as if we were in the helicopter with you. It livened up the place and gave us some important insight into an actual wildland fire water bucket drop."

The Colonel smiled as if that was his intention when he made that call.

"Thanks for making an extra set of photos," the Sergeant said to the Photographer. "I'm going to show them to my boys." He walked away as the Photographer turned back to the Colonel with a request. "I hope to get a picture of everyone standing next to the helicopter."

"After the drill. We can make sure everyone gets an opportunity to be in the picture."

"Yes, sir," said the Photographer as he walked off to snap a few more pictures of the assembling crowd.

An emergency medical technician shook the Colonel's hand next. "We're ready for any medical needs."

"Very good, Christina. I appreciate the extra effort you've been putting into these drills."

Billy stepped back for a second to disengage himself. How did the Colonel manage to be both friend and commander at the same time? Billy doubted his own ability to ever become this type of leader. He recalled the Colonel's words, "One must embrace diversity and allow this diversity to make team decisions, or be doomed to failure." And his own thoughts on the matter, "Diversity's a good thing? It's more like competing interests. Isn't it up to the Colonel, not the team, to make the decisions?"

But if he dared to be a leader, how could he pull it off? He joined in again, still content to listen, hoping for a suitable answer.

A state forest ranger in a neatly pressed, dark green uniform, grasped the Colonel's hand firmly, and grinned. "Got my plane tickets to fly to Washington, Colonel. We're looking forward to seeing you accept your environmental award at the Pentagon."

"That's an award I'll be accepting on behalf of the team," the Colonel corrected.

"Of course, sir."

"Why did the Colonel say that?" asked Sandy. She had just arrived, running over to Billy as soon as her mom parked her car. She moved closer to Billy whispering in disbelief, "My mom said the environmental award is being given," she paused to catch her breath and to say with added emphasis, "to him."

Billy leaned closer whispering nothing more clever than, "I dunno."

When Emma finally caught up with her daughter, she started their introductions.

Sandy looked at ease, but Billy could feel the back of his neck getting red, imagining what he would say when he was next in line to be introduced to the Colonel.

"Colonel, this is my daughter, Sandy."

"Mom, I already met the Colonel at the Sunrise Fire, remember?" Shaking the Colonel's hand, she said, "You're like part of the family. Mom's always quoting you because she says you're such a great leader." Sandy frowned and looked puzzled. She had expected him to acknowledge himself. What appeared was a dispassionate, stone face. The compliment seemed to have fallen on deaf ears.

The Colonel turned to face Billy. "And who is this young man?"

"Oh, that's Billy. He's in my fire department. He's going to be a Chief someday, right Billy?"

The Colonel shook Billy's hand firmly.

Much to Billy's surprise, he immediately confided, "I'm no officer, sir."

The Colonel's eyes twinkled. "There's no 'I' in team."

"T-E-A-M," Billy spelled it out slowly. "I don't understand. Isn't the officer essentially the 'I' in team which would mean there is an 'I' in team, but this makes no sense?" he asked puzzled.

"Yes and no," the Colonel said. Emma smiled at the familiar "Colonelism." With both military and civilian management skills effectively intertwined, the Colonel led by example and would rarely say anything more. In a soft voice, the Colonel commanded their participation in today's after action review.

"Sure," said Billy thoughtfully, feeling the power of command in his voice, but comfortable with himself as well.

A startled Sandy thought otherwise. "Me? Why should you listen to me? I'm new to firefighting." She brushed the hair from her face and waited. He gave her an expecting glance. Not wanting to disappoint him, she changed her mind, "Of course, I will participate."

The drill began. The team formed a circle around the open field to face the Colonel who stood beside them, not in the circle's center. He commanded, "We will attach the water bucket and fly over the lake to do a water pick up and then a drop off. The assigned ground crew will need to be in constant touch by radio to signal the drop off point." He paused and scanned the circle, "Any questions?"

"What if hikers wander in?" asked the Photographer.

The Colonel swiftly answered, "The park police know the trails. We've got them on patrol to make sure no one enters the fly zone." The fly zone area included both air and ground space, as the drill was all about air to ground coordination.

He looked around again, "Any other questions?"

Billy spoke up. "Colonel, is there an observation area?"

"After the helicopter takes off, take the trail down to the lake and observe from there."

He directed his attention to Sandy and Billy. "Verify that we hit the mark when the pilot lets go the drop."

"Yes sir," they both said.

The Colonel's eyes made one last informative scan of the circle to ensure everyone was attentive and not giving him what he often said was a, "deer in the headlights" stare.

"Let's do it," he commanded in an authoritative tone.

The group dispersed.

Billy went back to his truck to get his backpack and Sandy did the same. Her mom had parked beside his truck. The Blackhawk helicopter powered up. The Colonel had flown the Blackhawk in for the day. Now Sam, his second in command, lifted the sleek black helicopter. Billy had never seen a helicopter close up. As it rose, loose dirt and sand kicked up violently. The three of them dashed behind his truck to take cover.

Chapter 10

You Mean They Fight?

When the noise and wind subsided, Emma, Sandy and Billy crossed the open field to a foot path. It led to a dirt road where tall pitch pines created dappled sunlight. "Why the water bucket training drill is so unusual and so important is a story unto itself," Emma began with optimism for the future. "In the early 1900s, forest rangers relied on fire towers to watch out for smokes and paid locals to fight wildland fires. But by the 1930s, the tables turned. Local firefighters fought fires within designated fire districts, and forest rangers complained about the way local fire departments suppressed wildland fires."

"Mom! Billy! Look and see how these trees are spaced apart. That's probably a sign of past stump jumper damage. They knock down trees, leaving behind a wide path. The forest never grows back quite right. They make a mess of the Pine Barrens." Sandy raised her hand and pointed.

Up until now, Billy had found the walk in the woods appealing. He had never spent any time in the Pine Barrens and found the forest very different from hiking upstate. But now, it was as if fingernails scratched a chalkboard. Irritated by her remarks, his voice rose up in defense of local firefighters, "If you don't like the way we fight fire, then we just won't put the fire out."

"That won't do at all!" Sandy cried out alarmed. She tightened her day pack hip belt, determinedly. Thinking back on her most recent brush fire experience with wildland fire use, she visualized raking the path clear, allowing the fire to reach the path and how the fire burned out on its own. "Billy," she added in a more reasonable tone, "it's not that much extra work. I did it, by myself when . . . "

Sandy put a hand to her mouth, alarmed. Billy would say she was freelancing. She knew he was already upset about Kim showing up at a fire scene unannounced.

Billy eyed her suspiciously. "The Chief's in charge of fire suppression operations, not you. What were you thinking? What were you doing?"

"O.K. you two," interjected Sandy's mother. "As you two so eloquently pointed out, there's definitely a need for improved undertanding among us. But it's like we're talking different languages. Worse still, we get polarized and don't engage in intelligent discussions. Instead, we rely on sayings that define us, like, 'I'm in charge', and 'They're just a bunch of cowboys.' That's why this cross training drill is so important."

Sandy glanced down at her feet and said, "Sorry Billy."

Billy tousled her hair playfully.

She looked up at him and smiled.

In a purposely subdued tone, Emma said, "As Long Island developed, the number of fire districts expanded, and the number of forest lands outside of these districts dwindled. The need for forest rangers became less and less, and so the forest rangers left to go work upstate. Yet they returned in the 1970s, after the state acquired this land and Rocky Point."

"Acquired?" Sandy asked as they continued their walk to the overlook.

"The Radio Corporation of America, RCA, sold the land to the state for a dollar," commented Billy. "I wrote about it in a paper for physics class because fifty years earlier, RCA bought Marconi's radio communication company. Marconi set up a series of large radio towers for transatlantic communication. I knew his experiments were on Long Island, but I never realized they were in the Pine Barrens."

"Me either!" said Sandy, amazed at how adventures into the Pine Barrens always taught her something new.

At the observation point, gazing down at Wildwood Lake, Emma concluded, "The forest rangers patrol these lands and now want to expand their role in fire suppression too. But forest rangers prefer to use less intensive firefighting tactics whenever possible for forestry conservation. Local firefighters are much more aggressive, relying on heavier equipment. We need a way to work out their differences, and that's why this training drill is so important."

Sandy sat on a log and took out her baseball cap and sunglasses from her pack. She was proud of her mother for being so concerned and dedicated. Sandy wanted to help work out their differences. Billy leaned up against a pitch pine tree and turned on the radio the Colonel had given him. How could decades of differences be resolved? Emma settled in. If Wildwood Lake came to be from the movements of glaciers thousands of years ago, maybe things just took time.

"There's the Blackhawk!" shouted Sandy.

The lake whipped up as the helicopter approached. A red and yellow bag, known as a water bucket, hovered by cable below the Blackhawk. Gracefully, upon radio command, Sam lowered the Blackhawk, allowing the water bucket to dip gently into the lake.

Sandy squinted as she watched the Blackhawk fly upwards into the bright sky then neatly drop water in a sweep across the upper portion of the lake, a simulation of how water would be dropped on a wildland fire's head, its leading edge. It was easy for Sandy to admire the Blackhawk's movements as if it were a bird in flight and not a machine that required a skilled pilot.

Sam hit the mark, right on target.

Billy counted, "One for three . . . two for three . . . three for three."

With each drop a different approach was used.

"Rotating our crew, Colonel," Sam called back on the radio.

The next to fly the Blackhawk was Patricia.

"Hold it steady. You're doing fine. Bring her around," said the Colonel watching with the ground crew. As she flew toward her mark, he added, "Focus on your speed, altitude and approach."

She did the drop.

"Just missed the mark!" said a disappointed Sandy.

She missed the mark on her second try too. But as Sandy listened to the Colonel's steady voice calling instructions to her, she realized that it wasn't about messing up, it was about confidence building. She heard it in the Colonel's voice. She heard it in Patricia's unwavering response. Patricia picked up water for her third and final drop. Sandy caught her breath hoping she would hit her mark. With a swish of water, the red flag rocked back and forth.

"Right on the money," Billy exclaimed.

"Just like Sam, she did it," cheered Sandy.

The training drill lasted for about three hours as the crews rotated. The Colonel even had an opportunity to fly as the ground crew worked through various water bucket drop evolutions, exchanging ideas with the air crew. With the Blackhawk safely landed, the Colonel instructed Sam to place a can under the helicopter to catch any oil drip.

"Billy! Sandy!" shouted Sandy's mom. "The Colonel said it would be O.K. for you two to check out the Blackhawk's cockpit with Sam. Want to?"

"Sure," they said. Feeling important, they climbed into the cockpit.

Inside the Blackhawk, Sam showed Billy the instrument panel while Sandy checked out the back of the helicopter. "Sam," Billy asked, "How does the Colonel do it? How can he be in command of all these different people and still be their friend and not be the 'I' in team?"

"Let me share a secret with you," he said lowering his voice. "The Colonel keeps up his studies."

"Really?" asked Billy astonished.

"The Colonel also expects that of us too. Leadership is a trait to be developed."

"Yes, sir!" He mocked a solute, grinning. He called back to Sandy, "Come up front and take a look at the instrument panel." As he waited, he couldn't help overhearing Sandy's mother and the Colonel talking outside the cockpit.

"It's a good thing the water bucket training drill is being coordinated outside of the upcoming Wildland Fire Academy," Emma said. Confiding to the Colonel, she added, "I knew the team would be compromised in its decision making process — by him."

Billy studied the Colonel's face, and whispered, "T-E-A-M. There is no 'I' in team." He listened even more intently, wondering whom they were talking about.

"Yes," Emma nodded. "He chooses to go out on federal emergencies, while local firefighters with more relevant experience are told that they must start as entry level federal firefighters." Emma sighed in frustration. "This guy has figured out a way to work the system so that he can be part of federal command teams. I'm afraid this is setting a bad example."

The Colonel stood still and listened carefully.

Yet, maybe," Emma said hopefully, "we could set up an arrangement like the FDNY has with the U.S. Forest Service. They create shadow teams, pairing off local firefighters with federal response teams. But I would need to be at the Wildland Fire Academy to better arrange this, yet he's not being cooperative."

"You must do whatever it takes to achieve the mission," the Colonel advised. "Maybe you need to do what he suggests — if that's what the Wildland Fire Academy coordinator, Butch Gordon, wants of you."

Billy almost hit his head on the helicopter's door. The Wildland Fire Academy coordinator was Butch, Jim's Uncle! So that's what Jim's been up to! With mixed feelings, he swung himself out of the helicopter with his head down.

Emma dropped her pack. The Colonel knew that she had already gone out West for two weeks to build up her own credentials. Yet the Colonel was advising her to listen to Butch and be away from home for two more weeks. Even if she obliged Butch, there weren't many requests for Training Specialists on federal emergencies, and so how would she gain experience?

"Personally, I would have preferred being certified in a position more closely related to fire ecology. But now that I'm certified as a Training Specialist by the Colorado Wildland Fire Academy, I see no reason as to why I can't attend our wildland fire academy."

Calmly, the Colonel reminded, "You must always think to pull on the rope . . . "

" . . . in the same direction," Emma acknowledged, shaking her head, not willing to be open to the lesson. "Even if I did do what he said, who's to say he wouldn't just find another excuse. He's that kind of man. I don't trust him."

Sandy overheard the conversation too. Stunned, she thought, "Was Jim's uncle the main reason why my mom wants me to go out West?" Sandy stared at the Colonel wishing him to be the Wildland Fire Academy coordinator instead.

Emma saw the Photographer approach. "Sandy! Billy! It's time to get out of the Blackhawk. We're visitors today and shouldn't be part of the photo shoot."

While they stood by watching, Billy reminded Sandy of the after action review. "Sam says the Colonel always calls on the least experienced person first." He playfully tapped down Sandy's baseball cap, adding, "That will be you."

Sandy eyes widened.

"Don't worry. You'll do fine."

She hesitated just long enough for Billy to take her by the hand. He pulled her towards the circle of police officers, firefighters, emergency medical technicians, military personnel, forest rangers and park officers reassembling in the field.

The Colonel's eyes met hers; it was then that she knew she had to be open and honest. Quietly, at first, she said, "It was a perfect day for flying . . . and I learned a lot . . . and not to be telling you what you should do, but I think we parked too close to the Blackhawk. We had to run behind Billy's truck to get away from the dirt and sand being kicked up."

Calmly, he replied, "An excellent observation, Sandy. We shall define a safety zone between the helicopter landing area and the parked vehicles. 'Safety doesn't happen by accident.' Thank you for that observation."

Sandy was mystified that he wasn't bothered at all by her criticism.

The Colonel then went around the circle encouraging comments from each attendant, ending with Billy.

"Mom?" asked Sandy as she slid into the passenger's side of her mom's car.

"Yes, honey?" Emma asked.

"One of the forest rangers asked me if I was interested in signing up for the intro firefighter class at the Wildland Fire Academy. Do you think I should take the class, even if you won't be there?" Absently she played with a pine cone she had picked up on the way back from Wildwood Lake. The bristly, pitch pine cone pricked her fingers.

"Don't worry about me," her mother sighed in relief. At last her daughter was showing an interest in getting more training outside of her firehouse and the Structural Fire Academy.

"Well, O.K."

"Good. Then, I'll take you out to the Colorado Wildland Fire Academy next year for your refresher. You'll see. There are many more opportunities waiting for you out West."

"But I don't want to be a firefighter out West."

"You'll be fine. It's not that far away. I have some great contacts. The Planning Section Chief is also a professor at the University of Colorado. He will help you get into the U.S. Forest Service for a summer internship."

Instead, Sandy was thinking about how she had applied to community college at her guidance counselor's urging. She studied the closed pitch pine cone in her hand intently.

"Hon, why don't you and I go out to dinner?" Emma asked as she drove into their driveway.

"I'm going to the beach," Sandy announced, swinging open the door. "Be back later!"

Ignoring her mom's dejected expression, she hopped into her truck and sped off.

With a bathing suit always waiting behind her truck seat and a wetsuit in a milk carton in the truck bed, Sandy quickly changed behind the locked beach bathhouse. She knew she wouldn't feel right again until she plunged into the calm, cold water of the Long Island Sound. Overhead, the sky was pale blue. The only changes at the beach were cyclical: seasons, weather, storms and tides, something to be depended upon. And this spring was no different. In some way, time stood still at the beach.

After swimming, she pulled off her wetsuit, toweled off and changed out of sight. Walking back to her truck, a few of the regular fisherman nodded hello to her. Climbing up onto the hood of her truck, she leaned back on its windshield. She heard the waves breaking gently upon the shore line. The wind was behind the bluff, coming out of the southwest. She finished putting on the light jacket she had stashed in her pack from this morning and leaned back again. Dreamily, she stared up at the clouds. She knew the water would soon wake up from a long chilly sleep and be filled with mating horseshoe crabs.

Feeling guilty for running off to the beach and being so sharp with her mom, she lingered. She didn't want to be so mean to her mother. "I want to stay on Long Island with my friends and the places I love, the water and the Pine Barrens, and not go out West! But that would mean more trouble at the firehouse and at home." Hopelessly, she stared up at a passing cloud, thinking, "What would the Colonel do?"

Chapter 11

You Gotta Do What You Gotta Do

Tina furtively caught Sandy's attention in the high school hallway before morning classes began. Taking hold of Sandy's hand, she pressed, "What's the news? You never told me about your special day with Billy."

"Tina! Why are you always thinking about guys in that way!?" Sandy pulled away, blushing despite her best intentions.

"Ah ha! I knew it!" Tina gave her a wink.

"Shhh!" Sandy scolded, pulling her hand away. "It was nothing like that!" Composing herself, Sandy brushed her hair out of her face. "It was a serious wildland firefighting drill," she said remembering the day. Dreamily, she added, "Someday I'll respond by helicopter to a Pine Barrens fire."

Kim popped up out of no where and shook her head in astonishment. "Honestly, Sandy! You missed a gas leak in one of the main lines downtown. Pay attention! There was no fire, but the potential for an explosion was real."

Sandy defended her case, "Just a real as the eight hundred brush fire alarms the Pine Barrens gets in one year!"

Kim impatiently groaned, "Do I have to spell it out for you? We don't live in the Pine Barrens. We live on the North shore."

"But the Pine Barrens is only fifteen minutes away. The Pine Barrens is in Suffolk County and so are we."

Tina interceded, taking Kim's side, "That's not the way it works. You know that, Sandy. We don't normally get called out to Pine Barrens fires."

Kim laughed, "Hah! Most brush fire alarms, well, you could spit on them and they'd be out!" She turned to Tina, and even more confidently said in a serious tone, "Did you know that traffic was blocked off on East Main Street and several buildings were evacuated, including the library? They even searched the apartments above the retail shops to make sure everyone was out."

"What if there really had been an explosion?" Tina asked horrified.

"We'd lose half the village! People would get hurt! Fire would spread from building to building."

Tina put her hands over her ears not wanting to hear anything more.

Kim placed a hand on Tina's shoulder. "Don't you worry. You've got firefighters, like me, to set things straight." Lowering the tone of her voice, she added, "That's why firefighters have to take gas leaks very seriously. People do the stupidest things during an emergency, like insisting on driving down the road when there's a real big fire engine blocking their way. And they even hide out in buildings, thinking they're safer inside. During the gas leak alarm, people did just that. They hid. A police officer had to escort them out. It was a good thing no one lit a cigarette before the leak was located and the valve shut off. Everyone went back to business, and the firefighters all returned home safely."

Sandy interrupted, "Just you wait and see. We're due for another big wildland fire like the Sunrise Fire. It's not a matter of if — it's a matter of when." With no response from either of them, Sandy left to get to her morning class.

She wished she was more like the Colonel with a commanding voice that would force respect. The Colonel didn't have to force people to respect him though. They just did. This made Sandy even more discouraged. Before entering her class, she glanced up the hallway and saw Tina and Kim laughing as they headed upstairs. Sandy stood there for a moment, watching them until they turned the corner of the staircase and were out of sight.

By lunch time, Kim was on her way out of math class engrossed in adjusting her portable fire pager. She wore it like an MP3 player, clipped to her jeans, using earbuds to listen to the toned out fire alarms. It was a kind of music to her ears, a sequence of periodic calls: "Bepa, bepa, ta ta ta . . . powa, powa powa powa. Commack Fire Department reported a structure fire . . . 81 Lincoln Road, cross street Woods Trail. Repeating for Commack, a structural fire on 81 Lincoln Road, cross street Woods Trail. 11:34 hours, Fire Com out."

"Kim!" shouted Billy stepping directly in front of her and waving his hands.

"Oh sorry," she turned down the volume. "What's up?"

"Just checking in to see how you're doing."

She looked at him oddly.

"I mean, how's it going?" He paused to stare into her eyes. "You know with Rick, err, your Captain, I mean, you know, your Dad."

Kim reacted instantly. "Did you say anything?" she asked sharply glaring at him. She knew Billy knew she was freelancing. She eyed him suspiciously; not knowing what to make of the boy her father took under his wing to train to be a firefighter.

"No, I'd never . . . of course not," he said shocked. "Of course not," he repeated, quieter this time. The Colonel would step closer and offer her some respect. Billy did and offered, "I think you've really got what it takes to be a decent firefighter."

Kim took off her earbuds.

More confidently he added a "Colonelism," "That is if you keep at it and study hard." In a hushed voice, he cautioned, "And keep in line!"

Kim let the warning slide by. She smiled with relief. He wasn't going to talk to her father. "Sure, Billy, if you think so."

"Why not? I see the makings of a great firefighter. You just need a fair shot at it."

Just then Sandy walked by and gave them both an icy stare before heading off to the cafeteria for lunch. She hadn't spoken to Billy since the water bucket training drill. It looked as if he had forgotten all about her and was getting awfully close with Kim. Sandy felt her cheeks redden. Why should she be jealous of Kim in this way? But she was!

Neither Billy nor Kim paid any mind to Sandy's stares, if they noticed them at all.

Instead, Billy spoke to Kim just as he would talk to Jim, "Ever since we got those new pagers at the firehouse, I only get local fire calls and truck to truck communications. That's really somethin' that you've got your pager rigged up to hear county wide calls too."

"Yeah. And I got a scanner rigged up at home too."

"Was it expensive?"

"Nah, I got it online as a trade."

"Can I try it? Your pager, I mean?"

Kim grinned slyly and handed it to him.

He clipped it to his jeans and adjusted the earbuds. Nodding approval, he listened intently for a while before whistling excitedly. "Wow! There's a Signal 12 . . " He cupped his hands over his ears to listen harder. " . . . and it sounds like a heck of a big brush fire! It's in the Pine Barrens. There's already been three calls for mutual aid." He pulled off the earbuds and unclipped the pager from his jeans. "Here, thanks."

"Sure. No problem."

"You know, maybe Sandy would like to hear about it. Do ya think?"

Kim's eyes squinted. She stared back at him, realizing how wrong she was about him being her father's "preferred son." Out loud, she said, "Gee, You're right."

Some days, Billy thought, being a leader was easy.

Negotiating her way through the crowded cafeteria, Kim waited in line. She grabbed a grilled chicken burger and a red raspberry yogurt. Tina had already settled into their regular lunch spot off to the side under a sunlit window. She looked for Sandy and spotted her grabbing some hot food at the self serve buffet. Kim was so absorbed in listening to her fire pager; she didn't notice Sandy taking the seat across from her.

Sandy tapped Kim's plate with her fork. "You know Kim, there's something I need to tell you."

"What?" Kim asked hardly listening as she gobbled down her grilled chicken burger.

"You shouldn't be showing up at fires by yourself. It's very stupid …. and dangerous."

Tina looked up from eating her salad wondering why Sandy had decided to make an issue of it now.

Kim gave Sandy a devilish smile. "Oh, well. It's time for a lecture. Go ahead, then. I guess my news will have to wait!"

"What kinda news?" Sandy asked feeling jealous and uncertain.

Kim purposefully opened up her yogurt, eyeing Sandy. "Oh," she continued casually. "Billy thought you might be interested in knowing . . . "

"Knowing what! What were you two talking about?"

"We were talking about firefighting, Sandy. What did you think we were talking about?" Kim tilted her head in a questioning glance, but Tina eyed Sandy knowing full well what she was thinking.

Sandy's shoulders relaxed, "Never mind."

Kim impatiently continued, "Billy thought you might be interested in knowing that there's a brush fire in the Pine Barrens." She stared into Sandy eyes, "Do you want to know about the Signal 12 or not?"

"Of course, I do. Spill it!" Sandy pushed her tray of food away no longer interested in eating.

"South of Route 25A in Rocky Point. Wait . . . " She listened. "Yaphank's responding. That'll make ten departments called in for mutual aid."

"It must be on state forest land!" Sandy said, jumping up excitedly. "Maybe I'll go wait at the firehouse to see if we're called out!"

Tina grabbed Sandy's arm. "Don't get your hopes up. Remember, mutual aid is called out in sequence even if we're only fifteen minutes away."

Sandy sat down again and pulled back her tray of food taking a bite to eat, dejected. "What's the use of waiting at the firehouse. I was bumped off the Brush Truck last time anyway."

"You can expect that, you're still on probation," Tina reminded Sandy. Leaning forward, she reassured, "Don't sweat it."

"The County just called out a police helicopter!" announced Kim.

"That does it!" Sandy dropped her fork and pushed back her tray again. "I'm heading out."

"You don't mean by yourself without being on an engine?" Tina put her hand to her mouth, plainly scared.

"Now who's acting out?" Kim admitted in hopes of dissuading Sandy.

"This is totally different," countered Sandy.

"How? You're chasing fire . . . I'm chasing fire!"

"But I've always been chasing fires!" Sandy exclaimed, realizing too late how absurd it sounded.

Tina didn't want to hear it any more. She knew how crazy they were getting, being confined by the rules of the fire department. To her, she was just happy responding to minor alarms and helping Sandy with Fire Awareness Reports — after the fire was out. "Sandy, why must you go now?"

"Once the fire's out, it's hard to find as all the engines are gone. And it's also hard to see the fire's behavior. You know that. Guessing at it doesn't work." In a hushed voice, she added, "You'll take notes for me in Chemistry class, thanks."

Before Tina could say anything else, Sandy said, "Don't worry! I've gotta go!" Standing up, Sandy glared at Kim remembering their morning conversation, "At least I care about the Pine Barrens."

"Are you implying I don't?" Kim pushed back her tray and stood up.

Sandy flicked her hair out of her face and emboldened by the excitement of chasing fire, said in a dismissive voice, "After all, you're just a firefighter."

"Ah, Sandy, so are you," interjected Tina who had picked up her fork and pointed with it.

Kim's red freckles stood bright red. She snapped back, "Daydreaming about wildland fires is one thing, but running out there on your own?!" There was no response from Sandy. Kim reached out for Sandy's hand and pleaded, "Don't go!" "You could get hurt and no one would know." Still Sandy didn't respond. Making a last ditch attempt to dissuade Sandy, she offered, "Firefighters do a good job putting out fires and they will save the animals, too."

Sandy shook her head sadly. "You don't get it Kim. Fire's as natural as a thunderstorm or a snowstorm. It's what makes the Pine Barrens special. However, firefighters," she sarcastically added, "do too good a job at putting out fires."

Kim made a face, but kept on searching for a way to change Sandy's mind. "Missing Chemistry again? You know how teachers feel when it comes to cutting class." Too weak she thought. Bringing up the forbidden subject more directly, she added, "And remember how the Chief already warned you about freelancing? You can't just go off chasing fires now that you're a firefighter."

"You should talk."

Kim's temper flared. Her right fist banged the table. She had already decided to take matters into her own hands not satisfied with what was offered her. And now, there was no turning back. Freelancing gained her more experience. The excuse she gave as she faced Sandy was to the point and stark, "You gotta do what you gotta do."

Sandy nodded approval.

Billy passed by; realizing his attempt at leadership was working as Sandy and Kim were both smiling.

"So where's the cross street?" asked Sandy in a pleasant tone.

Kim's face revealed a sneaky in cahoots smile. "Route 25A east, off Radio Avenue."

Sandy bussed her tray and called back, "I'm off."

Chasing fire for the first time on her own, Sandy rapidly drove out of the village. By the time she reached 25A, she spotted several brush trucks on their way to the fire. She stepped on the gas to catch up with them and found herself trailing an ambulance. As cars pulled off the road, she kept pace with the ambulance. She even switched on her blue lights; giving the cars she passed the false appearance that she was responding to the alarm. She took a left knowing that firefighters would realize the trick and not let her go directly to the fire scene.

The street was filled with modest homes, a quiet neighborhood until Sandy sped through it.

Sandy cut off a black SUV pulling out of the driveway; the driver's horn blared in annoyance.

Racing on, despite a neighbor's nasty look, she hit an empty garbage can, and then swerved and drove over its lid. When a postal service delivery truck appeared out of nowhere, she hit her brakes and the old red pick up truck jerked forward and stalled. She restarted the engine, drove further east, and downshifted at the last moment to make a sharp turn into the rear of an evacuated shopping center where smoke from the wildland fire filled the air.

Two Fire Police vans blocked off its front entrance, but Sandy easily slipped out the back exit and even dared to drive on the wrong side of Route 25A to reach an empty golf course parking lot. She parked, jumped out, and reached behind the driver's seat. Finding the clipboard of blank Fire Awareness Reports and the pen tied to it, she readied herself.

The smoke from the fire was intense. Sirens and engines were everywhere transforming the normally busy commercial road into what looked like a scene from out West. She almost laughed at the thought, but started coughing instead. The smoke stung her eyes. She made a dash across 25A. Desperately wanting to run towards the orange glow of fire, she held back.

She wasn't wearing protective gear. But she wasn't there to fight fire; she was there to report what she saw.

The Pine Barrens she encountered was more oak trees than pitch pine. There were no leaves yet as it was early spring. She felt the wind on her face, touched the ground to find the soil damp and took a moment to fill out the Fire Awareness Report. She then headed towards the responding Chief's SUV, parked off the road on the grass. He was too distracted giving orders by radio to pay a bystander any attention. "We're fighting fire twenty feet over our heads," she overheard.

Additional fire engines and brush trucks kept heading toward the fire scene including the Brush Truck from her firehouse. "I guess we were finally called in too," she muttered not concerned. There was too much confusion for anyone from her firehouse to spot her. Over 40 fire departments with multiple resources had responded. When a forest ranger pulled up in his patrol car and a bulldozer unloaded, Sandy whispered, "Uh, oh, trouble."

"Look, I'm not disputing who's in charge," said the forest ranger in a reasonable tone to the Chief. "Why run a perimeter with a dozer now? The fire's out. All you need is a hand crew to patrol and do mop up."

Sandy recalled her mother's lesson on the day of the water bucket training drill. The Chief was responsible for fire suppression and not forestry conservation. Yet despite what her mother had explained, Sandy hoped the Chief would listen to the forest ranger and be one of Long Island's forest friendly firefighters.

"I have no time to argue tactics with forest rangers or anyone else." Pressing the radio clipped to his shirt, the Chief called, "Thirty to Thirty-Two, we've got a second dozer instructed to run a perimeter around the fire." He walked off.

The Forest Ranger shook his head and turned back to his patrol car.

Sandy stepped forward reintroducing herself. She had met him at the water bucket drill, "Can you take me in?"

"I've really got to go back to the office," he said apologetically.

She watched him drive off. Going in on her own, she felt more alone than ever. "Maybe this is how my mom feels when she gets no help from the fire departments or the forest rangers." She considered what the Colonel would say; "They need to pull on the same rope — in the same direction."

"Oh, no!" Sandy said out loud.

She had tripped over a fallen pitch pine. It still bristled green. Moving her head slowly from left to right, she couldn't believe what she saw. Dozens and dozens of trees had been uprooted, indiscriminately tossed aside like matchsticks.

She forced herself to move despite the sinking feeling in her heart. Where blueberries and huckleberries once grew lush underfoot, it was bulldozed tracked dirt. Who will remember what was once Pine Barrens?

"Wouldn't it have been easier to use existing roads?" Sandy thought. But that would've meant thinking more like forest rangers to become forest friendly firefighters. For now, she realized, more fire line rehab had to be done because the bulldozers bypassed existing dirt roads to run exact perimeters around the fire. Without rehab, they'd just say these new bulldozed roads had always been here.

"Major bulldozing," she feverishly wrote down. They mustn't forget.

Caught off guard by a returning bulldozer, she reacted without thinking of her own safety. She darted in front of it and waved her hands frantically. The returning bulldozer groaned and skidded to a halt. A man climbed out.

It wasn't uncommon for him to meet locals hiking, biking or riding horses on public parklands. "I work for the Town," he explained. "We started using heavier dozers to get at the trees."

"Great," said Sandy sarcastically. But he was just a regular guy, a town worker. How could she be upset with him, she considered. As if reading her thoughts, he explained, "I'm just doing my job. Normally, I move garbage around."

"At the landfill," Sandy forced a conversational tone to learn more.

"Yes, but I've been responding to fire calls for more than ten years. I try to steer clear of trees as best I can, but I do whatever the Chief orders." Climbing back up on the bulldozer, he commented, "I have to take trees down. It's not my intention. I get paid either way."

There was nothing more she could do. She kindly waved at him and said, "See ya."

Moving deeper into the forest, her sneakers and jeans picked up the new forest color: black. The silhouetted stems of burnt blueberry and huckleberry stood naked and bare. With a dusting of ash on the forest floor, the crunchy sound of her footsteps left slight impressions. The air smelled dry and charred, familiar smells that reminded her of being in the Pine Barrens with her mom.

Walking silently, she found a dead box turtle.

Box turtles were land turtles, with mottled orange and black shells. Individuals lived long lives, thirty to fifty years, if lucky. To increase population survival, Sandy visualized more natural areas acquired like Rocky Point had been. When finding a box turtle, Sandy couldn't resist picking it up to say, "Hello." Then she would wait patiently for it to poke its head out again and stare back at her. Carefully, she'd place it back in the same direction that it was heading and watch it walk off.

But this particular box turtle hadn't escaped the fire.

Despite what she said to Kim in a moment of anger, it was hard for Sandy to accept that wildland fires played an important role. Coupled with spring rains, the blackened Pine Barrens would green up again, and other box turtles would replace the ones lost in the fire. Yet she felt sorry for this particular turtle and moved ahead quickly.

Most of the burn appeared to be no higher than four feet. How would the plants recover after the fire? Which ones would fair better? Would there be more blueberries or huckleberries? Random thoughts filled her mind, intermixing a naturalist's

FIRE AWARENESS REPORT

Date: _4/30/06_ Report by: _Sandy Lewis_

Fire Danger: _Moderate_

Fire Location: _Rocky Point - NW Fire_

On Site: Fuels, Topography, Weather - Fire Behavior

Fuel Type _trees & shrubs_ Live Fuels: _none_

Topography: _flat_ Temp: _warm_ Humidity: _sort of dry_

Wind Direction/Speed: _SW, windy_ Severity: _light burn; hot spots_

Rate of Spread: _can't see fire to tell_ Flame Lengths: _4 feet mostly - ?20 feet_

On Site: Response

Size Class of Fire: _C (10-99 acres)_

Resources: _many fire departments bulldozers, brush trucks, stumpjumpers, engines_

Fire Line Rehab Needs: _major bulldozing_
thousand of trees needed for replanting
block off access; use fallen trees

desire to understand the world with the new knowledge gained from being a firefighter.

A stand of tall pitch pines with yellowing needles indicated a troubling pocket of heavy fuel. Could this have been where the fire was reported to be twenty feet over the firefighters' heads? Was this just one hot spot in the center of the fire or one of many? Not being there during the time of the fire, she filled out the Fire Awareness Report as best she could.

By the time she got back to the main road, traffic had returned to normal. With school being done for the day and with free time on her hands, Sandy drove over to Whiskey Road to find last week's fire. Usually, it was hard to find the fire once the emergency vehicles left the scene but from her mother's description she found it easily. She headed up a hiking trail near where they had planted trees with the 9/11 Planters and found the treaded bulldozer cut and the fire scar at the same time.

It was as her mom described. But one particular strong and healthy pitch pine caught her attention. Ripped violently apart by the blades of a dozer, she stopped and gently put her hand right through the belly of the tree, right between the splintered white wood and the droplets of oozing sap. Not knowing what else to do, she pulled her hand out quickly and reached for her cell phone to take a picture, and then called her mother.

"Why do fire departments use bulldozers? It's awful," complained Sandy.

Emma was home in her office making notes about this very same brush fire. Irritated by the lack of a preplanned conservation response, Sandy's question pushed her over the edge. She leaned back in her chair, stared at the ceiling, and began a pointed, running commentary. Her voice resounded loudly on the speakerphone in the otherwise still forest.

"I've been told by firefighters that there are three reasons for using bulldozers. One, to stop the fire from running underground in the roots or through the canopy. That's all well and good, but it makes no sense when the ground's cold and damp. And it's not effective when the pine trees are touching above the bulldozed cut, either."

"So this bulldozed cut wouldn't have stopped a running canopy fire?"

"If it had been that kind of fire, that's right."

"Reason two," Emma continued, "is for stump jumper access and to pull them out when they get stuck. They should be using existing roads to fighting fire. But no! And to think of all the times I heard stump jumpers don't need roads."

"And reason three?" asked Sandy feeling a knot in her stomach as her mother's voice sounded very strained.

"To create more roads to fight future fires. That's crazy! We'd have no Pine Barrens left. It's better to preplan access needs before fires occur!"

The sun turned yellow in the western sky. Sandy quickened her pace, talking to her mom about what she saw, only briefly stopping when she met a hiker. He told her about a stump jumper that got stuck in an old sand pit. It had to be pulled out by a winch.

"Where?" asked Sandy.

"Where they've been planting those pitch pine tree seedlings."

Sandy's jaw dropped and she raised her cell phone back to her ear. "Mom, I have to take a look before it gets dark! I'll call you right back." Charging down the path to the planting site, it didn't take Sandy long to find where the stump jumper had mistakenly plunged into the 9/11 Memorial.

Sandy reached for her cell phone again. "Mom! I can't believe it!"

"Where are you?" said Emma having had time to wonder about where her daughter was calling from.

"I'm at the 9/11 Memorial. One, no two stump jumpers got lost. They ran over our planted pine tree seedlings. Will they survive?"

"They're young trees, Sandy. They should be fine, but the soil may not be! It's been slowly recovering with lichen and moss. Arrgghh!" Emma took out another piece of paper to take notes, commenting, "They should've stayed on the main trail. Sandy, any other damage on the rim?"

Sandy traced a path back along the ridge, detailing the downed trees in that area too. Emma made some more notes, thinking out loud, "Those firefighters need to be accountable." Sandy kicked some of the dirt back into the empty hole the stump jumpers had made. "Mom, did my wildland firefighting gear come in the mail today?"

"Yes, it did."

"Oh good, I can't wait to take the class now."

Emma sat straight up, "Wait a minute...what are you doing out there? I heard there was another fire in progress. Are you sure you aren't anywhere near that fire? Sandy! They didn't call you in as a firefighter, did they?"

"No, I'm out here on my own, but I'm not near that fire." She bit her lip, admitting, "Not now anyway. But . . . I . . . I just wanted to see and test out one of your Fire Awareness Reports — and shouldn't there be an after action review, like what the Colonel would do?"

What have I unleashed in her? Emma thought inwardly, upon realizing that her daughter was safe. But she blamed herself for Sandy's foolishness.

"Mom, I'm not in any danger, don't worry!" Firmly, she added, "isn't that what you wanted? That I should take an interest in being a wildland firefighter?"

"Not in this way!"

"I don't want to be a firefighter out West," Sandy snapped, a knee jerk response, realizing her mother was about to mention Colorado again. "Give it a rest," she muttered.

Emma still hoped she would reconsider, "You may think otherwise when you attend a nationally recognized wildland fire academy.

"Gotta go. I'm on my way home now. Bye!"

Chapter 12

Know The Ropes And Keep Your Mouth Shut

With more than a dozen staff and parkland officials attending the Wildland Fire Academy meeting, Jim pictured his uncle impatiently waiting for him. They would all be sitting around his uncle's office staring politely at each other. It was a stark room with one institutional window. Its white blinds would be pulled up, taut and uneven. The meeting room's air ducts would hum with the noise of circulating trapped air. Meanwhile, Jim was nervously checking his watch. It was late when he finished talking to his teacher about doing an extra credit report on firefighter protective gear.

Jim dropped off his textbooks at his school locker, and ran down the hallway with only one thought on his mind. That was when he collided into Billy. "Oh sorry! I'm late! Gotta go! Can't stay for lunch." Jim spun around. "I've got a meeting with my uncle. I'll catch up with you later."

But Billy had turned away.

Jim stared back with a questioning look, shrugged, and ran out. There would be one large table in the room, a big desk and a swivel leather chair, Jim pictured. His uncle would think, "That's it," and lean forward then sit back again, muttering, "This is my meeting, not to be run on his schedule. If this kid wasn't my nephew . . . " Jim ran up the steps of the government building three at time, and exploded into the meeting. "I've got a good reason," he offered breathless.

"Close the door, son," Uncle Butch said, shaking his head, reaching for the pen he had placed squarely on top of a blank yellow note pad. Butch Gordon, the Wildland Fire Academy Coordinator, was a charismatic man with a flaring mustache. He cleared his throat. "Last year, over four hundred students attended twenty-five classes. This year, we already have nearly four hundred registered. And we've added on five new classes."

Everyone nodded, and a few applauded.

Jim went to the back of the room and pulled out a stackable plastic chair. He collapsed in it as two guys made room for him at the table. Pulling out a pencil from his back pocket and doodling on the Wildland Fire Academy brochure someone had handed to him, he was vaguely aware that his uncle was credited for starting up the academy. It was the first one on the east coast and it was on Long Island.

Jim should've been impressed, but he wasn't. He was already bored with sitting still and listening. He stared out the window at the parking lot, and drummed absently with his pencil on the table, until his uncle spoke at length about being part of the federal emergency team responding to the space shuttle crash in Texas.

"Gosh." Jim whistled, staring in envy at his uncle.

Butch pointed around the table making sure everyone had their assignments for this year's academy. When he got to Jim, he took a deep breath, "Jim, I expect you to be there on both weekends, on any days off from school, before school to attend the morning briefings, and after school for at least an hour. No excuses." Flipping to the next page of his yellow pad, he added, "You're assigned to Logistics. You'll get your identification badge and orders on registration day."

"Logistics? I thought I'd be helping in Finances selling hats and T-shirts like I did last year."

"That's not for you to say, son." Turning his attention to the rest of his team, he elaborated on Wildland Fire Academy details.

Jim raised his hand.

Butch stopped talking and making notes. Muttering to himself, "He will be assigned to Logistics and organize classroom equipment needs." Long seconds passed as the room filled with uneasiness. Twirling his mustache, he spoke directly to Jim. "I will not accept insubordination."

With a totally surprised and questioning glance, Jim wondered why his uncle was acting as if he were still his baseball coach. That was a long time ago. Now, Jim considered himself to be on more equal terms with his uncle.

"Son," his uncle said. "If you want to play with the big boys you must know the ropes and keep your mouth shut." Swiveling in his leather chair to face everyone else, he ended with, "No matter what you think."

Jim looked around. Everyone was staring at his uncle. Jim squirmed in his chair, banging his knees against the bottom of the table. He felt incredibly out of place and self conscious.

"And here I was setting you up in Logistics to give you a head start in your career." Everyone nodded their approval. This prompted Butch to stand up and pace the room, explaining to his team, "You need to get in tight with the guys running the academy. Logistics is the better way to go. That's the way it works." Standing directly behind Jim, Butch put his hand on his nephew's shoulder. "Son, I don't need to be wasting my time with you on this, no matter what your mother thinks."

Jim winced at his uncle mentioning his mother. He felt the back of his neck getting hot.

"So you must tell me now and not waste my time." Moving to the front of the room, he sat down and in a jocular voice, added, "Unless, you think you can manage your life on your own. That would mean, of course, you have friends in higher places than I do."

Everyone laughed at Uncle Butch's joke except Jim.

"It's your choice, son." Uncle Butch picked up his pen as if nothing had happened and began taking notes again.

Jim slunk back into his chair and shut up. At first, Jim was just doing his mom a favor. That's what she expected of him because his uncle owned the house that they shared with him, and his uncle also offered to help pay for his college tuition. Stewing in his chair, Jim directed his anger out on Tina instead.

Jim visualized how dumb she could be. She couldn't even handle the fire hydrant! He even had to yell at her once, "Wait until the engine is completely backed into the bay before going into the firehouse," then sneered at her when she gave him a dumb look, and he was forced to say, "Isn't it obvious? You see it every day." But Jim never realized how Tina lost many opportunities to gain fire experience during minor alarms. Jim was often picked to go with the officer instead of her.

"That's it," Butch snapped waving his hand. "Everyone out, see you in two weeks." As the room emptied, he coolly stared at his nephew, expecting an answer.

Jim broke the pencil he was toying with, and in a stifled voice said, "Logistics is the way to go, sir." He filed out of the office like everyone else. He never gave his uncle any more trouble until he found himself running late, of all days, on the day of the Wildland Fire Academy.

"Of all days to be late," Jim muttered to himself, driving faster, keeping half an eye on traffic and half an eye on his brown sedan's dashboard clock. He drummed his fingers against the wheel, anxiously waiting behind a stream of cars entering the Wildland Fire Academy. "I'm not going to make it." Fortunately he passed through security without a hitch. He parked as close as he could, rushed in, and located the registration desk. Not caring about the line of students waiting their turn, he announced to the attendant, "Jim Gordon, I'm staff."

The woman behind the counter handed him a registration packet, badge and meal tickets. Taking hold of his material, he was about to ask where his uncle was when a firm hand grasped his shoulder and spun him around. Jim cautiously stared back at his uncle, expecting he had done something wrong. Instead Uncle Butch pounded him on the back and paraded him around the room proudly.

"Kathy, glad to see you made it back this year. You've met my nephew, right? Last year, of course. Well, he's already well on his way to becoming a highly regarded firefighter." And to another, "Yes, this is my nephew, Jim Gordon."

Up and down they marched, from the cafeteria to the conference rooms. At each turn Jim met more academy staff. Butch, who was giving directions here and there, expertly introduced his nephew to the right people, the important people.

Jim felt more at ease and even confident enough to add in a few pleasantries of his own.

Uncle Butch introduced Jim to a woman in her middle twenties who wore wildland firefighter colors, a bright yellow shirt with pockets and dark forest green pants with a smart belt and leather fire boots. Jim said hello. Georgeann's brown hair was neatly trimmed short. Her dark eyes were steady and calm. "As the Incident Commander's daughter," Butch further explained to Jim, "she grew up on the fire line and knows her stuff. She's running Logistics." To Georgeann, he added, "I want you to take special care of my nephew, Jim. Take him over to the cafeteria for some coffee. Introduce him to some of your friends."

Before the two were out of earshot, Butch called back, "And, Jim, don't be late for the Saturday morning briefing at zero seven thirty."

"Yes, sir."

"Come on Jim," said Georgeann. "Let's get some coffee. I'll set you up tomorrow, after the morning briefing."

"Doing what?" Jim asked while they walked into the cafeteria.

"Basically, you'll keep track of requested equipment. I'll show you the forms you need to fill out. You can help me with organizing the supply area too."

Jim reached for the meal tickets he had stuffed in his pocket to pay for coffee, a pile of eggs, and two pieces of toast. They took a seat in the middle of the cafeteria, around a table which held half a dozen firefighters dressed as Georgeann. She easily joined in on their conversations. As promised, Georgeann introduced Jim to her friends, of which there were many young men and women.

Loudly packing the Wildland Fire Academy, Sandy saw emergency responders dressed in uniform with insignias from the U.S. Fish & Wildlife Service, National Park Service, Forest Service, and State Forestry Services. Some wore wildland fire gear; others wore T-shirts picturing famous fires like the 2002 Colorado Hayman Fire and the 1994 South Canyon Fire.

But unlike Jim, who was well received on the day he registered, Sandy had walked in unannounced. Despite wearing wildland fire gear, she felt vulnerable and out of place. Aimlessly, she stared at the flashy souvenir pins, hats, and brochures filling table tops.

Nearby, a rugged firefighter was comfortably sprawled out in a lounge chair reading a book about the 1949 Mann Gulch wildland fire in Montana. Another young firefighter with curly hair and a Southwestern drawl said, "I was on the Cedar Fire in California and the Cave Creek Complex in Arizona." With a wide grin, her buddy answered, "I hooked in with a crew organized out of New Hampshire for the Cave Creek."

Sandy eyes opened wide. How could they be so relaxed and happy? Could she really be one of them? Until now, she had fixated on protecting the Pine Barrens. How exciting would it be to fight fire elsewhere! Friends and her time at the beach seemed distant. She wanted more. An unaccustomed tug, a yearning of her heart, urged her to do so. "But am I ready?" She wavered. The Colonel's advice, "Whatever it takes," and his stature, gave her the confidence she needed. Pacing excitedly to the registration line, she waited her turn.

The woman at the registration desk reached behind her seat and pulled out copies of the <u>Firefighter's Guide</u>, a textbook for fighting wildland fires, the <u>Incident Response Pocket Guide</u>, a handbook useful in a wide variety of emergencies, and the <u>Fireline Handbook</u>, a field guide for fighting wildland fires. "There are meal tickets inside your registration packet for the days you'll be attending class; check the class schedule for time and locations," said the woman as she passed the materials to Sandy.

"Thank you," Sandy said almost choking on her words due to her excitement. "Excuse me." Sandy brushed the hair out of her face, and swallowed hard before politely asking, "I was told I could go to the morning briefing tomorrow." She continued, "Is that okay?"

"Yes it's open to everyone attending the academy. It starts at zero seven thirty."

The next day, Sandy entered the large auditorium, a few steps up from the common area. Sandy took a seat up front as Butch took center stage. She eyed Butch suspiciously and wouldn't clap for him as others did. "Why hadn't he let her mom attend the academy as a Training Specialist?"

"I'd like to welcome you to our fifth academy," Butch began. For those of you returning, thank you for coming back. For those of you attending for your first year of classes, glad to have you on board." There was another round of applause welcoming everyone. Butch cleared his throat and motioned with his hands to quiet them down. "We have a busy and well attended academy this year. There are many new faces, new classes, the annual banquet, and more. Check your daily IAP to keep current on what's happening."

Sandy flipped through her copy of the daily Incident Action Plan. The IAP contained staff contact phone numbers, class information, upcoming scheduled events, daily weather forecasts, general announcements, and short articles.

"Now, I'd like to turn it over to the Incident Commander," announced Butch.

Sandy voiced the words, "Incident Commander." The academy not only trained firefighters, it was also organized as an incident, for additional emergency training. Incidents were planned events with standardized positions and procedures. How these standards meshed with her own fire department's terminology wasn't clear to Sandy. She'd just have to figure it out later.

There was another round of applause.

It took a while for Sandy to recognize him. Rocking on the heels of his boots, the Colorado Firefighter looked the same except for a few new grey hairs. She had met him the day of the Sunrise Fire. In a loud voice, he announced, "It's great to see you. Glad you all made it here safely. Butch and his team have done a great job organizing this academy and we're looking forward to an educational week." He then quickly said, "It's the Planning Section Chief that really runs the show," and sat down in the front row.

The Planning Section Chief, a tall, soft spoken man, simply said, "Glad to be back this year." Then he kindly, but firmly announced the ground rules for the meetings. "Cell phones off and no side conversations." With the projector turned on to review class schedules for the upcoming week, he apologetically explained, "It may be hard to read this chart, but it is in your IAP and will be updated daily." Wrapping up he added, "There will be section meetings after breakfast at ten hundred hours. Classes will begin today as well."

Sandy had learned from her mother that when he wasn't attending wildland fire academies and federal emergencies, he was a biology professor at the University of Colorado. Just like volunteers at the local fire departments came from all walks of life, this was also true when it came to training and responding to federal emergencies. As a Training Specialist, her mom would've reported to him.

Next came the Operations Section Chief who made sure the classrooms were up and running. He was a burly man with sleeves rolled up and steady eyes. "We need two more projectors."

"We'll be ready," announced the Logistics Section Chief. She organized equipment needs for the academy. She pulled Jim up to stand beside her, "Jim Gordon will be handling supply requests." With a coffee cup in his hand, Jim stood next to Georgeann wearing a dark navy blue staff T-shirt with an American flag patched on his sleeve.

Sandy briefly glared before turning her head away. She'd seen his name listed under staff in the IAP. She figured he was helping his uncle, but as staff?! Jim looked different, more relaxed perhaps, even more grown up.

The next report came from the Finance Section Chief, who announced, "T-shirt sales are already doing well. If you want to purchase some extra ones for your family members, stop by and see me."

One of the designs had already caught Sandy's eye and she planned to buy it for Tina. Tina was the most artistic of the three girls, contemplating a degree in fashion design.

Next came the Command Staff. "The key to becoming a good firefighter is recognizing that safety is not just something we talk about at meetings; it's what we do." The Safety Officer continued, "What issues could possibly affect people at this academy?"

Someone complained about the traffic driving out from the airport. "Dodging cattle in Montana was as hairy as it got for me until I drove out here."

Another cried out, "I've got the bends."

Sandy giggled at the good natured teasing, especially comparing altitude sickness to what one couldn't possibly get along the coast at sea level.

"More seriously folks," the Information Officer said, "there's a bulletin board just outside the auditorium room. I encourage you to check it daily. And we'll be taking pictures, so don't be surprised if you see yourself in the daily IAP, but I promise to delete the bad ones," she offered, smiling.

Just before the morning briefing ended, the Liaison Officer stood up. "We're working closely with the agency hosting the academy, and we will be coordinating a room for the upcoming Pine Barrens Wildland Fire Task Force meeting."

There was a flurry of activity as the large auditorium room emptied.

Sandy's class started in a few days. On her way out, she felt compelled to introduce herself to Butch, reconsidering what the Colonel had said about pulling on the rope — in the same direction. She introduced herself as being in the same fire department as Jim.

Butch briefly shook her hand, saying "Glad you can be here. Always good to see another firefighter attending the academy. Don't forget to buy your banquet tickets." Then passing by Jim, Butch slapped two banquet tickets in Jim's hand, saying, "Here's two free tickets to the banquet. Go invite your friend Billy to attend. It's a real good time. We've got a raffle going and we give away door prizes."

Sandy stood there astonished. Even though she had dressed the part, she realized she wasn't really one of them at all.

"Thanks, Uncle Butch," said Jim smiling. Turning to find Georgeann, Jim's face soured immediately upon spotting Sandy. He whispered something to the group of firefighters surrounding him. They stared back at her and a few snickered.

Many of the young firefighters had well worn gear. Hers was brand spanking new. Feeling flushed and embarrassed, Sandy made a beeline to the door thinking it had all been a mistake. What was she thinking? Who was she kidding? The pilot in training under the Colonel's command, Patricia, who amazingly hit the mark at the water bucket training would have looked them all in the eye and boldly taken a stand. Sandy couldn't. She didn't have the confidence to stand up for herself. She wasn't strong enough to prove her worth and was irritated by this.

Driving off, she couldn't settle down. Images of high school graduation filled her mind. If she didn't focus on her firefighting, what else would she do next? Not until she passed by Rocky Point, did she also recall her purpose for participating in the Wildland Fire Academy. She gripped the steering wheel harder. How could she let them get the best of her? Didn't she want to learn how to be a forest friendly firefighter?

"I can't face them again. But I must. Time is really running out for me, and for the Pine Barrens too!"

Sandy's woodchuck Parsley, with pine cones

PART C
PROTECTING LIFE, PROPERTY &
THE ENVIRONMENT

Spring peeper with pine cone

Chapter 13

Smokey I

Idly staring at the Smokey Bear poster in her bedroom, Sandy thought, "I'd better study." She got up and reached for the wildland firefighter textbook on her desk, then plopped down on her bed again. Thumbing through it, she lingered over a picture that explained what to do when a fire spreads into brush. Captivated, she realized how much she enjoyed the subject matter despite issues with Jim embarrassing her at the Wildland Fire Academy.

"Definitely, I'll leave my helmet behind and wear a pair of jeans and a T-shirt I'll buy at the Wildland Fire Academy." Satisfied with her decision, she let herself become more absorbed in the wildland firefighting textbook.

Two hours later, her pager beeped and announced a Signal 12, bush fire, near the railroad tracks uptown.

"Enough studying!" she jumped up and ran out her bedroom door, down to her pickup truck and sped away. By the time she made it to the firehouse, the Brush Truck and engines were already gone.

"Oh, man," Sandy whined to no one in particular.

"You missed it, too?" A familiar voice came from behind her.

When she turned around, she saw Billy. They could do nothing but wait at the firehouse on standby until extra resources were needed or until the fire was out so they could sign for their point. They heard nothing more from the firehouse's radio.

Sandy milled around the engine bay, staring absently, until she noticed the posted newspaper article. "Way to go, Mom," she rooted.

Billy looked up and read, "Should taxpayers buy new trees? Activist seeks funding when chiefs send in bulldozers."

"Billy! My mom's quoted in this article for wanting firefighters and their fire districts to be accountable when putting out brush fires," she exclaimed. But then bit her lip as she read the angry scribble off to the side of the article, in dark red ink, "It will never happen!"

Billy kept still, reading the article intently. "Chiefs have no time to bicker with park rangers or anyone else about where to send trucks when they're fighting a blaze. The goal is to save lives and property, not scrub pines. Whatever environmental damage is caused by bulldozers and stump jumpers running through the woods is nothing compared to the importance of keeping people safe and wildland fires under control." Skimming through it again, Billy reread, "paying for the cost of planting trees would set a precedent in structural firefighting."

A firefighter next to Sandy muttered, "If she wants us to pay for the trees, then we just won't put out the fire." It felt like an eternity to Sandy before the "525," was announced and they could sign for their point.

Sandy pulled Billy outside behind the firehouse.

She mocked, "If you want to fight wildland fires, you'd better go out West. Well, doesn't that fire count as a wildland fire? And to think our fire department is talking about spending $150,000 on a new brush truck? And so what if fire districts have to pay for the trees? Firefighters would think twice before making a mess of the Pine Barrens!"

Billy felt conflicted. The Colonel would say: "One must embrace diversity and allow this diversity to make team decisions or be doomed to failure." Billy thought about the water bucket training drill and how those firefighters were working together, benefiting from their differences.

He put a hand on her shoulder and said, "I know it's tough being, like you say, a forest friendly firefighter, who's also on probation. But you're almost done with your classes, right?"

"Yeah, I just have the Firefighter Hands-on left." She nodded, breathing easier.

"And I'm sure you want firefighters to be safe and that you want people's homes protected too, so there must be a better way." He dropped his hand off her shoulder and pointed his finger at her, "Knowing you, I'm sure you'll figure it out."

Looking in his eyes, she realized she had never confided in Billy about her situation at home. "Did you know that my mom's been pushing me to go out West too — to college in Colorado? She thinks I'm wasting my life here, trying to save the Pine Barrens. She makes me angry and I don't mean to be." Staring into Billy's eyes, she shrugged, "Maybe I'll just take a year off and waitress."

He laughed. "I'm sure you'd do a good job at it — eventually. But waitressing ?"

She pretended to take orders and carry dishes out to waiting customers, and then to get confused as to who ordered what. She shrugged, "Waitressing doesn't really suit me, does it? I daydream too much. I'd forget who ordered what." She giggled playfully.

"Take it easy then. You've applied to community college, for an Associate's degree? Then why not take a class at the Wildland Fire Academy? These are steps in the right direction, you know, baby steps."

In a more reasonable tone, Sandy told him about the basic wildland firefighter class open to firefighters and how her mom had already set it up for her.

"Sounds like you're set."

"I guess I am," her voice trailed off.

"By the way," Billy said, "I just started getting involved in Technical Rescue. It's advanced training in confined space, high angle rope, trench collapse rescue and . . . "

"But what has that got to do with me?" she interrupted.

"You may like it because of the training in ice water rescue, *and* wilderness search and rescue."

It took Sandy a moment to realize what he was saying. Her eyes sparkled at a chance to link her love of water with the Pine Barrens. She had heard about the wilderness search and rescue training from the forest rangers, but never thought much about it. After all, she knew the Pine Barrens well and had no reason to take the class. She never got lost in the Pine Barrens. It would be like getting lost in her bedroom.

"Do you think I would be good enough at Technical Rescue?"

"Whatever it takes." Billy's eyes twinkled.

She grinned understanding the hint.

Billy impulsively pulled Sandy behind the firehouse, near the picnic pavilion. "You know," he said to Sandy in a half playful, half serious tone, "There's talk about all these brush fires. Maybe a firefighter has been setting them on purpose."

Sandy recoiled at the thought. She kidded, "Well, I once called myself a fire bug and not a lady bug, but that was before I understood that firebug was slang for an arsonist."

"Hmmm," Billy said thoughtfully.

Sandy's eyes opened wide, and a knot formed in her stomach. Would he take her stupid joke the wrong way?

"You know maybe it's also the kind of firefighter who is jumping out of their skin to get onto a brush truck to see more action." He gave Sandy a sideways look to tease and a disarming grin.

Sandy smiled easily as the tension in her melted away with Billy's joking. "Well, don't look at me. I'm not starting those brush fires."

Billy leaned closer to whisper, "I wasn't accusing you. I just wanted to see that shy smile of yours."

She looked up at him with an even bigger smile.

Billy leaned down to kiss her.

Sandy turned away shyly, leaving Billy to take an awkward step back. She could feel her heart pounding but wasn't sure why. All she knew was that kissing Billy right now was a lot scarier than fighting fire. She tried to give Billy a smile but he was still staring down at his shoes. He wouldn't look at her.

Having returned from the fire alarm and signing for his point, Jim spotted Billy's truck and went around to the back of the firehouse to find him. Eager to offer Billy a banquet ticket for the Wildland Fire Academy, his face soured upon finding the two rather close.

They both looked up embarrassed. "Hey," Billy said trying to regain his composure.

"Her again?" Ripping Billy's banquet ticket in half, Jim allowed it to flutter to the ground. He stomped off.

Billy called out, half-heartedly, "Jim, wait."

"Why is he like that?" asked Sandy startled, as Jim drove off. "Maybe we should worry about *him* starting a fire," she pointed emphatically. Turning back to Billy, she brushed her hair aside and confided, "He almost did the other day at the beach."

Billy gave her an incredulous look. "Jim would never do such a thing. He might be angry at me now, but that's different. He's the kind of firefighter you'd run into a flaming building with. I trust Jim with my life," he said somberly. "It's just that . . ." he hesitated not used to being so open about his inner thoughts.

Sandy looked deeply into his eyes, "It's just that . . . ?" She pressed gently.

Reassured by her trusting look, Billy leaned closer. "Jim's uncle used to be our little league coach, your best friend until you offered his team advice. Jim's uncle had it in for me ever since. It's a sore point between us."

Sandy imagined a boat steering recklessly in the harbor and how Jim's uncle was just like that, leaving a wake of trouble behind him and Jim falling overboard. "Maybe, Butch is too much for even Jim to handle."

"Jim's a tough dude."

"One things for sure, I bet they're not pulling on the same rope — in the same direction." She pretended to be Jim, having a lengthy tug of war with his uncle. But Billy looked so worried, Sandy flashed a smile and beckoned, "Walk me back to my truck."

"Sure." His dark mood vanished. Ss they walked over to Sandy's pickup, he said, "Good luck with the wildland fire class."

Sandy reached for his hand, "Thanks," and giggled.

Did she want to be kissed now? Should he try again? Feeling the heat of humiliation rise up the back of his neck, his face was probably red too. "She must think I'm a complete idiot; I mean, I can't even manage to pull off a kiss!" he thought to himself.

Pulling his hand away abruptly, he said, "Hey, you better go study." He couldn't afford to slip up again.

By early Saturday morning, Sandy found herself in the middle of a crowded classroom which seated about fifty students. She had been right in her choice to wear jeans and a recently purchased wildland firefighter T-shirt. Yet her classmates looked more worldly and experienced. Their talk of far away places and their use of jargon to describe federal fire positions gave them an aura of expertise. She took a seat up front feeling intimidated, yet ready to learn from the instructor who seemed amiable enough.

He began with a round of introductions. Only a few firefighters were from Long Island; most had either taken courses in fire science or had plans to be fighting fires out West over the summer.

"Before we start on getting all of you guys trained as wildland firefighters, we're going to talk about forest fire prevention. How many of you have been in the woods sitting around a campfire? Don't bother answering. I know most of you have. Worse still let's say you're out there when it's dusty hot from lack of rain. And even more so, there's a strong drying wind. What do you think is going to happen, boys and girls, when you or one of your buddies starts smoking, jabbering on and flicking ashes?"

"Fire," shouted half the class, while the others laughed and said, "A really big fire!" And a few more exuberantly added, "We'll get to see some action."

"Hold on there. Let's not get so crazy. Calm down. Besides flicking your cigarette ashes directly into the fire and making sure that when you're done smoking you put the cigarette out, what else would you do?"

"Clear a five foot diameter ring around the campfire to mineral soil," said an older boy.

"Yes, I see someone's been reading the textbook. Good." He looked around at the youthful faces, "What else?"

Bravely, Sandy called out, "Build the campfire away from overhanging dead branches."

"Very good," her instructor nodded in acknowledgment. He continued to survey the room for other respondents.

Sandy felt more comfortable. Maybe this wasn't so bad after all. What was the big deal? Fighting fire out West or in New York, it was still fire, she thought proudly.

"This is pretty basic stuff." The instructor suddenly added. "Now what else?"

Instantly deflated with his patronizing comment, she and the rest of the class fell silent.

"Let me give you a hint. How about the size of the campfire?"

"Keep it small, so it's easy to put out," said a girl behind Sandy.

"Right," the instructor said, adding, "And don't add heavy wood that's going to take some time to burn down. Because you probably won't have enough water to put out too big a campfire either." The instructor cleared his throat to make sure the class was listening. "Final point about fire prevention. Not all fires are set by lightning. If you love fire, and that's why we're are all in the firefighting business, what we need is more firefighters and not firebugs." He slammed the firefighter textbook he'd been holding down on the desk to make his point heard.

The room silenced completely.

"Now," he whispered, "Let's get started."

"Inside your copy of the Fireline Handbook are the ten standard wildland firefighting orders for firefighter safety. He went around the room selecting different students to read out loud. When he pointed to Sandy, she read, "Base all actions on current and expected behavior of the fire." Another read, "Identify escape routes and safety zones, and make them known." And so on.

It was hard for Sandy to keep all of these in her head, including LCES (lookouts, communications, escape routes, and safety zones). She was grateful to hear the instructor announce that it was time for lunch.

The cafeteria was jammed with firefighters. Sandy took a plate of food and sat down in the corner beside a window. As she ate she stared out the window at some white pine trees. It seemed like everyone knew everyone else at the Wildland Fire Academy. She couldn't help but hear some of their conversations. A few were planning summer jobs at names of forests she only dreamed of: Yellowstone, the Tetons, and the Grand Canyon.

"Excuse me, want some company? You're Sandy, aren't you? Jim mentioned you were taking a class."

"He did?" she asked, not sure if she was more surprised about Jim's mention of her or that someone was taking the time to notice her. She looked up and recognized Georgeann from the day she had come to register for the Wildland Fire Academy.

"How do you like your class so far?" asked Georgeann.

"It's okay. There are a lot of really experienced firefighters in my class."

"Ahh, you're used to swimming in a small pond. You're just shy 'cause it's a big lake you're in now."

"Well," Sandy admitted, "I don't really think they're so much more experienced. They just look like they stepped out of a movie."

"Don't be intimidated. They're learning, just like you. And don't worry so much about being from the east coast. Did you know a huge number of firefighter injuries and fatalities are motor vehicle accidents, which can happen anywhere? Every fire has hazards. A firefighter from Florida may take a few days to adjust to elevations of the Rockies, but a firefighter from Montana has to learn that what appears to be solid ground in Florida may be the back of a gator or a thin film of plant matter over a nasty hole. Getting complacent can get one hurt or killed, no matter where a person fights fire."

"I never thought about it that way." Looking up to Georgeann, she added wistfully, "You're really smart."

"Don't be so quick to put me on a pedestal. I was one of the newbies once," Georgeann confided. "My dad's been firefighting all his life and I grew up living it. Give it time and you can become just as knowledgeable." Trying to make Sandy feel less isolated, she added, "You know Long Island's part of the fire community too. It's not the first time my dad was on Long Island either. He may be IC at the academy this year, but he was an Operations Chief at the Sunrise Fire."

"The IC is your dad?"

"Yeah, the apple doesn't fall far from the tree."

Sandy laughed. "I guess that's true with me too. My mom's a Training Specialist."

"Really. How come she's not at the academy?"

"The Wildland Fire Academy coordinator says she needs to get more experience by going out West; her credentials from the Colorado academy don't count unless she goes out on a western fire."

Georgeann frowned explaining, "Support staffs for an academy don't have to be credentialed let alone experienced. Academies are good opportunities for giving local people a chance to become familiar with federal firefighting terminology. An instructor's qualifications, however, are very important. If your mom's qualifications were properly earned, she can be a Training Specialist throughout the country as well."

"Really?" Sandy's eyes widened. So it had nothing to do with her mom's qualifications. Reminded of her mother's conversation with the Colonel, she asked, "Did you know, an U.S. Army Guard Colonel is also helping to train firefighters? I just went on a water bucket drill with him. Your father actually worked with him during the Sunrise Fire."

"He sounds like a cool person for me to meet someday." She smiled and stood up. "Guess I better get back to work. And you'd better get back to class."

Glancing at her watch, Sandy sighed, "Yeah, you're right. Thanks."

Back in class, the instructor had donned his wildland firefighting gear, complete with helmet and gloves. He explained to them the importance of the safety equipment he carried and lectured them about their need to watch out for their own personal safety as well as keeping an eye out for others.

"I'm trying to give you the experience to realize the need to protect yourself. Don't look to others to protect you! They can get sloppy. You can't afford to be sloppy with your own personal safety."

Sandy thought about swimming in cold water. She knew what to expect and knew how to be prepared. It was natural for her to suit up in a winter wetsuit with boots and a hood from years of growing up near the water. But with firefighting, admittedly, she was already much more careless. The instructor was right about offering them the experience to know better. Making a promise to herself, she vowed to suit up more carefully when responding to fire alarms.

For the last hour of class, the instructor spoke of being on a federal fire. "You boys and girls will start as hand crews and be part of a squad of twenty with two squad bosses and one crew boss in charge. Here's a handout explaining ICS terminology and another on incident transitioning as fire complexity expands."

Sandy stretched. She was tired of sitting so long. By now the ICS terminology was familiar to her. She turned her attention to the second handout. Many conditions were common to the Pine Barrens, including residential homes mixed with unique natural resources, wildland fires spreading across fire districts, and the potential for Fire Danger to be VERY HIGH or EXTREME.

Sandy raised her hand to ask, "So transitioning means that the responding Chief wouldn't be in charge as the fire complexity expands?"

"Possibly. It depends on the Chief's credentials, the geographic spread of the fire, and the number of fire districts involved. Type 5 incidents have the lowest complexity, meaning a single resource, like an engine, will do. Type 4 incidents need multiple resources usually called from outside fire districts. Type 3 incidents are more regional and more complex. And so on . . . There are different skills needed at each level. The goal is to resolve the incident the best way we can."

Sandy nodded.

The instructor attentively spoke to the entire class, "We will break early today, so you will have time to read your textbook. See you tomorrow, bright-eyed and bushy-tailed. We'll start off with map and compass work *and* an added surprise to keep me amused."

Chapter 14

Smokey II

Sunday morning, the wildland firefighter instructor eyed his students over the rim of his glasses and said, "There are two kinds of people in this world. Those who have faith in electronic gadgets and those who have faith in pencil and paper."

Sandy guessed the type of instructor he was. He seemed very old fashioned she thought. But this is what the instructor said and so she tried to keep an open mind.

He ranted, "How many of you are carrying a GPS?" He smiled, saying wryly, "So you didn't think I knew what a GPS was did you? For those of you who don't know, a GPS is short for Global Positioning System. It's a hand held electronic, mapping device."

Tentatively, about a dozen hands were raised.

"How many of you are carrying electronic calculators?" he derided.

The entire class of about fifty students raised their hands.

He shook his head and frowned back at them. "In this class, you are going to learn with pencil and paper. What are you gonna do if you run out of batteries?"

The young firefighter next to Sandy commented, "Solar power, man."

Some students in the class stifled laughter, but the instructor just glared. Making his point clear, he retorted, "A GPS is all fine and good for finding your location on the Earth, but when it comes to navigating, even the most sophisticated GPS user needs to know basic map and compass skills. Now take out your compasses, and put away those electronic gadgets. If you don't have a compass or a pencil," he grabbed a box off his front desk, "Here, you go."

Rustling papers and tossing compasses, the students packed away their electronic devices and found or borrowed a pencil and paper.

"Before a firefighter can set foot in the backcountry," the instructor began again more subdued, "you need to know where you are and where the fire is. These basic skills also increase your understanding of fire behavior: the manner in which fuels ignite, flames develop, and fire spreads."

Dimming the lights, he turned on the slide projector. "We begin by looking at topography, fuels and weather, respectively.

When a fire begins at the bottom of a slope, the fuels located uphill are preheated by the rising air, so that they easily catch fire when they come in contact with flames." The instructor took a pointer pen out of his shirt pocket. "Know your terrain. Note potential barriers that would serve as a firebreak as well."

That made Sandy think about the Sunrise Fire. The highway hadn't been an effective firebreak.

He next pointed to a slide picturing a mountain pass. "This mountain pass is otherwise known as a saddle." Changing slides the next image pictured the same area as a topographic map. Squiggly lines encircled each mountain top. "These varying elevations also influence overall fuel groups, which we will discuss later. Finally, if the fire is on a slope exposed to sunny weather, the fire spreads even more quickly because the sun is also preheating the fuel. "

Staring blankly at the mountain pictures, Sandy thought about Long Island's topography, to some boringly flat in comparison. "Yet our weather isn't!" she thought. Long Island's off shore and on shore breezes, drying north winds, hot westerly winds, and humid southerly winds, created frequently shifting weather patterns. She had wanted to ask the instructor about fire behavior during the Sunrise Fire, but the instructor had already shut off the projector and was handing out compass exercises.

The morning passed quickly with Sandy too busy to think about her missed Sunday morning drill at the firehouse.

"You've got an hour for lunch, and then I've got that surprise for you. So get back here on time!" the instructor warned.

Returning from the cafeteria with a yogurt, Sandy took her seat.

The chatter quieted down as the instructor dimmed the lights.

"We're taking a siesta," the young firefighter sitting next to Sandy whispered.

She laughed.

The instructor didn't look amused.

Sandy gobbled down her yogurt mistaking his continued stare to mean that she wasn't supposed to be eating in the classroom.

Grumbling, he pointedly commented to Sandy and then to the rest of the class, "Lunchtime distractions are common to many tragic fires because firefighters lose their focus on the fire and its behavior." He hoped they would heed this lesson.

With the lights dimmed, he turned on the speakers and the roaring rumble of a distant plane filled the silence.

"Imagine," the instructor's voice dramatically confided, "You've finally made it. You're the smokejumper you've always wanted to be. Assigned to do initial attack, parachuting in, you settle in for a long day of hard work. The fire has already been burning for several days, persistently with creeping flames. The winds are light. Out comes your trusty hand tool. You lean into it as you, along with others of your crew, cut line between ten foot tall shrubs. Tools chop, cut and clank in unison as the fire break slowly advances uphill to flank the fire. Yes, there are occasional interior flare ups. No problem. It's heavy work at high altitudes. The day gets on, warms up, and the crew gets spread out."

The mountainous terrain images were steep and rocky, but this time Sandy could relate; the shrubs looked just like the ones in the Pine Barrens. She listened more intently as he described the general fuel groups, from grasslands to woodlands to forests, and the way they burned.

"What watch out situations do we have here?" he asked.

All of a sudden there was a chorus of answers.

"Safety zones and escape routes not identified."

"No communication link between crew members."

"Weather getting hotter and drier."

"Can't see the main fire. Not in contact with anyone who can."

"What about your predictions on changing fire behavior?" pressed the instructor. "The fire has been burning for several days and spreading slowly. If the fire's still not going out despite your best efforts, what will happen if an alignment of worst case conditions occur?" A hollow, whistling wind, filled the classroom air. "Wildland fires are also capable of generating their own wind, bringing fresh air inward from below and hot air rising above. What now?" he shouted over the wind.

Turning the lights on, he caught them by surprise.

The class broke up in an explosion of excited chatter, each of them comparing notes on fighting fire under these circumstances.

"Think about this tonight. And study your textbook."

But by Monday, their third full day at the Wildland Fire Academy, they were told to pull out their textbooks and follow along with the instructor instead. A few of the students moaned, but he ignored them. He had the students decide which fuel group best matched the projected pictures of mountainous terrain.

"After lunch, we'll discuss fighting fire under potentially explosive conditions," he concluded with a wry smile, hinting a return to the firefighter story.

Sandy called Kim on her cell phone as she ate lunch. "Kim, what's it called when, in a house fire, the fire is explosive? A flash, something?"

Kim was having lunch in the high school cafeteria with Tina.

Tina put down her sandwich. "Are you on the phone with Sandy? How's she doing? Did she meet any good-looking guys yet?"

"Shhhhh! I can't talk to Sandy and listen to you at the same time. Sandy! It's called a flashover, when a fire grows to involve all combustible surfaces."

"Kim, I think that's what our instructor was getting at!"

"Wildland fires acting like structural fires? No way!"

"Why not?" Sandy said. "Maybe that's what those firefighters were thinking about when they bulldozed Rocky

Point. Did you know, they kept on saying that it was the Sunrise Fire all over again?"

"There you have it then. The bulldozers were needed to prevent those Rocky Point fires from turning into a Sunrise Fire — a flashover."

"No. I think the Rocky Point fires were very different."

"So how do you know? We're taught to anticipate a flashover. We use the fire hose to not only hit the fire but to cool the air above the fire. Bringing bulldozers in was just like that, a precaution, for firefighter safety."

"There's got to be a better way to protect life, property, and the environment." Sandy said as if it were a puzzle she was trying to figure out. Billy's confidence in her: "Knowing you, I'm sure you'll figure it out," helped too.

"Well, then what?" said Kim getting impatient with Sandy, despite their recent truce and promise to help each other out.

"That's what I've been working on . . . Hey, I gotta go. I want to check out something online."

"Sure."

"By the way, is Tina there?"

"Want to talk to her?"

"Don't have time. Just tell her there are lots and lots of cute guys here! Bye."

"Bye." Kim laughed as she conveyed the message to Tina.

When Sandy got back from lunch, she tentatively raised her hand.

"Yes?"

"The weather service has issued a red flag warning for today because of high winds. So that might tell us to fight fire aggressively. But the red flag warning reads more like a Fire Danger." She handed the printout to the instructor with a confused look on her face. "And I know today's Fire Danger is MODERATE."

The instructor took hold of the paper Sandy handed him and approvingly said to the classroom of students, "Thanks to Sandy, we have an example of what a red flag warning would say." He cleared his throat, "THE COMBINATION OF GUSTY WINDS . . . AND LOW RELATIVE HUMIDITIES WILL TEAM UP TO CREATE A HIGH FIRE DANGER FOR THIS AFTERNOON ACROSS MUCH OF THE TRI STATE REGION."

Hmmmm," the instructor considered, "I see the confusion . . . the occasional misuse of terminology. The report should say increasing fire risk or elevated fire potential and not use the words, moderate, high or extreme as those are Fire Danger terms with special meanings."

"Remember Fire Danger is a forestry term for predicting wildland fire risk," he continued. "This information is posted on Smokey Bear signs. Red flag warnings are issued by the weather service to also indicate wildland fire risk. In theory, they should be the same forecast. Hopefully with improved communication and coordination this trouble spot will be cleared up."

Handing the paper back to Sandy, he emphasized to the class, "Be sure you listen to the right information for your fire district. Understand what your district's predictions are saying and how your district prepares and responds to elevated wildland fire risk."

He eyed them intently.

The room filled with nodding heads.

"Now, let's get back to the fire scene in Colorado."

As the lights dimmed and the speaker came alive with a whistling wind, hollow and chilling, it stirred Sandy's imagination.

The instructor began, "What happens to the fire behavior when the wind picks up?"

A student called out, "It's windy, which means longer flame lengths and the fire will spread faster."

Another student added, "The fire would run uphill at a faster rate of spread."

"Good. That's weather and topography. What about the fuels, the live fuels?" The instructor asked. "So far you've got two out of three. Weather, topography, now what about fuels?"

"The live fuels would dry and catch fire, and the flames would extend higher," said Sandy excitedly.

"That's exactly what they were unprepared for," the instructor added somberly in contrast to Sandy's jubilance.

"With flames over their heads, engulfing the trail on both sides, they made a dash uphill. But so did the fire. Fourteen firefighters lost their lives that day."

Pictures of the memorial instantly quieted the room. One after another, he displayed their pictures on the projector's screen. Each of them looked just like everyone else in the classroom: youthful, rugged, and happy to get out on an adventure. It was then that the students realized their lesson had been based on an early July, 1994 wildland fire known as the South Canyon Fire of Storm King Mountain, Colorado.

The instructor shut off the projector but not the speakers. In the darkness, they sat reflecting on what they had just seen, listening to the speakers as they replayed the sounds of howling wind and the crackling of fire, imagining the trail engulfed by flames. Turning off the speakers, the instructor somberly concluded, "Respect their lives by respecting yours. Be safe."

Flicking on the lights, and in a much lighter tone, he said "That's it for today. Go home, have some dinner, and get some sleep."

Sandy broke the silence. "Does every wildland fire have the potential to behave like a flashover?"

"That's a structural firefighter's term," the instructor clarified. "We call it a blowup. Given the right conditions, any fire can have areas of high intensity."

"Even when the Fire Danger is MODERATE? Does that mean a blowup can still occur?"

"With MODERATE Fire Danger, a blowup shouldn't happen."

"But at the Rocky Point fires, Fire Danger was MODERATE, and firefighters observed flames twenty feet over their heads. How can they both be right?"

"You can still have MODERATE Fire Danger with flare ups in heavy concentrations of fuels. Keep in mind, on-site fire behavior determines fire suppression strategies and firefighter safety."

Sandy raised her hand.

Checking his watch, the instructor said, "A question for another time."

Sandy looked disappointed as she gathered her belongings.

"That's it for today," the instructor said "And don't forget to keep reading your textbook."

On her way out of class, Sandy's instructor caught her attention. "You really have taken an interest. Take the intermediate fire behavior course next year to learn more."

Her face lit up. She had wanted to show the class her latest Fire Awareness Report. Instead, she put it away, satisfied for now.

After dinner, Sandy settled down to read and study. She shut off her cell phone, not wanting to be interrupted and fell asleep with the wildland firefighter textbook beside her. Sandy's mother smiled as she put the textbook on her desk, shut off the light, and pulled a blanket over her daughter.

The next morning, the instructor quickly went over the subjects he missed the day before. Nonstop, the class followed along silently in their textbooks. After each section, they had to work on open book quizzes. "It's time for lunch. Be back in 45 minutes, sharp. We'll be testing your skills with belt weather kits, fire shelters, and hand fire tools."

The facility cafeteria bustled with both new and experienced firefighters, in conversations around lunch tables or standing about in groups. Many nodded their heads at Sandy walking by. She enjoyed being part of the crowd. On her way back from getting a hot meal, she went to find a seat.

A jovial Jim was eating lunch with Georgeann. He had convinced his mom to get him a permission slip to miss a few days of class during the week.

Georgeann waved at her to join them.

Jim's expression soured, "Oh, it's Smokey," he mocked. "I read that tree hugger article at the firehouse." He hoped she wouldn't sit next to them.

Sandy raised her eyebrows and snapped back angrily, "My mom was right!" She sat down. "And I'm proud of what she said about firefighters being accountable."

"Nonsense, we're firefighters, not tree planters." Jim sneered, raising his hand, brushing her off.

"I bet you don't treat house fires in the same way."

"What's a few dead trees?"

"Actually," Georgeann leaned forward between them to point out, "Wildland firefighters also have a conservation mission. When the flame lengths are over four feet, bulldozers are called in. Afterwards, hand crews rehab the fire line."

Sandy's anger turned to surprise. "They do?"

Georgeann nodded.

Sandy leaned asking, "They don't bulldoze an exact perimeter around the fire, do they?"

Georgeann took a sip of her coffee. She calmly offered, "A more insightful question would be to ask what is the anticipated fire behavior before you jump right into tactical decisions. You need to monitor the elements of fire behavior, like changes in wind speed, wind direction, fuel temperatures, sun and shade conditions, and so on. Remember the fire itself will also impact each factor, causing even greater variation. Your fire suppression strategies, escape routes, and safety zones must dynamically change with the anticipated fire behavior."

Sandy calmed down enough to finish her lunch. She chewed her meat loaf while deep in thought, not the dreamy thought of her youth, but in a much more informed, concentrated manner. Finally, she admitted, "What I heard was the Chief and the Forest Ranger arguing about bulldozing, and then saw what the bulldozers did in contrast to the wildland fire."

Georgeann smiled. "Now you're thinking more openly. It would also be quite useful for Long Island to establish after action reviews for such incidents."

Sandy's eyes lit up. That was just what the Colonel would say.

"As there are a range of tactics available," Georgeann continued, "from width and placement of control lines of which the fire line is part of, to the kinds of bulldozers or fire line plows used, firefighters serve the conservation mission as well."

Jim impatiently cleared his throat. "Time to get back to Logistics, right Georgeann?" How easy it had been for Sandy to move right in on another one of his friends, he silently fumed.

"Oh! I better get back to class," Sandy realized and jumped up from the table.

"Jim you can handle supplies for this afternoon. I'll be joining Sandy's class today to help the instructor," replied Georgeann as she went to bus her tray and down her last bit of coffee. By the time the two entered the classroom, the instructor was making an announcement.

"All right, boys and girls," the instructor said, welcoming them back to class with an announcement. "We're going outside for our field training drills."

"Yes," Sandy cheered. She sprung out of her chair, glad to be doing something more active.

"Break out into three groups," the instructor called after them. "You'll be rotating once through each drill."

Georgeann worked with the first group. "Let's say you're on a wildland fire use management team. You're using wildland fires to meet ecological objectives. Firefighter safety is your primary concern and you have been assigned to monitor fire behavior conditions." She showed them how to measure wind speed first, and then humidity with a sling psychrometer. Each student took a turn with the belt weather kit, while Georgeann kept a watchful eye. When they were finished, she briefly showed them how to use the <u>Fireline Handbook</u> to estimate one hour fuel moisture."

Sandy was in the second group. A young forest ranger handed out encased practice fire shelters, and explained, "Fire shelters are tents designed to protect a firefighter from smoke and heat but not from direct flames. In a real fire situation," he continued, "you must deploy away from forest fuels, especially the fine grasses and any thick brush."

Sandy held the case behind her back pretending it was clipped to her belt for easy deployment. In anticipation, she watched him pull out a stopwatch.

Raising his hand, he said, "Get ready," he shouted. "Go!"

Students pulled out their tents.

Tents unfurled, and flapped in the wind.

"Come on. You've got twenty seconds," the young forest ranger yelled louder.

Sandy held on to her tent despite the wind.

"Fifteen seconds! Get moving. Hurry up!"

Placing the heel of one foot then another into the corners of the tent, Sandy backed in and twisted her body into the formless fire shelter all the while thinking, "I'm not going to make it!"

"Ten seconds!" the forest ranger shouted. He stood over her, waving the stopwatch and yelling, "Fires getting closer, hurry up!"

Hitting the ground hard face forward, she continued to extend her legs and arms outward to the corners of the tent. She kept her nose close to the ground and waited.

"Don't get out no matter what happens!" he shouted. "It'll be hot in your tent, and you'll probably feel as if you're getting burned, but you won't die, not unless you get out of the tent too early."

The light was dim inside and it was starting to get stuffy. Sandy held firm even when the young forest ranger rattled her tent to catch her off guard.

"Stay put," the young forest ranger announced as he moved off to another student. He kept a watchful eye as an older forest ranger handed out fire tools to the third group.

"We can better protect the forest with hand crews as long as fire conditions make this possible. When key fire attack points are selected, you are ready to think about control line locations. The width of the line depends on fire behavior."

He briefly went over sharpening techniques and care before organizing them in a line to clear a simulated fire line in nearby wooded area. The first two cleared leaf litter. Those next in line chopped roots or cut down overhang branches.

"That's it. Keep moving. Don't forget, when flame lengths get over four feet, fire lines are constructed by bulldozers, but be watchful of excessive blading. Better to use existing roads coupled with a burn out to complete the control line."

After about thirty feet, he had them exchange tools and rehab the line by reversing their actions, pulling back roots and debris, and raking back leaf litter. Cut branches were scattered across the fire line.

"That's it. You guys did a great job. Any questions?"

The students standing in the tool usage training area were silent.

"Good. Return your tools and go to fire weather training with Georgeann. Over there," he pointed.

After the three groups rotated through each drill, they returned to class, settling in with their textbooks open. But the instructor surprised them. "That's it for today. Study fire suppression tactics tonight. There will probably be a question or two about fire suppression tactics on the final exam. Those of you taking the physical, get a good night's sleep. We'll plan to start the exam at zero eight hundred and the pack test at ten hundred."

On her way out, Sandy chatted with several classmates.

As they broke up in groups of two and three, Sandy headed out the door. Her mind drifted back over the lessons she learned. Halfway out the door, her eyes lifted. She spotted her mom briskly approaching, with a determined look on her face.

"Mom, what are you doing here?"

Chapter 15

The Team Of One

Emma stared blankly at Sandy. They stood in front of the Wildland Fire Academy entrance. Instead of feeling exhilarated from time planting trees, Emma felt exhausted. Tree planting was now done in a hurry so that she had more time to tend to all the players involved in the politics of fire in the Pine Barrens — players, no longer friends. To remain in the game, Emma had to understand motivations, positions, and positioning.

"Mom! What are you doing here," Sandy repeated. "You can't be here as a Training Specialist. Even if you are qualified, it doesn't matter. Jim got to be part of Academy staff because of his uncle." Nervously fidgeting, back and forth on the heels of her boots, she continued, "I should've told you about Jim sooner, but I was afraid it would've made you upset. Did you know that Wildland Fire Academy positions can be filled with nonqualified individuals? Please don't make a scene!"

"I'm not here to talk about the Wildland Fire Academy," Emma hissed. "There are many players, not just firefighters. There are hikers, bikers, hunters, horseback riders, dog runners, and birders, national organizations, county, state and federal park agencies, and individuals, just like your mother." Emma's eyes became distant. Her friends had become mere players, but it was all part of the game, except lately, she realized, she was having a hard time coping.

"Sandy," she said in an edgy whisper, "The cat's out of the bag. Why didn't you tell me about freelancing?"

"What about it?" Sandy asked. Avoiding her mother's eyes, she brushed her blond hair out of her face.

"Sandy!" Emma snapped. "Word is getting around that my daughter, the firefighter, is showing up unannounced at a series of Rocky Point brush fires. Suspicious eyes are now being cast at me too! Worse still, every available forest ranger, park police officer, and even the county police are on patrol watching out for arsonists. They ask *me* who has been setting these fires!"

Sandy pulled her mom to the side of the entrance, away from the firefighters streaming in and out of the Wildland Fire Academy. "Don't worry so much Mom! I'm chasing fires like we always do," she whispered excitedly. "I just went to one off of Rocky Point Road. There was no wind and the blueberry bushes were greening up and damp with live fuel moisture. With no wind to spread it unevenly, the fire burned out from the point of origin into a ten foot diameter circle! It was so perfect! I filled out a Fire Awareness Report on it too, just like you showed me."

FIRE AWARENESS REPORT

Date: _5/10/06_ Reported by: _Sandy Lewis_

Fire Danger: _Low_ Red Flag? _no_

Fire Location & Name: _Rocky Point - Green Ring Fire_

Coordinates: Lat: _40.929175_ Lon: _-72.941988_

On Site: Fuels, Topography, Weather - Fire Behavior

Fuel Type _trees & low shrubs_ Live Fuels: _spring leaf out_

Topography: _flat_ Temp: _72°_ Humidity: _55%_

Wind Direction/Speed: _no wind_

Severity: _light burn_

Rate of Spread: _creeping_

Flame Lengths: _few inches_

On Site: Response

Size Class: _A_
A(spot-.25) B(.26-9.9) C(10-99) D(100-299) E(300-999) F(1000-4,999) G(5000+)

Resources:_____
brush trucks, stumpjumpers, not sure what else

Fire Line Rehab Needs: _minor stumpjumper damage_

no rehab needed
_____

"You're a firefighter now, and chasing fires is not acceptable – matter of fact, that's freelancing. It's dangerous to show up at an emergency unannounced, alone . . . without a brush truck or fire engine," her mother said firmly.

Determinedly raising her chin and her voice, Sandy said in defense, "I'm always careful. I keep out of the way. All I've been doing is collecting data like you taught me. Tina's even helping, and she's getting really good at it. And Kim found an old GPS for me. I know the teachers at the Academy want us to use maps, but it's useful too. I even borrowed a belt weather kit — until I can get one on my own. I won't forget to give it back, I promise!"

Her mother's stern expression softened. Sandy's Wildland Fire Academy T-shirt, dark jeans, fire boots, and even the beginnings of that facial expression of rugged individualism and adventure made her look more and more like the Western firefighter Emma always imagined her to be. However, Sandy had become a double edged sword, both a strong young woman interested in pursuing fire as a career, and despite her best intentions to keep her out of the politics of fire in the Pine Barrens, a perceived troublemaker. Emma feared her daughter would be stuck with that stigma for years.

Pulling Sandy even further away from the front entrance, she warned, "You must be careful mixing forestry conservation and firefighting. The things we do are . . . are better suited for out West."

"But Mom!" Sandy protested.

Emma took a deep breath. To resolve the immediate dilemma, Emma had spoken with their county's structural fire coordinator. Accidentally, she overheard his annoyance when speaking with his staff, "Please answer her. I know you don't want to, but neither do I." Not willing to accept defeat, she said to Sandy, "Tonight, I will settle this with the Pine Barrens Wildland Fire Task Force."

"By yourself?" Sandy's eyes widened. She knew a little bit about the meetings her mother attended. Her mother had once told her with a wry smile, that a task force was a group of people assigned to do a task and then forced to get it done. As diverse as the water bucket training had been, the Pine Barren's Wildland Fire Task Force included many more fire departments and government officials. Most of her mother's direct involvement, however, had been through smaller committee meetings.

"Will the Colonel be there?" Sandy asked hopefully.

"No, he's on assignment and isn't coming tonight."

"Then I can help!" Before her mother had a chance to say no, Sandy swung her backpack off her shoulder and rummaged around for her full binder of Fire Awareness Reports. "Even if you don't approve of what I'm doing, show them this!" She paused and added, "I want to go to the meeting too, can I?"

Her mother took a moment to leaf through the binder. Despite her misgivings, she was quite impressed by the data collected. "It's about time that the need for this kind of data is discussed openly." She glanced at her watch. "Join me in the cafeteria for a snack, before we go to the meeting."

"Thanks, Mom!" Sandy said grasping her mother's hands.

An hour later, they walked into the meeting room. It was being rearranged, with chairs organized into rows and tables pushed off to the side. They took a seat. Before the meeting started, they stood to recite the Pledge of Allegiance, and to take a moment to remember departed members.

With the minutes from the last meeting were, committee reports came next, including talk of the recent water bucket training drill and their plans for next year. Public Education talked about getting funding for a video on wildland fire prevention and education. And so on, until Sandy's ears perked up when the Fire Danger Committee took center stage. "Hey, Mom that one's your committee, right?"

"In a manner of speaking."

"Aren't you a member of that committee?"

"Shhhh ..."

A slender woman faced them. Behind her was a large table where several of the higher ranking task force members sat. Describing the daily Fire Danger, she said, "We consider red flag warnings, fire weather station data, and fire activity. When there's an increase in brush fire activity being reported, we know we are approaching higher Fire Dangers."

"Taking it to the next level," a firefighter in the middle of the room questioned, "Who is going out on the fire line to get the information back to you?" He understood the woman calculated the daily fire danger from inside an office in front of a computer screen.

A firefighter sitting at the table interceded, "I assist with that. By phone call, several times a week, and if I know someone is having a fire, I call them. 'Look, what do you have?' But you can basically tell by the radio chatter. We try to be on target with our Fire Danger calls, not crying wolf too fast."

"I see," said the firefighter in the middle of the room.

"Mom," Sandy whispered, "why didn't he mention that you also monitor fire activity, fire weather station data, do field checks and call in when you think something's wrong?"

She put a hand on Sandy's shoulder to quiet her.

Sandy fell back in her seat, discouraged. A moment later, she leaned forward and tugged on her mom's sleeve, insisting, "At least tell me why he doesn't call on you?"

"Shhhh . . . " With experience gained from counseling clients, though it was often hard not to take it personally, it was all about the communication on top of the communication – the double meanings of troubling conversations. She had to pay attention, yet what she lacked was public recognition. With recognition came power, influence, and acceptance of one's knowledge.

"But why doesn't he mention your work? They should be giving you credit."

"Keep your mind focused, Sandy, on going out West."

"Why are you bringing that up now?" Sandy snapped.

Several firefighters turned their heads to stare at them.

"Shhhh . . . or we will have to leave."

Stewing until the meeting ended, Sandy rose eagerly to follow her mother to the large table in the front of the classroom. Emma spoke to one of the high ranking task force members directly, introducing them both.

But the recently retired Arson Investigator was a cagey man.

Eyeing Sandy suspiciously, he growled, "Yes, I guess it runs in the family. I know people like you. People who get a kick out of fires, people who chase fires."

"We are interested in studying fire behavior," her mother explained again.

Reluctantly, he said, "O.K., keep going."

"My daughter's a firefighter who can respond to an emergency scene to collect fire behavior data, including the fire's location. I also need to be notified so I can coordinate fire line rehab."

"First of all, let me get this straight. In terms of this meeting, who are you representing?"

"No one."

He gave her a dismissive grunt, picking up his papers and placing them in his briefcase.

"Wait," her mother's voice rose, "You're not understanding me. Maybe I'm not using the right words."

"No," he said harshly. "You listen to me! I've been through this before. You're not going to use our meetings for your interests."

"Whoa! We're not doing this for our own interests," she explained. "It's for the Pine Barrens."

"I don't care about your interests," he said dismissively, ignoring her mother's previous comment.

"Wait a second," her mother called after his fleeing figure.

He turned back, "You're not listening to me. I've seen this before."

"You never, never have," she said defensively, her voice rose, flustered. "No fire department collects this kind of data," she flipped through Sandy's binder full of Fire Awareness Reports. "I'm sure of it!"

"You don't represent any agency. You have no voice here. I've been through this before."

"But my daughter, she's a firefighter."

His turned to stare back at Sandy. "So, she is representing a fire department?"

"No," Sandy said awkwardly.

"I see," he said rudely, and glancing at them, concluded, "Just what I thought."

Sandy felt guilty and hid behind her mom.

"As I told you before, we're not going to support your interests. If her department hasn't been called to the scene, she's not sanctioned to be there either."

"Wait a second. She'll soon be a federally qualified firefighter. Will that do?"

Sandy watched them go at it again. Round two, three, four, neither gave an inch. They spoke two different languages: one spoke about forestry conservation, and the other spoke about emergency management response. Sandy could see both sides of the issue, but couldn't resolve it. Perplexed, she watched them while they argued.

"You're not listening to me. You don't represent anybody. And your daughter isn't sanctioned to be at a fire scene without her fire department. It's a liability issue." He shifted his eyes to Sandy and toned down his voice. "I'm trying to explain to your mother that during fire suppression, the Chief has supreme authority. So when he decides that there needs to be an investigation . . . "

"What do you think I'm asking my daughter to do?" Sandy's mother interrupted, moving in closer. Exasperated, she threw her hands up in the air. "We're only interested in collecting data — something you should be interested in too."

"The only thing that I can tell you," he pointed his finger directly at both of them, "is that if either of you are seen at the scene of an emergency, unsanctioned, you're both going to be arrested!"

Sandy blinked, not knowing if she could be arrested for being at a fire on her own but his threat scared her into thinking that she should be more careful. While her mother, believing that he did have the authority, pulled her daughter away from him in a protective manner.

A fire marshal stood by. He wore a stiff, white shirt and a shiny badge. Considering each side to ease tensions, he warned Emma, "You're opening up a can of worms. What you want can't be easily done. And I can tell you if the Chief at the scene doesn't know either of you, it's not going to work."

"That's why we have a regional task force so that we can figure out a way to include forestry conservation into a firefighter's response protocol. Once resolved, no more fire chasing is needed," Emma concluded.

But the task force leader answered instead, "We're not going to support this. That being said, I understand your daughter interfered with one of the Rocky Point fires. She said she was part of the firefighting operations and went in. Let me tell you something, I have the proof! I will get back to you on that. You better believe it."

"Mom, that's not the way it was!" she whispered. "I asked permission first, and I was dressed in my wildland fire gear."

Frantically, Sandy's mother looked about for support realizing she couldn't fight this battle alone. Butch, whose full time job was managing Rocky Point and the properties around Wildwood Lake as well as many other parcels of state forest land, stood unusually quiet in the back of the room. Though she despised him, the lure of his power and authority took hold of her. She ran over to him.

Sandy eyes opened wider. What was her mother doing?

Butch twirled his mustache and said, "You need to get permission from me and not the fire departments. When there's a fire on state lands and they call for more resources, they have to work with us anyway under a unified command. Your daughter would work under me to collect data."

Emma's eyes opened wide and hopeful, yet Sandy could see her mother's hands were shaking. It was late. The meeting had broken up some time ago. Sandy pulled her exhausted mother out of the classroom and followed her home.

At home, Emma dropped off Sandy's Fire Awareness Reports on her desk. Emma's mocking grew louder. It filled up her office and the living room with nervous barking fits of words. She paced and took on the various roles of the attendees. To Sandy, she sounded like one of those propane tanks on fire, getting hotter and hotter in danger of exploding.

"Mom! Have something to drink!"

Emma went to the kitchen and kept her hands busy turning on the water, and then turning it off, looking for a clean glass in the sink, and then opening and closing cabinets. Sandy went into the kitchen to help. They both drank water for some time before Sandy asked deliberately, "Mom, why did you ask Butch for help?"

"To protect you from being accused of freelancing, sometimes you have to team up with the wrong people."

"But he hasn't ever thought about you before. Do you think he'd really call now, Mom? Like if there's a really big fire, even if it's under a unified command with him being part of it, do you think he'd really call?"

Emma shrugged. "This is what happens when you stand alone and speak out for what you know is right. You know it is right in your heart and in what you research. Yet, you take what you can get. They listen sometimes. They involve you at other times. That's the way it goes for an environmental advocate." With a crazed look in her eyes, she said with twisted pride, "Did I tell you how the state forest ranger now listens to the person I trained, but not me?!"

Sandy thought about the Colonel. What would he do? Why did her mother always stand alone? She reached for her mother, but Emma pulled away. The phone rang. By the time Emma navigated her way to her office, the caller hung up. In frustration, she shouted, "I hate the Pine Barrens," and swept her hand right across her desk. Papers, pens, books, binders and field guides clattered to the floor. Sandy rushed in and raised her hands to her head.

Feeling the pressure in her head ease, Emma turned to Sandy explaining, "I study. I think. I evaluate. I offer my knowledge to make the Pine Barrens better. What for? Finely crafted instruments should never be played the way I've been played! You deserve better. That is why I am sending you to college out West."

Tears rolled down Sandy's face. "I don't want to go to Colorado. Billy's going to be a firefighter in New York and live on Long Island. Tina and Kim will be staying here too. Most of those firefighters I've met at the Wildland Fire Academy drift from place to place. I don't want to be that way. And besides," she bit her lip, "I got accepted to community college. I've been meaning to tell you."

Without skipping a beat, Emma said, "For your first year that will be fine. Colorado will have to wait until the following year. Meantime, we can sign you up to take your refresher out there and we'll visit colleges together."

"Mom, you're not listening to me. The Colonel says, 'Whatever it takes.' I want to live on Long Island and be a forest friendly firefighter."

"Have you been training for the pack test? It won't be as easy for you as you are a smaller woman. I should've ordered you a professional weight vest and got you a trainer."

"Mom," Sandy said softly, "I'll be okay." Then with a twinkle in her eye, she lowered her voice in imitation of the Colonel and made up her own Colonelism, "There are no teams of one."

Emma looked deeply into Sandy's eyes.

Sandy placed her hand upon her mother's shoulder to offer comfort. "There must be a way to recognize the many who stand alone like you. You need not stand alone anymore."

"Sandy," her mother responded, "You're not a child any more, are you? And now you're teaching me."

Sandy smiled in relief.

Emma fondly picked up her daughter's binder full of Fire Awareness Reports. Sandy reached down to help her pick up the rest of the papers, pens, book and field guides that had scattered on the floor.

"Beep ... Beep ... Beep ... " Sandy's fire pager sounded, "Signal 13, 112 Sexton Street."

Sandy dropped the book she had been holding. It hit the desk hard. She recognized the address.

"Mom, that's Tina's house! Will you be okay?"

Urgently, her mother said, "Yes. Go, hurry!"

Chapter 16
Girly Girl

Not knowing that she would soon be facing fire for the first time in her life and that it would be in her own house, Tina's morning life went on as usual. It was Sunday. Sandy was doing map and compass work at the Wildland Fire Academy. The Pine Barrens Wildland Fire Task Force hadn't met yet. Tina's younger brother, Jeffrey, thought it would be funny to put a rubber cockroach in Tina's breakfast bowl. Tina let out a squeal pretending she was horrified, as she knew this was the reaction he wanted. He almost fell out of his chair giggling. Jeffrey laughed so hard, milk started to come out of his nose.

"Eewwww . . . " squeaked Tina, "You're so gross."

"At least I'm not a girl," said Jeffrey, throwing another rubber bug at her.

Tina ducked and it hit Jack, their older brother as he came into the kitchen for breakfast.

Jeffrey and Tina howled with laughter.

"Knock it off, Jeffrey!" said Jack.

Jack looked at Tina with a serious expression on his face, "Tina, can't you even handle your stupid little brother?"

Jeffrey went back to eating his breakfast.

Tina carried her dishes to the sink as tears welled up in her eyes. Compared to her older brother's words, Jeffrey's pranks were easy to endure. She forced a sweet smile, strode back to her younger brother to scruff up his hair, "Well at least I know how to make him laugh. I should be better able to handle him, but he's so irresistible."

Tina twirled around the kitchen, singing the lyrics to the song, "Simply Irresistible." The two boys laughed. More at ease again, Tina carried the rest of the dirty dishes to the kitchen sink and washed them. Making sure Jack had his fill of breakfast, she settled into their Sunday morning routine.

"Here, Tina," Jack handed her his empty bowl. Grabbing an apple off the table's fruit bowl, he went into the living room to their family computer set off on a table in the corner.

"You'll watch after Jeffrey, won't ya Jack, until Mom wakes up?"

"Sure, Tina." Chomping on his apple, he called back, "Have fun at the firehouse," and in the gossiping tone Tina used with their mother, added, "with the guys."

"Don't worry yourself about that," she said.

The drill was uneventful. It was an engine check.

On Monday, Tina eagerly listened to Kim relaying Sandy's chatter about the Wildland Fire Academy during lunch. Later that evening, Tina drove down to the firehouse with the black sedan Jack had rigged with blue firefighter lights. Being the sister of an auto mechanic had certain advantages, she realized.

The ferry whistle blew and she caught a glimpse of it pulling out of the harbor. Sandy was home studying for her wildland firefighter class and Kim was studying for an exam. Reluctantly, Tina got on her gear and met Company Two in the parking lot behind the firehouse. Being a probationary firefighter meant she had to rotate through the companies and this was a required drill.

The ladder drill was already underway. "Remember to watch out for overhead electrical lines," warned the Captain. Two firefighters positioned the ladder below the window of the annex building. A cute guy came out of the village grocery, and Tina stared, distracted. "Tina," the Captain said. "Is the ladder at the right angle?"

"Oh, sorry." She faced the ladder and extended her arms. "For the ladder to be at the correct angle for climbing, one's arms need to be resting level on the ladder rung . . . Yes, sir."

"Good."

Five guys took turns handling the ladder. Next was a firefighter who painted houses for a living. He flung the ladder up and positioned it easily.

"I bet he's got great arms," commented Tina, but no one was listening except the Captain.

"Come on Tina," the Captain said.

With the butt of the ladder against the building, she went to the other end. She squirmed her way under the ladder. Easy at first, she walked toward the building with the ladder over her head, rung by rung. But by the time she reached the halfway point, she cried, "I can't do it!"

The firefighter who painted houses for a living took her place. Up went the ladder. He hefted it lightly against the wall. Tina bent down to pull out the butt of the ladder away from the wall, and stood up. Feeling overpowered and helpless, she commented, "I guess I just need to start working out with the guys at the gym." No one paid her any attention.

When it was her turn again, the objective was to stand on the butt end of the ladder which was sticking out from the wall, grab a rung, lean back, and lift the far end of the ladder which was now pointed at the wall. With both hands she held on to the ladder rungs, grunted and leaned back as hard as she could. Two firefighters were waiting to guide the ladder upwards against the building. She fell backwards onto her rump, "Ouch."

No one laughed.

She felt like a fool anyway.

Glad to finish the drill, she left for home, not wanting to speak to anyone. Before her brothers noticed, she went upstairs and closed her bedroom door for some peace and quiet. Her bedroom walls were painted in a soft shade of pink. The furniture was white wicker with pink rosebuds painted on it. Fluffy teddy bears, in pastel colors of light pink, blue, yellow, and white, were piled on the bed and the dresser.

Tina undressed, discarding her sweaty clothes into a white wicker hamper beside her dresser, and grabbed a towel hanging behind the door slung over a full length mirror. She went off to take a shower and returned feeling much better. In her walk-in closet were neatly hung dresses, skirts with floral prints and designs, pink and white sneakers, and lots of sandals. She picked out a spring dress and a pair of sandals. Reaching into her vanity table drawer, she took out her makeup and combed her hair using the lighted makeup mirror on the vanity. She spent some more quiet time putting on makeup, carefully selecting the shades of pink for her eye shadow, cheeks, and lips.

Firefighting wasn't on her mind for the rest of the evening nor on Tuesday, the day Sandy practiced the deployment of her fire shelter. By the time Tina got home from school and Sandy was just about to meet her mother at the Wildland Fire Academy, Tina took off her shoes to feel her room's soft pink shag carpet. She had a subscription to several girly magazines since she was ten. She picked one of her favorites from the bottom of her closet, and flopped down on her bed, hugging the white teddy bear.

"Beep!" rang her pager. It was another boat fire down by the marina.

She deliberately ignored it.

About an hour later, her cell phone rang.

"Hey," said Tina.

"How'd it go?!" asked Kim excitedly.

"How did what go?"

"You heard the pager go off didn't you?"

"Yeah, but I was busy."

"What?! You mean you didn't go to the boat fire?!"

"Well, no."

"Oh Tina, you were probably just reading one of your girly magazines again."

Tina closed the magazine on her lap.

"Gotta go. I'm at the firehouse. Billy just signed for his point. I gotta talk to him. Bye."

"Right," said a relieved Tina.

Some time ago, Tina began to openly admit, to herself anyway, that she was really afraid of fire. She stood up and paced. Most of the alarms were false anyway, but the odds were starting to go against her as she'd been responding to so many minor alarms. One day it would be a real working fire. What would she do then? It was scary running into a building knowing how quickly fire could spread.

Modern homes were air tight and filled with plastics instead of old fashioned wood furniture. The fire would be five hundred times hotter, she learned. And there was such a thing as black fire: smoke so hot it could burn without the firefighter ever seeing the flames. Unlike fanatical Kim and Sandy, she was scared of facing a real fire. Sometimes, when her pager rang, she waited to see if the fire was real or another false alarm before responding. It was working. But what if she guessed wrong?

Picking up the magazine on her bed, she flipped through it again. She didn't know how to back out of being a firefighter because Sandy needed help with her Fire Awareness Reports, and Kim needed help coping with her dad at the firehouse. Despite her loyalty to them, nagging thoughts of quitting continued. Firefighting was the last thing she'd ever thought she'd be doing.

Staring at the pinned up magazine cover of the hottest teen heartthrobs on the wall, she dreamed of romance instead of firefighting until her mom called to her.

"Tina, it's time for dinner."

Sitting down to their usual Tuesday night macaroni and cheese dinner, Tina complained to her parents about Jeffrey's little prank.

"Mom, Jeffrey put a cockroach in my bowl Sunday morning."

"A what? Where did he get that?" asked her mom, sounding alarmed.

"Oh, come off it. Tina. It was only a FAKE bug," spat back Jeffrey.

"Well, it was still gross," said Tina.

"Jeffrey," their father considered. "Aren't you getting a little too old to be teasing your sister?" Winking at Tina, he teased, "When are you gonna get a girlfriend?"

"I hate girls," snapped Jeffrey, who was only nine.

Jack decided to say something while he took a second serving of macaroni and cheese. "You should have seen these kids Sunday morning. I wish I had my own apartment!"

Pouring himself another large glass of milk, he added, "I'm over 21, it's time for me to have my own space."

"I need you around the house," said their mother. "Besides, you know what kind of trouble you would get into on your own."

Tina thought it would be great if Jack moved out. The older he got, the more he acted like he was the man of the house when her parents weren't around. When the meal was done, Tina put the dishes away and went back to her room. Sometime in the middle of the night the pager went off, and she shut it off. She buried her head under the blankets, not getting up, feeling guilty. When she finally fell asleep, she dreamt she had responded to a fire call carrying her teddy bears instead of fire tools. She even smelled smoke. Dreamily, she considered why she should smell smoke if it was only part of her dream. She stirred in bed, yawning and realized she smelled smoke for real!

She jumped out of bed, tossed off her pink nightgown, and grabbed one of Jack's hand-me-down flannel shirts and sweat pants, set aside for her responding to alarms. She slipped into a pair of sneakers and went to open her bedroom door. She remembered to touch its surface. It felt cool to the touch. No fire in the hallway she thought.

"No fire in the hallway," she repeated and woke up completely. "What am I saying? There's a fire in my house!" Immediately her heart started pounding as she imagined the worst. Her mind played tricks on her. Flames would soon engulf her and her family. Somehow, she managed to find her cell phone to call 9-1-1.

Out in the hallway, without her air pack and mask, the smoke was intense enough to make her eyes tear up immediately and sting. She dropped to her knees and crawled over to her young brother's bedroom and felt the coolness of the door before yanking it open.

Crawling into the room, she felt for him in his bed, but the bed was empty!

"Jeffrey! Where are you?!"

"In the closet."

"What are you doing in the closet?"

"I smelled smoke and got scared."

"Come out!"

"It's not safe!" He cried.

She pulled open the closet door and grabbed him.

"Tina, you won't be angry with me, will you?

"Why should I be?"

"I think I started the fire! I didn't mean to. I woke up hungry and put some pizza in the toaster oven and went back to my room to wait until it was done." He coughed. "I fell asleep. Don't get mad. I'm sorry."

"Don't worry about that now," she said, forcing herself to be calm. Out in the hallway, she told him, "Stay low and follow me. Put your hand on my back so you won't lose me."

"O.K. Tina," he whimpered.

She went into her parents' bedroom next.

Her dad jumped out of bed.

Her mom sobbed, "A fire! We'll lose everything."

"Dad, we have to get out of the house," Tina shouted. As she gently pulled her mom out into the hallway, Jack reached his parent's bedroom.

Their father followed quickly behind.

Jeffrey was still clinging to Tina's flannel shirt.

"Jack," shouted Tina to her older brother. "Get behind and follow us out!"

Down the stairs, the family fled.

"Tina," her father said. "There's the fire. It's the toaster oven!"

"Uh . . . oh," confirmed Jeffrey.

"It's not his fault," sobbed her mother, "I heard Jeffrey in the kitchen."

"I did too," Jack admitted, cursing at himself for not watching after his little brother.

As they got closer to the fire, Tina grabbed the industrial sized fire extinguisher in the hallway, the one her brother had given to her as a present the day she went on probation. The fire in the toaster oven lit the corners of the empty pizza box on top of the toaster oven and was about to climb higher. Her heart pounded. In an otherwise dark kitchen, the flames lent a dull orange glow. The heat and smoke intensified. Sirens blared in their driveway and emergency lights reflected in the hallway mirror.

Tina shouted, "Everyone out! Follow me!" They crept into the living room as Tina let go of the fire extinguisher, making the decision that it was more important for her to get her family out of the house safely.

Outside, Kim left her hiding place to stand by Tina. "Are you O.K.?" Her father was out on a date with her mom. She was supposed to home watching her younger brother.

Holding on to her family tightly, Tina couldn't look Kim in the eye. "I couldn't face the fire. I saw it, and I had the fire extinguisher in my hand and let it go," she mumbled.

Billy and Jim went in as first and second man on the hose.

Moments later, while the six of them stood waiting in the front yard under a moonlit night, the officer radioed back to the Chief, "The fire's out. I need mop up crew to check for any fire extension." Sandy was about to rush over to Tina, when her

Captain told her to stop feeding hose line and help with setting up the exhaust fans.

Half an hour later, a Signal 8, refreshments, arrived in the Fire Police van. Only then did Sandy find an opportunity to rush over to Tina, as did Billy who grabbed four drinks. By then the Chief had announced it was safe to go back in, but Tina lingered outside with her friends.

Jim glanced over at the four of them chatting. Continuing to pack hose, his eyes turned back to stare at Tina astonished. Without her make up and perfectly styled hair, he was strangely attracted to this natural, real Tina wearing an oversized flannel shirt over baggy sweats.

"Tina," Billy said in admiration. "You kept your head, called 9-1-1, and got everyone out safely."

Kim added, "Wow. Tina. You're one up on me now. You've been in a real fire."

"Me too," chimed in Sandy who pulled Kim off to the side, reminding her that she had shown up at the fire scene on her own. "You should go home," she warned.

Billy stayed with Tina.

"Don't you guys understand, Billy? I'm not like any of you. Even tonight in my own house when I could've used the fire extinguisher in my hand, I dropped it and ran out. You know," she finally unloaded her dark secret, "I've been missing fire alarm calls, getting there late just to sign for the point, and only riding the engine when it was probably a minor alarm. I'm not like you guys. I'm not a firefighter! Who am I kidding? I was thinking about quitting." Tina gave Billy one of her girly girl looks, an involuntary helpless response when feeling overwhelmed.

For the first time, he realized that her good looks were as much of an impediment as his. Billy's face got serious. "Lots of firefighters are afraid of interior firefighting."

Tina eyes opened wide. Her jaw dropped. "Really? I thought it was only me."

"No, it's not only you, Tina."

"It doesn't matter. I won't ever think of myself as a real firefighter, like you guys."

"Tina . . . " Billy said, momentarily lost for any more words to say until his eyes twinkled with a lesson he could pass on from the Colonel. "There's no 'I' in team."

"T-E-A-M," Tina spelled out. "No 'I' in team," she repeated. Glancing back at Jim who was busy packing hose, she told Billy, "But *some* guys at the firehouse don't think of me that way. They don't trust me as a firefighter. And I wouldn't trust them with my life either."

Billy winced. "I trust you," he said. "You kept your head and did the right thing during this working fire . . . As for firefighting, pick something you feel comfortable with and get good at, like getting water to the fire. That's an important job. Study hard and practice at it. Train with both engine companies. Real firefighters don't always have to be on the nozzle. You can learn to work the hydrant and get better at understanding the pump on the engine."

Tina gave in. "I'll think about it." She yawned. "Sorry, it's late."

Let's go," Sandy's Captain called. "Billy, you can ride back with us on Engine Two. The Ladder Truck has left."

On the way to the engine Billy said to Sandy, "I'll help with filling the air bottles and cleaning the masks back at the firehouse. You've got your tests tomorrow."

"Yeah, you're right," she yawned. "It's been a long day for me too."

Jim couldn't help himself. He eyed Tina once more before climbing into Engine Three. Surprised by the way he felt; he was also embarrassed. "What if she noticed?" he paused to think.

Chapter 17

9/11 Revisited

The following day, Jim forgot about Tina. He and Georgeann, busy with coordinating resources and supply needs for the Wildland Fire Academy, took a needed breakfast break. Georgeann spotted her father and Butch in the cafeteria and took a seat. Calling out to Jim, she said, "Come on over." They sat around a large table with plenty of room. "We've been talking about next year's classes. Thought you might want to listen in."

"Sure thing," Jim said. He sat down in front of his plate stacked with pancakes and eggs.

"I don't know where you put that," Georgeann's father said, eyeing his skinny frame. "Back when I was your age I was already showing signs of a tub around the waist."

Jim laughed, at ease. He could see it now, getting in tight with her, her father and others. In a few years, he would be fitting in just like Georgeann at the wildland fire academies and federal emergencies. It was just as his uncle had promised. Already he felt that he was more than a kid in high school.

Georgeann patted her father's belly, "That's why I'm really here. It's to keep an eye on what you eat for breakfast."

"Never mind that," the Incident Commander said as he pushed away his partially eaten bowl of cottage cheese and fruit. "What I was saying, Butch, is that you've got to teach these local fire departments how to respond to forest fires. You got to keep offering the wildland urban interface course despite the low enrollment. The structural guys protect the homes and the wildland firefighters will protect your Pine Barrens."

Jim gave him a considered comment, "Long Island firefighters respond to both. We risk our lives to get brush fires out fast. Wildland fires are out West. The Sunrise Fire was an exception."

The Incident Commander shook his head. "What you do get here are some pretty decent wildland fires. But you've got stump jumpers knocking down trees for access. You could use some training in burn out to a designated fire line. You mop up with stump jumpers instead of having firefighters getting off their butts and use hand tools to go easy on the land. And you don't pre establish transition teams or a unified command system. Sounds like a cluster . . ., uhmm, a bad situation waiting to happen."

Jim wasn't really into wildland fire suppression tactics. But it soured him to hear Long Island firefighters being put down. He opened his mouth, "The Chief's in charge, not cowboys with Western ideas on how to fight Eastern brush fires."

"Jim! Watch your mouth!" Butch snapped and apologized to the IC, "Please excuse him. He's a bit hot headed."

Jim pushed back his chair and stood up to leave.

"Just talking tactics, son — sit down," commented the IC. Turning to Butch he added, "You do need that wildland urban interface class. I can see that. Long Island needs to learn how to fight fires like the rest of us. Their methods didn't work during the Sunrise Fire. Lucky no one got killed staging at the head of the fire that way."

Georgeann could see it in Jim's eyes, and then in his entire body. Though his remarks to her father had been rude, he was still just a kid expressing old school thinking. But her father, he should know better! She quickly interceded, "Dad, it's really different on Long Island. Stump jumpers work well in areas without topography, at least most of the time. Maybe rework the class to get better alignment between forestry conservation and local firefighting tactics?"

Begrudgingly, her father admitted, "Well, maybe. Long Island has a damn good record on safety and house protection. We could sure learn from them. They just got to get their forestry firefighting tactics squared away." Taking a look at his watch, he said, "Oops, gotta go."

"Me too," said Georgeann.

Butch faced Jim squarely. His face gnarled with anger, "What makes you think you're such a hotshot as to embarrass me in front of the Incident Commander?"

"I was just clueing him in on what we think of those guys from out West," said Jim. He couldn't help it if his uncle was no firefighter and missed the point. Jim shrugged.

Butch pointed his finger directly at Jim. "Who gives a crap about what you think? As I told you before, you're to keep your mouth shut. I tell you what to think!" Butch took a long breath, "Being my nephew is one thing, son, but insubordination is another. I've already explained this to you before . . . You get in tight with these boys and you're set."

Jim shoved a bite of pancake in his mouth to ward off his anger. Chewing furiously for several long seconds, he calmed down. His uncle was no Chief. And even if he were, he'd be lousy at it. Jim wouldn't be the only one complaining. Sooner or later, he'd get the point. Thinking of Georgeann who had spoken up for him during breakfast, he now considered that he should do the same for her. Begrudgingly, he admitted, "Yeah, I guess you're right. I'll make it right with the guy. It's no big deal."

Butch's anger didn't subside as easily. "You . . . you just guess I'm right?" he stammered. "Maybe I should drop you from my Wildland Fire Academy, if you really feel that way."

Jim stopped eating and pushed his food away. "That's a bit extreme!"

"You'll have to fend for yourself in the fire service as you see fit." He turned to leave.

"Uncle Butch! That's not fair! Please don't do that . . . "

"I'll tell Georgeann the assignment was too much for you and that she should go ahead and find someone else," he announced as he walked off.

Seeing that Jim was following him, Butch kept at it. "We don't need you in Logistics. We'll work on getting someone else for the rest of the week."

Jim eyes opened wide when his uncle turned around. His long arms fell awkwardly to his side, and his confidence faded at the thought of being isolated from the decent firefighters he had already met with Georgeann's help.

Momentarily resting his arm over Jim's shoulder, he confided, "Show me how well you can do what you're told, and I'll think about it."

With hands in his pockets, Jim bowed his head and took off to Supplies, while his uncle stopped by the registration desk to speak with his staff. But no one ever gave Butch advice he didn't want to hear. They absolutely assured him that he was right about Jim. Satisfied, his next stop was T-shirt sales.

"I think we should be offering last year's T-shirts at a discounted price."

"Yes sir, that's a great idea, Butch. Why didn't I think of it?"

"Good, set it up," Feeling more at ease, Butch went outside to supervise the pack test as planned.

Sandy finished her Wildland Firefighter Academy written exam and handed it in. Relieved, she went outside to get a change of clothes and her backpack. For the pack test, each student was required to carry 45 pounds on their backs for three miles in 45 minutes.

"Hey! Billy! I didn't expect to see you!"

"Oh, I was just driving by," he teased. "Anyhow, it's Teacher's Professional Day." Walking over to her, he asked, "So how was the exam?"

"Piece of cake."

"Sandy, did you speak with Tina this morning? How's she doing?" Billy asked. He took hold of her backpack weighted down with the bags of sand.

"Tina called before I left. She's doing fine."

Sandy reached for her change of clothes and a pair of sneakers.

At the Wildland Fire Academy's entrance, Billy offered, "I'll leave your weighted backpack by the doorway. I know you can't eat anything now, but I'll get us some drinks and sandwiches from the cafeteria for later."

"Thanks, Billy. I'll meet you back here in a few minutes."

As Sandy went off to change clothes and then to check in with one of the forest rangers, Billy had returned from the cafeteria and spotted Jim. "Hey! I'll see you at the boat drill later, right?

"Yeah, sure."

We can check out the new boat deck gun." A boat deck gun was a water nozzle that delivered large amounts of water.

"I gotta work, Jim answered, expressionless, showing none of his prior enthusiasm or interest in discussing firefighting tactics and equipment with Billy. He held a slide projector for the wildland urban interface course in his hands.

"What's up? I was really looking forward to the boat drill," Billy said alarmed. He had always assumed Jim would be there for him.

Shifting the projector he carried, his shoulder slumped discouraged, "Same old, same old."

Before Billy could think of anything else to say, Jim took off to the classroom. Billy turned away too, and headed back outside to watch the pack test where Sandy was getting her pack weighed along with her classmates. When they assembled at the starting line, wearing an assortment of sunglasses, caps, running shorts, T-shirts and weighted backpacks, Billy wished Sandy a brief, "Good luck."

Butch raised the stop watch. "On my mark, ready, go."

And they were off. The taller, leaner guys took the lead. Everyone else spread out. Sandy fell behind. Pounding the ground, she strode faster and faster.

"Sandy, no running," shouted one of the attending forest rangers, "or you will be disqualified!"

She readjusted her pace. Women passed her by too. Their walking strides were quick, long and natural. Sandy tightened her backpack straps and readjusted her stride again.

"Go Sandy, keep on going," shouted Billy waving his arms a few blocks ahead.

Sandy bowed her head down and strode on even harder, shortening her stride, doubling her pace, and making sure she kept walking.

The route went from the Wildland Fire Academy down the main road which was closed to traffic for three blocks, and then to the right for two blocks, back onto a dirt road. After passing a tall white pine and one more turn, it was a straight shot to the finish line. The students had to lap the route four times.

It was a sunny, dry day. Windy too, maybe a good day for a wildland fire, Sandy considered. There wasn't much more to think about. Forty-five minutes was a long time. She focused on her stride. By the end of her second lap, she was just a short distance behind. It was grueling. "I must keep pushing . . . forward . . .faster . . . faster." These thoughts, now ever present, kept her feet moving. She had been practicing for twenty to thirty minutes a day, not forty-five. Halfway into her third lap, the exertion was taking its toll. She had fallen back, but so had several others. It was difficult to gauge how she was doing.

Butch had repositioned himself by the finish line, shouting out lap times, and words of encouragement, "Doing good. You need to keep up that pace, keep going."

Sandy couldn't tell if she was doing fine or if she had to speed up. She was just behind a tight pack of four students when all of them entered into the fourth and final lap. Sandy had no trouble with the weight on her back. It felt light, contrary to her legs. Today her legs handicapped her much more than the forty-five pounds could ever do. Every time someone passed her she felt like giving up. Onto the dirt road and now under the tall white pine, two more firefighters strode confidently passed her. She could go no faster. Her knees hurt from putting so much pressure on them.

Billy jumped out of nowhere to race the final block with her. Encouraging her to keep moving, he yelled, "Go, go, go! Don't stop!"

Sandy strutted, sweated, and gritted her teeth. Concentrating on the last stretch of road, Butch clocked in her final time. "I finished," shouted Sandy unclipping her backpack and dropping it to the ground. She clung to Billy, exhausted.

"Did you hear your time?" Billy didn't quite know how to break it to her. Butch was off congratulating those that passed the pack test.

"Well, no. I made it right?"

"Your time was 47.23."

It took a moment to register. She was still breathing hard. Oh no, 47 was greater than 45! "That can't be right! I didn't make it?"

Billy shook his head, "But I'm sure you can train and retake the pack test when you're ready."

Sandy wasn't listening. She wasn't used to failing. She was used to winning. How could she have failed at this? She knew she aced the final exam. Failing the pack test meant she wouldn't be qualified to fight wildland fires out West. To her surprise, instead of disappointment, she felt relieved. All the fret and worry about going out West lifted away. And there was Billy. He stood by her side, encouraging her regardless. She reached up to kiss him.

Startled, Billy wrapped his arms closer around her in an embrace.

"Let's get out of here," whispered Billy when they pulled apart.

Aware of her surroundings again, Sandy agreed, "But where?"

"Why don't you show me where you've been planting?" He asked playfully.

"We plant all over the Pine Barrens," giggled Sandy. "Wherever it's needed."

Billy reached down for her weighted backpack. He waited for her in the parking lot while she changed. When Sandy returned she was much less giddy. Billy thought that the moment they had shared was gone. He struck up a conversation to ensure otherwise.

"So when you plant these trees, you're doing a sort of emergency response operation?"

Sandy was relieved to have something else to talk about. "We call it fire line rehab."

She tossed her clothes in the back of her pickup.

"Do you still want to go?" Sandy asked shyly in the momentary awkward silence.

"I've got the drinks and sandwiches, ready and waiting."

"It's on the way back. It won't take long."

They stopped at the planting her mom recently organized. Dozens of dead trees were thrown across the bulldozed fire cut and in between, volunteers had planted thousands of pitch pine seedlings. Walking along, Sandy took on the role of a naturalist without thinking, "Pitch pines are all around us. Three needles are in a bundle, see? A white pine has five. And here's a blueberry bush. Green stems identify them now because they aren't in flower yet, nor with fruit."

"You mean like the same blueberries we buy in the store? Are you sure these aren't poisonous?"

"Of course they aren't," she laughed. "I've been eating them all my life, and I'm strong and healthy!" He followed her as she ran lightly along the trail, jumping over a fallen tree. "Oh, look, some trailing arbutus, and it's in flower! See the tiny pink flowers tucked in between the furry green leaves." She pulled Billy down to smell the sweet blossoms.

"Such a tiny flower! What a strong sweet smell. It's as pretty as you," Billy chanced to say.

Sandy flashed a smile. "Oh, I'm not pretty. Pretty blondes are tall, and I'm short."

"Your smile puts those tall girls to shame."

She laughed, "Come on, silly!" She grabbed his hand and pulled him along the trail to the 9/11 Memorial. The young trees looked healthy and strong. "See how these older planted trees are doing? This one already has pine cones? And this one is standing so tall! And these little guys must be three years old already!" She knelt down to study them more closely.

"Did you plant them all with your mom?"

"No. We have help. I missed this year's planting 'cause we were at a department drill. But last year I was with my mom. Mostly, for this site, we get help from the 9/11 Planters. We call them the 9/11 Planters because this is the 9/11 Memorial."

Not feeling Billy's presence, she looked up and said, "Billy, what's wrong?" Surprised to see his sullen expression, it made her stop and think. She brushed the sand from her knees and stood up. It was then that she remembered.

"Billy, I'm so sorry I took you here. This is one of my favorite places, but I could've showed you dozens of others we've planted. I wasn't thinking."

"That's O.K.," he said quietly, but he continued to distance himself, taking long strides down the slope to the bottom of the hollow.

Sandy felt stupid for being so insensitive. Billy's father was actually in New York City, responding as a firefighter, on September 11, 2001. She tried to imagine the empty space where the towers had been in the same way she felt about the Pine Barrens being bulldozed. She ran closer to him.

Billy finally confided, "I've never really talked to anyone about it."

Sandy walked with him, leading him gently away from the hollow to the overlook.

"I was confused at first. My dad wasn't killed. He just kinda faded."

"What do you mean kinda faded?"

"After the second plane hit the Twin Towers, my dad led his men into a parking garage before the full force of the collapsing towers could hit them. Even so, it knocked them all the way back into the garage where my dad hit his head. He said an angel helped them find a safe way out." Billy paused to look at the large solitary tree swaying in the wind. "Hey, that's a pitch pine?"

"Yes. And that grass below is actually a sedge."

"The trees you planted will get that tall?" Billy asked quite impressed.

"Hope so, but go on. What happened next?"

Billy laid on his back with his arms under his head. He closed his eyes briefly listening to the wind blowing through the trees. It sounded very much like the changing tide, rhythmic but with variations. A passing car would be a steady sound rising and falling as it passed by. In the Pine Barrens, the wind began as a whisper gaining strength, from a slight rustling of oak leaves to a vast sighing of pitch pines. The wind would then lessen in time to a whisper again.

At last he spoke, "My dad lost his nerve."

"What do you mean?" Sandy asked sitting beside him, knees up and arms wrapped around her legs.

"After they got out of the garage, he stopped to rescue a downed firefighter and told his crew to wait for him back at the engine. He made it to the ambulance, only to collapse. It wasn't supposed to happen that way. He meant to get back to the engine. But the ambulance carted him off too — with restraints. As it turned out, he had a head injury."

Sandy put her hand on Billy's shoulder, "I don't understand. His crew was safe. He made the right decisions."

"That's not what he thinks. He blames himself for letting his men down. He said he would come back for them and he never did. That's the way it is. If you're in command, you never let those under your command down. Jim was so distant today at the Wildland Fire Academy, because of what I've done." Billy turned to her, saying, "I know how frustrated you are at the firehouse. I feel responsible."

In the shared silence, still bothered by the fact that she didn't pass the physical part of her course, Sandy drew a stick figure in the sand and put a pebble on it for its backpack.

"Hey! I've got an idea!" Billy felt the Colonel's confidence, authority and friendship, as if he walked out of the 9/11 Memorial to the overlook with them. Billy pointed to the stick figure. "You can train for the pack test as if it were a race. Did you know that a runner's stride is less determined by his height? There's ways to improve your stride if you think of it from a runner's point of view. Some say short runners are even more efficient."

"Really?" Sandy brushed aside the stick figure and stood up. "Okay, I'll try."

"I shouldn't be afraid to lead again either, right Sandy? . . . I mean, he'd say, 'Leadership is a trait to be developed.' The Colonel expects us to keep up with our studies."

"Yes, sir!" Sandy saluted.

They both laughed at Sandy's silly salute.

Turning back, they held hands.

Unlike the North shore with a gusty cold front passing through, the sheltered hollow faced south and was quite warm. Billy and Sandy ate their lunch in the hollow of the 9/11 Memorial.

As they climbed back up to the main trail, Billy leaned down to set straight a planted pitch pine run over by one of the lost stump jumpers. He packed the soil firmly around it.

Sandy took a pen and strip of paper out of her pack and wrote, "in memory of those departed." She buried it beneath the little pitch pine.

Billy broke the silence, reluctantly saying, "I have to go."

They retraced their steps back down the trail to their parked trucks. Before driving off, Billy briefly kissed Sandy. They held on to each other, until Billy pulled away.

Sandy's eyes dimmed.

"Hey, I'll see you later at the firehouse."

"Sure thing." Sandy flashed a happy smile. She hopped into her pickup and drove off.

Moments later, Billy drove off confidently thinking, "I told Jim I'd be at the boat drill. He'll turn up. He always does."

But Jim would never make it to the boat drill.

Chapter 18

Boat Drill

After brushing off Billy and dropping off the slide projector requested by the wildland urban interface course, Jim overheard two instructors laughing. It was another sideways comment about the Sunrise Fire and Long Island firefighters. Jim clamped his mouth shut, not knowing who to be loyal to as he headed back to Supplies and took a seat. The last thing on his mind was the boat drill. He stared aimlessly at the ceiling. Georgeann eventually caught up with him.

"Hey, I thought you quit."

"I was delivering a slide projector," he said not making eye contact. In a pleasant voice, Georgeann responded, "It's the rumor mill around here. You know how it gets. I should have asked you directly." She sat down next to him. "Are you getting the hang of which forms need to be filled out?"

"Yes." He pointed out the one he just completed for the slide projector request.

"Seems like we're caught up here. I was heading out to make my rounds. Interested in connecting with the rest of the medical and communications units? They'd be happy to go over any questions you might have."

"Nah. I'm busy." He busied himself with straightening some forms and boxes. All he could think about was his uncle. "Son," his uncle had said. "If you want to play with the big boys you must know the ropes and keep your mouth shut — no matter what you think."

"Suit yourself. Later."

Jim felt like an idiot and was grateful when Georgeann left. Hanging around, doing nothing, he started sorting supplies. But that made him feel even more incompetent. He restacked boxes, not caring and not thinking. After an hour of feeling miserable, he couldn't take it anymore. Impulsively, he left a note for Georgeann, making up some lame excuse, and took off.

Cranking up his brown sedan's stereo, he drummed his fingers on the dashboard. What's his mother going to say when he tells her what a jerk his uncle really is. But Jim wasn't ready to give up the promise of getting on a federal response team. His uncle had been right about that. Stopping at the village grocer to grab some lunch, he eyed the cigarettes behind the counter remembering how foolish he had looked not being able to take a puff without choking. He bought a lighter, and headed down to the beach. While watching the water, he ate lunch. Rummaging through the glove compartment, he pulled out a disheveled cigarette. Fingering the lighter in one hand and the cigarette in the other, he finally tossed out the cigarette in disgust and put the lighter in his pants pocket. An hour later, he drove home.

"Jim, is that you?" his mother called out to him.

Not answering, he took off for a walk.

Expecting Jim, it was Kim who stood on the dock when Billy arrived. "What are you doing here?" he asked.

"I know my way around boats," she answered confidently and climbed on board with the other firefighters attending the drill.

"Junior Firefighters don't go on boat drills," he commented.

"Oh, Billy. Don't be so serious. It's fine. I won't get in the way."

Not knowing what else to do, he said, "Oh, all right," and climbed on board as well.

A stiff breeze blew a steady northwest wind into the harbor. The water was clear and choppy. The fireboat sped towards open water close to the bluff to practice with the deck gun. Billy stood off to the side and watched.

"What's the first thing you don't do when you arrive to a boat fire?" reviewed a boat crew member with Kim.

"Don't tie your rescue boat to the boat on fire," she said seriously.

"Very good," he nodded, offering her a chance to handle the deck gun.

Billy turned away. Despite Billy's warning, Kim was still freelancing, showing up at house fires unannounced, and now showing up at boat drills she shouldn't be attending. Kim was an accident waiting to happen. She would go around her father and the whole fire department, he realized, to see some action. And his buddy, Jim, who should be here, wasn't.

The cool air felt good on his face as he held on to the boat's rail. He could see the houses along the bluff. One was a gray house with large glass windows, another a stone cobble colonial near the shoreline. The pink mansion at the highest point of the bluff was the furthest out. It overlooked the harbor and the Long Island Sound. He could almost make out Jim's house tucked under dense oak woods. Where was he anyway? It was their first boat drill of the season.

The boat driver then took them on a tour around the harbor in a wide easy swing. They passed by the barrier beach on the west side of the harbor. It was a bird sanctuary and a favored camping spot by locals. They came back round to the bluff again.

Kim shouted, "Look! I see smoke. There, near the pink mansion!"

"I see it," confirmed the boat driver who steered the boat closer to shore. "I'll call it in."

Billy grabbed binoculars and scanned the bluff searching for more smoke. Spotting a fleeing figure, near Jim's house, he gasped. Was it Jim or were his eyes playing tricks on him? About halfway between the pink mansion and the ferry dock was another wisp of smoke.

The boat's engine sputtered as it neared shore.

Kim paced excitedly and grabbed a fire extinguisher filled with air pressurized water. Impulsively, she jumped off the boat, splashed through the cold water, and touched the beach with wet sneakers. Driven by adrenaline, the extinguisher felt light in her hands. She ran nimbly over the cobbled beach into a thick stand of pitch pines and disappeared out of sight.

Moments later the firehouse siren went off.

Showing up early to meet Billy at the firehouse, Sandy rushed for her turnout gear and hopped into the Brush Truck! The driver arrived, and she expected to be told to get out, but the driver took off with her! The ride was rough. The Brush Truck rattled as it sped through the village and raced up the hill towards the bluff.

Excitedly, Sandy recalled the Fire Danger to be MODERATE, not likely to become a serious fire and control would be relatively easy. But there could be some flare ups. It was windy, but no Red Flag warning had been issued. Continuing to size up the anticipated fire behavior, she knew the fuels and the terrain well. If the wind drove the flames uphill into a heavy pocket of fuel, she should be careful, especially near the more flammable pitch pine stands. She had the belt weather kit, a GPS, and a blank Fire Awareness Report with her, but had no time to stop and collect data.

Running behind the Brush Truck for the hose, Sandy pulled it out, and headed towards the fire. From her vantage point, the flames were about one to two feet high, burning in spotty fuels. She closed in on the flames and hit them hard before they could spread into heavier fuels.

Two engines arrived and hooked up. More hose lines were stretched.

"Sandy, get back into the Brush Truck," shouted the Brush Truck driver. "We're to watch out for any spot fires closer towards the village. The engines are taking over here." Sandy shut down the hose and reeled it back. They passed several responding engines, one of them being led by Company Five's Captain.

Fighting the fire on the bluff, above where Kim had jumped off the fireboat, Rick heard the radio chatter. His daughter was missing. He spoke directly to the boat driver by radio. "What about my daughter? Where is she? What were you thinking to let her on the boat drill?"

He had no answer for him.

Billy took the radio. Recalling Jim's fleeing figure, he asked, "Where's Jim? He wasn't at the boat drill."

"He's with me!" He snapped. "Billy, where's my daughter?"

"Sorry," said Billy, but what he really wanted to say was, "Billy kinda faded, just like his father. Don't you understand? Can't you see this?"

"Hey! Billy!" Kim splashed back to the boat, grinning. She had long since emptied the extinguisher. She ran back down the bluff to escape the fire's tremendous heat. Not wanting to admit how vulnerable she had felt, she climbed back on board, and nonchalantly took the radio handed to her.

"Kim are you safe?!"

"Dad, I'm fine."

"What kind of stunt were you pulling?" Rick yelled. "I've got a fire to put out. Who's in charge of the boat crew anyway?"

Kim dropped the radio into an outreached hand.

"Bring the boat back. The Chief's ordered anyone who's qualified to get up here. Ride up in the Police Van. And bring my daughter up here, so I can keep my eye on her!"

The Police Van repeatedly brought up fresh firefighters from the firehouse including Tina. Tina had been down the road helping her brother clean out her neighbor's rain gutters. It had been an easy task, a chance to get away from their mother who was still upset from last night's fire. There wasn't much left to clean up or do at their house except mope about the fire.

"Tina," their neighbor offered in a concerned voice, "You'll hurt yourself, climbing the ladder. Let Jack do it." Tina laughed. "Oh, I'm fine, really." It was the first time someone else was afraid for her and she wasn't. How odd, thought Tina. When the alarm rang, she borrowed her brother's truck, wondering what her neighbor would think of her now as a responding firefighter.

At the firehouse, she jumped into the Police Van, holding her fear in check. "I won't be alone," she realized. "If I'm faced with something I can't handle, I'll tell my commanding officer." Tina made it to the fire call with new found confidence.

Returning to Engine Five, Jim was rotated out for a rest. He leaned against the fire engine gulping water as two engines and several brush trucks arrived on mutual aid requests from nearby fire districts. Company Five's Captain went over to him. "You okay?" Jim nodded. "Good, then take Tina and grab some shovels. Go check for hot spots."

Jim and Tina headed off together, but it didn't take long for Jim to cut her off. Tina snapped, "Hey, watch it! What's your deal, dude? Why are you so obnoxious to me?"

"What are you talking about?"

"You know, exactly what I mean. Cutting me off just now as if I don't exist! Treating me like I can't do anything, like at the fundraiser when we were cleaning up in the kitchen, making fun of me at the beach when I was building a campfire, ripping the hydrant wrench out of my hand when I went to open the fire hydrant. You know I can pack hose as good as any guy."

"Huh!" Jim's mixed feelings about Tina surfaced. "How can a guy take you seriously, especially with your nails polished with some pink sparkly gunk? Firefighters wear gloves, remember. Put' em on!" Jim quickly jogged out of sight, hiding a goofy grin.

Tina hurried after him, pausing briefly to put on her gloves. When she did spot him, she saw Jim slip and tumble, head first, through a stretch of small pitch pines.

"Ouch!" Jim yelled. With his leg caught in a low lying branch he tried to free it, but his turnout gear and the steep slope made it impossible. Struggling, he removed his jacket. Yet he couldn't free his foot. He cursed. Gawky and all twisted, he made one last final attempt. Upon seeing the concerned look on Tina's face, he made a goofy grin, shrugged and laughed. He made Tina laugh too.

The radio called out a signal 4, everything was under control. Moments later, the radio called out for Jim.

Tina grabbed the radio, caught up in a branch.

She responded, "Captain, It's Tina. Go ahead."

"Now, Jim's missing?" Rick said annoyed.

"No! He's, uh, hung up at the moment." Tina pressed a finger to her lips, to quiet Jim's laughter. Composing herself, she responded, "I'll relay him the message."

"Copy that. Report back when you can. We're packing up."

"Yes sir," she said.

They worked together to get Jim untangled.

Finally standing, Jim slapped his forehead, "I've never done such a stupid a thing on a fire call."

"What got you so distracted?"

He didn't want to admit it was Tina, so he said, "My uncle! He threatened to throw me out of the Wildland Fire Academy. After all I've done for him! Maybe I'll quit first!"

"So quit then."

"I can't."

"Why not?

"Don't you get it," he snapped. "I can't say anything, including the way I think about firefighting. I thought getting in tight with federal firefighters was well worth keeping my mouth shut, but not anymore!"

Stunned, Tina realized his anger was directed elsewhere. "Tell it to him! You sure did a great job of yelling at me!"

"Oh, I'm sorry about all of that," Jim said as he went to untangle the radio. "But I must stick with it to get what I want. Then he'll use my connections to trade up for something else he wants or needs, like I'm some kind of baseball card. That's the way it is. I'm stuck."

"You need to untangle yourself from him too," she smiled.

His manner softened as he clipped the speaker microphone of the radio back to his fire jacket. "It's not as easy as you think. My uncle's been really good at helping me fit in. You know, I hate social scenes."

"No kidding." Tina retrieved their shovels as they headed back up the trail. Slowly, she admitted, "I hate social scenes too."

"You do?" He asked, surprised.

"It's not easy for me to fit in either. I put on an act."

"You're just fine, when you act normal. A guy could like that, you know." Jim gave her the same look he did last night at Tina's house while packing hose.

Tina gave him a look over; "You're not so bad yourself, when you act normal too."

Off in the distance the ferry was announcing safety procedures to its passengers as it left the harbor. Up on the bluff, Kim and Billy arrived with the Police Van. Before Rick could say anything, Billy felt obliged to intercede on Kim's behalf, Captain, "If it wasn't for me . . . "

"Grow up and stop covering for your friends."

Kim nodded angrily in agreement with her father.

A helicopter flew overhead. He looked up half expecting the Colonel. But it was only a news station coming to report on the fire. Bolstered by the Colonel's words of advice, Billy listened and studied the situation.

"As for my daughter, I've had enough of your community service!" Rick critically eyed everyone returning from the boat drill. "Whose arm did you twist to let you on the boat drill anyway?

The boat driver tried to speak on Kim's behalf too.

"Don't tell me she's got a hold on you, too?"

With no one else coming forward on Kim's behalf, father and daughter glared at each other until Billy stepped directly between them, decisively, to stop their tug of war. With clarity he said, "What if a daughter freelances because she feels trapped by her father? What if a Captain has failed to realize that his daughter isn't a little girl anymore? What then?"

Billy put his hand on Rick's shoulder, "Kim needs to be recognized for who and what she is. Solve this, and the freelancing will end." Billy paused, with a twinkle in his eye, he said, "You will both pull on the same rope — in the same direction."

Rick fingered the probationary shield in his pocket, not knowing what to do. Ever since Kim's birthday, the Chief was letting him decide.

Kim moved closer to her father, admitting, "Sure, I was angry. I took my training into my own hands. I knew I was freelancing."

"I should've seen it coming," Rick said. She was so much like him in her love of firefighting. Yet he didn't want to see her hurt. He remembered the day she had looked up at him with tears in her eyes. The day he had fallen through the roof, his little girl had stood proudly waiting for him in the firehouse. She knew full well that firefighting was dangerous. She had known this for years. He handed his daughter the probationary shield, cautioning, "Any slip ups and your out. No more monkey business."

"Yes, sir." Kim said. She polished the shield with her shirt and grasped onto it firmly. Her stubborn attitude vanished. In its place was calm nod. "Thank you, sir."

Rick slapped Billy proudly on the back.

Billy grinned, but wouldn't forget that he must continue his studies as well. Today, he had made the right decisions, after all.

In the din of firefighters pulling and packing hose, Sandy returned with the Brush Truck and grabbed a sports drink. She was drenched with sweat and thirsty. Billy beckoned for her to come over.

"Now, when it comes to Sandy's freelancing . . . "

Sandy's jaw dropped.

Rick crossed his arms and stared directly at Sandy.

The excitement of landing a seat on the Brush Truck quickly faded, as did the joy of fighting a wildland fire. Sandy gave Billy, and then Kim a questioning look.

To her surprise, Kim told her father, "Sandy's freelancing is another matter entirely."

"Yes," Billy said thoughtfully. "Sandy wants firefighters to be, as she calls it, more forest friendly. But we're not listening, so she freelances. Alternatively, if we embrace this diversity and allow this diversity to make team decisions . . . "

Sandy did a double take. She thought she heard the Colonel's voice, but it had been Billy's voice.

" . . . we would have her collect data at brush fires as a start which will make us all better firefighters," Billy concluded.

Both Jim and Tina had long since returned and dropped off their tools. Tina spotted her friends talking to Kim's father.

Something had changed in Kim's manner to her him. She walked over to find out what happened. Jim also noticed a change in Billy. He walked over as well.

Rick raised his eyebrow. "File a fire report on a brush fire?"

Tina explained, "Fire Awareness Reports are field notes for feedback on wildland fires. Sandy's mom studies wildland fires. We're helping her out. I'm also learning more about on site fire behavior and emergency response."

Billy nodded, having seen and heard of the report from both Sandy and Tina.

"I see." Caught between their determination and fire department procedures, Rick stepped back, "Guys," he said with a defensive smile, "this isn't my call."

Jim, Tina, Billy, Sandy, and Kim gathered around him, pressing for a response.

"Hmmm," said Rick, considering his options. "Well, being that you're all safe and the fire's out, an extra ten minutes wouldn't bother anyone concerned." He waved his hand at Sandy. "Go ahead. Have the Brush Truck wait for you, and if you need any help ask its driver. When you've finished the report, give it to me to look and to any else you need to. "

Sandy's voice couldn't hide her excitement. "Yes sir!"

"You okay?" Billy asked Jim as the two of them rode back on the engine from the bluff. Ever since Billy teased Sandy about who was starting fires in the village and she had mentioned Jim, in the back of his mind was something dark. "I mean, well, I saw you up on the bluff when the fire was spotted."

Jim gave Billy an astonished look. "I'll never hear the end of it. Ever since I blew off some steam and lit off the campfire, Steve calls me pyro. That's not funny. He's such a jerk . . . but," he handed Billy the lighter he had been fingering in his pocket, "I've been in a very dark place lately."

"Ridiculous for me to even think that way of you . . . Nah, we put fires out. It's just that when I saw you up on the bluff, and not at the boat drill, well . . . "

Jim went to punch Billy in the arm, but abruptly stopped. "Billy, you were right about distancing yourself from my uncle. I should've done the same."

"I've been a bit distant too. I've got a lot on my mind."

"You mean, Sandy . . . and on becoming an officer? I understand," Jim said as they walked into the firehouse to take off their gear.

"You do?"

"And you were right about me looking into a local fire service job. I've had enough of wildland fire academies."

"More likely you're getting to the point where you can recognize a bad leader when you see one, and know what to do about it."

FIRE AWARENESS REPORT

Date: _5/23/06_ Reported by:_ Sandy Lewis_

Fire Danger: _Moderate_ Red Flag? _no_

Fire Location & Name: _The Bluffs - Pink Mansion_

Coordinates: Lat: _40.963891_ Lon: _-73.075454_

On Site: Fuels, Topography, Weather - Fire Behavior

Fuel Type _trees & low shrubs_ Live Fuels: _spring leaf out_

Topography: _60% slope_ Temp: _63°_ Humidity: _21%_

Wind Direction/Speed: _8-10 mph_

Severity: _moderate_

Rate of Spread: _moderate_

Flame Lengths: _2 feet_

On Site: Response

Size Class: _B_
A(spot-.25) B(.26-9.9) C(10-99) D(100-299) E(300-999) F(1000-4,999) G(5000+)

Resources:_ brush truck, 2 engines, police van_
and 2 engines (mutual aid)

Fire Line Rehab Needs: _no rehab needed_

"My thoughts exactly," Jim chuckled. "I'll make it straight with Georgeann at the Wildland Fire Academy, and wrap it up for this year. Then perhaps, another time and place, I'd get involved again."

After they signed for their point, the two of them headed to the lounge for pizza. Finding a table off to the side, Jim struck up a tactical conversation with Billy as if nothing had happened between them.

"Tina," Jim called out, "Come join us. We're talking about water pressure. I thought you would be interested." He made room for Tina at the table.

Tina plopped down next to him and smiled, "Sounds good to me."

Billy eyed them oddly, wondering what he had missed.

The conversation got technical pretty fast and Billy had to pay attention. Recounting the number of engines used and hydrants tapped on today's fire, Billy realized they were conducting an after action review, especially when Sandy handed them each a copy of her filled out Fire Awareness Report.

"Sandy," Billy said. "Don't forget about the Technical Rescue meeting coming up in a few day. Are you still interested in going? They're setting up for a wilderness search and rescue drill this summer and, next year, an ice rescue drill."

"Sounds good to me." Sandy grabbed her second slice of pizza topped with juicy onions and peppers. Between bites, she asked Tina, "Where's Kim?"

"Just what I was wondering."

Kim ran in wearing her probationary firefighter gear.

"Looking good!" said Tina.

She dismissed the compliment. Instead, she called out, "Get ready guys! There's a Chief's investigation going on. Sounds like there's going to be an alarm."

A few seconds later, all five pagers went off.

Within minutes, all five of them got on their gear and jumped on an engine. As they waited for an officer and a driver, they did an unusual, impromptu, engine check.

Jim asked Tina, "Got your gloves on? "Tina nodded, and asked Kim, "Got your helmet on tight?" Kim nodded, and said, "Sandy's got bunker pants that still don't fit." Billy nodded, and said, "We'll have to speak to the Chief."

"Yes!" sighed Sandy relieved.

And the engine sped off.

The End

THE CONSERVATION BEHIND THE STORY: LONG ISLAND PINE BARRENS, NEW YORK

Photographer: Raymond P. Corwin

Photographer: Raymond P. Corwin

The Long Island Pine Barrens is the third largest park region in New York State. Encompassing approximately 100,000 acres, it protects the region's drinking water and a coastal pine forest. The Pine Barrens is known for hiking, birding, mountain bicycling, hunting, fishing, cross country skiing, horseback riding, studying nature, and picking blueberries. Left is the oak brush plains during a hazy day in Brookhaven State Park. Above are water reflections along the Carmans River.

Photographer: Gaven Christie

In exploring the Pine Barrens, you may find odd looking remains of the 1920's Radio Central. Left, the concrete base of a radio frequency tuning coil, wooden poles, and the base of a 450 foot tower. These artifacts are remnants of Marconi's trans Atlantic radio transmission experiments. To understand what Radio Central looked like, study the glass enclosed diorama pictured below. It is located at the Cape Cod National Seashore. Such prior land uses influence the Pine Barrens plant communities of today.

Photographer: Raymond P. Corwin

In 1980, when standing on this hilltop, the Pine Barrens view wasn't blocked by trees as it is today. Instead of cutting back the trees, fire tower historian Larry Paul and others plan to restore the view by building a climbable, historic fire tower (insert).

Photographer: Larry Paul

Photographer: Sonny Walker Turner, Jr.

In 1995, Long Island experienced a wildland fire as big as the ones out West. Left, firefighters staged in hopes of stopping the fire before it jumped Sunrise Highway. Below, the fire was so hot that they had to hose it down to make sure the roots wouldn't rekindle. Soon after, naturalist Glenn A. Richard used an old video camera to document how the Pine Barrens recovers from fire. Bottom, a green snake in the black ash, a box turtle finding its way home, and a blueberry resprouting from buried roots.

Photographer: Sonny Walker Turner, Jr.

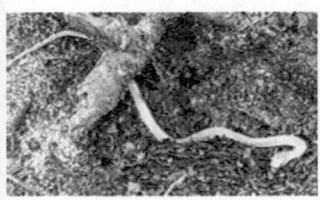

Photographer: Glenn A. Richard

Photographer: Raymond P. Corwin

By 1996, volunteers planted thousands of pitch pine tree seedlings in the fire lines created during the Sunrise Fire, and in the following years, in other disturbed areas. Below is a typical tree planting day at the Long Island Pine Barrens September 11th Community Forestry Restoration Project — a sandy, disturbed area located in the Rocky Point nature preserve.

Photographer: Raymond P. Corwin

Photographer: Colorado Wildfire Academy

In 1998, several people who were involved in the protection of the Pine Barrens began taking classes in wildland firefighting. Some even went to the Colorado Wildfire Academy. Left, firefighter check-in, marching, and clearing fire line with hand tools. Below, firefighters train in the classroom.

Photographer: Doug Campbell

Photographer: Raymond P. Corwin

Suffolk County Park Trustee Matthew Kruger came up with an idea. US Army Guard pilots could practice air maneuvers by removing abandoned cars out of the Pine Barrens. By 1999, water bucket training drills began at Wildwood Lake. A water bucket is dropped and released to simulate a wildland fire response. Many thanks to the Colonel who taught us: "There is no 'I' in T-E-A-M."

Photographer: Raymond P. Corwin

Photographer: Port Jefferson Fire Department

Photographer: Craig Jackson

In 2002, Mindy Block joined her local fire department to better understand why local firefighters didn't see the world as she did. Pictures on the left show a power plant fire drill, and county fire academy training drills: firefighters learning to control and direct a fire hose, and a fire drill conducted at a taxpayer. Below is a search and rescue drill.

Photographer: Port Jefferson Fire Department

Photographer: Ken Kindler

In late April 2004, fire suppression tactics upturned trees and bulldozed wide open paths. Quality Parks and others documented the damage. Village Beacon Record newspaper articles also described these events and were quoted in this story.

Photographer: Ken Kindler

Photographer: Raymond P. Corwin

In making a special map for the Pine Barrens, Mindy Block wanted it to be a combination of fantasy and reality. Left and below, we stopped at the Dwarf Pine Plains to explore a trail and to study the map. This is how Deborah Boudreau, our map illustrator, came to know the Pine Barrens on frequent travels with Parsley, the woodchuck, and his friends Raymond P. Corwin, the photographer, and Mindy Block, the naturalist.

Photographer: Raymond P. Corwin

FIRE AWARENESS REPORT

Date: _____ Reported by:_____

Fire Danger: _____ Red Flag? _____

Fire Location & Name: _____

Coordinates: Lat: _____ Lon: _____

On Site: Fuels, Topography, Weather - Fire Behavior

Fuel Type _____ Live Fuels: _____

Topography: _____ Temp: _____ Humidity: _____

Wind Direction/Speed: _____

Severity: _____

Rate of Spread: _____

Flame Lengths: _____

On Site: Response

Size Class: ___
A(spot-.25) B(.26-9.9) C(10-99) D(100-299) E(300-999) F(1000-4,999) G(5000+)

Resources:_____

_____

Fire Line Rehab Needs: _____

_____

_____

The Fire Awareness Report was created by Quality Parks after many years of field observations and data collection. Some of the data collected were used by a U.S. Forest Service scientist to improve fire danger prediction. In the story, the first three reports found on pages 130, 168, and 227 are based on real wildland fires.

Photographer: Ken Kindler

The Pine Barrens lives on.

Photographer: Raymond P. Corwin

Glossary

13-35 - a fire code for a working structural (house) fire

after action review - the review process done at the end of an assignment

assistant chief - 1st, 2nd, and 3rd, one next in command after, and helps, the Chief

blowup - sudden increase in fire intensity sufficient to preclude direct control

brush fire - local firefighter terminology for, often thought of as less severe than, a wildland fire

bunker gear - outer protective clothing traditionally kept by the firefighter's bunk

burn out - setting fire to consume fuel between the edge of the fire and the fire line

can man - a firefighter assigned to carrying a fire extinguisher

captain - the officer in charge of a company and its fire vehicles; for example, an engine and crew

chief or fire chief - responsible for fire suppression and the running of a fire department

colonelism - a saying that defines a good leader such as: "There's no 'I' in team."

command staff (ICS) - public information officer, safety officer, and liaison officer

dead out - referring to a wildland fire when the ground and the fuels are cool to the touch

deck gun - a mounted nozzle on a fire vehicle or boat, that provides large amounts of water

deploy - to arrange in a position of readiness, or to move strategically or appropriately

driver- under captain, responsible for fire vehicle and is the driver and water pump operator

engine check - weekly maintenance check of fire vehicles

evolution - a sequence of events that firefighters use to practice their suppression tactics

EXTREME - a fire danger rating indicating wildland fires that start, spread, and intensify furiously

ex-chief - a person who has been a chief in previous years

federally qualified firefighter - one who has passed national wildland fire training and performance standards

finance section chief - ICS staff position in charge of incident expenditures fire awareness report - field notes useful for feedback on a wildland fire, its conditions and the response

fire behavior - description of how fire reacts to the influences of fuel, weather, and topography

firebreak - a natural or constructed barrier for stopping a wildland fire; also called fire lane or control line

fire danger - from LOW to EXTREME, a word identifying protection needs if a wildland fire happens

fire ecology - the study of how fire changes wildlands

fire hazard - anything that encourages a fire to start or increase

fire lookout or fire tower - a tall structure traditionally used to spot wildland fires from a high vantage point

fire line - part of the control line that is scraped or dug to mineral soil

fire line rehab - fire line and possibly firebreak repair caused by suppression activities

fire line plow - a heavy duty disc plow usually pulled by a tractor to construct a fire line

firefighter hands-on - field classes taken by a firefighter to compliment classroom training

flake it out - to deploy hose in a snake-like manner

flame length - distance between the flame tip and base, indicator of fire intensity

flashover - complete incineration of all combustible materials within an enclosed area

freelancing - emergency personnel acting alone without assignment

fuel group - a wildland categorization that helps predict fire behavior; general groups are grass, shrub, timber, and slash

fuel load - how much wildland can potentially burn, given the right conditions

fuel model - a mathematical description of a fuel group's behavior during a fire

global positioning system (GPS) - an electronic device used to pinpoint a location on the Earth

halligan - a multipurpose structural firefighter tool invented in 1948 by FDNY firefighter Hugh Halligan

HIGH - a fire danger rating indicating wildland fires may become serious, unless attacked while still small

hot spot - a particularly active part of a wildland fire

hundred hour fuels - an arm-sized dead branch that takes 100 hours to match current humidity conditions

minimum impact suppression techniques (MIST) - firefighting tactics used to reduce damage to wildlands

incident - an event using emergency service personnel and the incident command system

incident action plan (IAP) - daily report detailing how an emergency will be controlled

incident commander (IC) - ICS position responsible for overall incident management

incident command system (ICS) - a process for organizing people to respond to emergencies

incident complexity - how hard it will be to manage an emergency: Type 5 (minor)- Type 1 (major)

public information officer - ICS command staff responsible for releasing information

interior qualified firefighter - a firefighter who is qualified to enter a burning building

irons man - a firefighter who carries an axe and a halligan tool, also known as "married" tools

LCES - wildland fire safety: look outs, communications, escape routes & safety zones

liaison officer (LOFR) - ICS command staff who coordinates with external agency representatives

live fuels - living plants, such as trees, grasses, and shrubs

live fuel moisture - the amount of moisture in living plants

logistics section chief - ICS staff responsible for organizing equipment and people

LOW - a fire danger rating indicating wildland fires creep or smolder, with little danger of spotting

maze - a drill to test a firefighter's ability to find one's way in a confusing network of passages

MODERATE - a fire danger rating indicating wildland fires aren't likely to become serious, but heavy fuels may burn hot

mop up - making sure a fire is completely out and is safely controlled

mosaic - one snapshot of how wildland areas change in time

mutual aid - formal agreement enabling outside resources to lend assistance when requested

one hour fuels - primary carrier of fire, dead needles/twigs, only takes an hour to match humidity conditions operations section chief - ICS staff that takes specific actions to control the emergency

pager - a device carried by volunteer firefighters alerting them of a fire call

pack hose - to put hose back onto the engine's hose bed

pack test - fitness test used to determine the aerobic capacity of a wildland firefighter

planning section chief - ICS staff position that works out the next steps in controlling the incident

point - all active firefighters have to respond to a certain amount of fire calls. Each fire call is a point.

probationary firefighter - a probie, a firefighter who has recently joined a fire department

rate of spread - how fast the wildland fire moves (creeping, moderate, fast, very fast, furiously)

red flag warning - a weather service statement indicating conditions are ideal for wildland fire ignition and growth

saddle - a mountain pass or a low spot between hills

safety officer - ICS command staff responsible for assessing and dealing with unsafe situations

scanner - a device that repeatedly searches for, and broadcasts, radio frequencies

search and rescue - an orderly procedure for finding and removing victims from danger

severity - the degree to which a site has been burned; the amount of soil damage caused by a fire

signal 4 - a coded fire department call meaning the incident is under control

signal 8 - a coded fire department call for refreshments

signal 12 - a coded fire dept. call for a brush fire alarm

signal 24 - see mutual aid

shadow team - local firefighter groups who go to see how a federal emergency response is organized

size class of fire - number of acres burned: Class A(.25), B(10), C(100), D(300), E(1000), etc.

sling loading - transporting materials by external net or other device attached to a helicopter

sling psychrometer - a hand operated instrument for obtaining temperature and relative humidity

smokejumper - a specially trained firefighter who arrives by aircraft and parachutes to the wildland fire smokes - wisps of white smoke in leaf litter indicating that the ground is still hot and the fire could rekindle

spot fire - a wildland fire that is no larger than 1/4 acre (size class A)

spotting - a fire behavior where the wind carries sparks or embers to start new fires beyond the main wildland fire

staging area - sector of an incident where responding resources register for assignment

structural triage - procedure for evaluating structures in a wildland fire to minimize risks

stump jumpers - modified trucks specially designed to fight fire in heavy brush

supplies - minor items of equipment and all expendable items assigned to an incident

supply line - large diameter fire hose that transports water from the hydrant to the fire engine

taxpayer - one to two story store, usually with a residence attached: deli, cleaner, pizza, etc.

technical (tech) rescue - a group of firefighters trained to save people in difficult places to reach

ten hour fuels - a finger-sized dead branch that takes 10 hours to match current humidity conditions

toned out - a method of alerting firefighters of a fire call through a pager

topographic map - a graphic of landforms showing elevation contours

training specialist - ICS planning staff responsible for coordinating firefighter training opportunities

turnout gear - see bunker gear

unified command - ICS method for enabling shared responsibility

vent - to release enclosed smoke and heat from a building by hacking a hole in the roof

VERY HIGH - a fire danger rating indicating wildland fires start, spread and intensify rapidly, and spot fires may occur

watchout situations - reminders to firefighters to rethink LCES and fire suppression tactics

water can - a fire extinguisher filled with air pressurized water

water hammer - backlash of water pressure from the nozzle to the engine pump, if the nozzle is turned off too quickly

wildland fire use - the management of naturally ignited fires to achieve resource benefits

wildland urban interface (WUI) - where buildings intermingle with wildlands

The Making of Sunrise Fire

Mindy Block and Gretchen Saule started this firefighter story around 2004. It is based upon Mindy's experiences as a naturalist, conservationist, and firefighter. But instead of a memoir, they decided to explore various aspects of firefighting as seen through the eyes of young adults.

Characters illustrate various growing up themes as well. For example, readers can explore what it takes to be a good leader. In terms of fire, they compared and contrasted the love of fire (how it changes the Pine Barrens and how fire behavior is both exciting and dangerous) with the love of firefighting (being good at what you do, saving life and property, and the evolution of wildland firefighting tactics).

The plan was for Mindy to write the content behind the story, and for Gretchen to write the dialog. Character development and story scenes were based on their in depth phone conversations. However, an unexpected turn of events made it more difficult for Gretchen to participate as she was returning to college for high school teacher certification.

With Quality Parks underway as a charity working on conservation projects, Mindy turned to its volunteers to fill in for Gretchen. The response was overwhelming, and soon Mindy realized that in creating opportunities to participate in the publication process, volunteers would also learn more about the Pine Barrens and nature conservation.

While volunteers worked to balance content and character to create an educational yet entertaining story, Mindy found new ways for them to contribute to Sunrise Fire. As with independent films, but with different roles, the Production Team grew. It divided and expanded into chapter reviewers, editors, producers, production assistants, illustrators, and more.

Sunrise Fire is a joint effort among Mindy Block, Gretchen Saule and Quality Parks. This is why Mindy prefers to consider Sunrise Fire a book production. Proceeds from the sale of this book will be used for charitable purposes. To ensure this, this book isn't sold in for profit stores.

On the following pages, please view the Production Team. Then learn more about Quality Parks, upcoming productions, conservation projects, and park news at www.qualityparks.org .

In appreciation of their contributions to fire education
and forestry conservation, Quality Parks recognizes:

The Production Team

EXECUTIVE PRODUCER
Mindy Block

PRODUCERS
Jennifer Smith
Judy Emily Soh
Mindy Campbell

EDITORS
Andrew Tetreault
Angela Suba Natarajan
Bipin Roy Lekshmanan
Daniel Pollard
Ellen Bogardus-Szymaniak
Fred Von Mechow
Gloria Block
Janet Ilacqua
Jennifer Smith
John Black
Judy Emily Soh
Julie Radachy
Leonard Schwartz
Mindy Campbell
Ray Calabrese
Raymond P. Corwin
Sophie Downes

INTERIOR GRAPHIC DESIGNER
Judy Emily Soh

COVER GRAPHIC DESIGNER
Zak Ettlinger

FRONT COVER ILLUSTRATOR
Lillian Ulman

BACK COVER PHOTOGRAPHERS
Raymond P. Corwin
Sonny Walker Turner, Jr.

PINE BARRENS MAP ILLUSTRATOR
Deborah Boudreau

PART A ILLUSTRATOR
Winford Jones

STORY PHOTOGRAPHER
Raymond P. Corwin

CONSERVATION PHOTOGRAPHERS
Colorado Wildland Fire Academy
Craig Jackson
Doug Campbell
Gavin Christie
Glenn A. Richard
Ken Kindler
Larry Paul
Port Jefferson Fire Department
Raymond P. Corwin
Sonny Walker Turner, Jr.

ADDITIONAL ILLUSTRATORS
Dana Moss
Meredith Mollohan
Zak Ettlinger

GLOSSARY EDITORS
Andrew Tetreault
Raymond P. Corwin
Suechu (Julie) Taing

ORIGINAL FIRST DRAFT WRITER
Mindy Block

ORIGINAL STORY CREATORS
Gretchen Saule
Mindy Block

SENIOR PRODUCTION ASSISTANTS
Barbara Sabatino
Benlin Alexander
Denise Rodriguez
Horace Corwin
Katherine Coleman
Valerie A. Molinaro

PRODUCTION ASSISTANTS
Anna Shpitsberg
Ashleigh Jones
Ashley Preece
Dayanna Arriola
Doug Campbell
Fred Edel
Jon Hoydic
Laura Perez-Harris
Ken Ettlinger
Renee Ryan
Steve Barreres
Suechu (Julie) Taing
Sweet Image
Tonya Barnard
Zak Ettlinger

CHAPTER REVIEWERS
Akua Abu
Amy Browne
Amy Goldschlag
Andrei Nomerotski
Anna Verticchio
Ashley Stiel
Barbara Stewart
Brennen Holmes
Bruce Johnson
Caroline Paul
Dayanna Arriola
Denise Rodriguez
Donna L. McCormick
Doug Campbell
Edwina Carr-Jangarathis
Flora Kohane
Frank Intini, Jr.
Fred Edel
Gabrielle Cyr
Gary Wood
Harriet Cassidy
Janice Molloy
Jay & Rebecca Spillmann

Jazzmyn Arrington
Jenna Cavelle
Jennifer Somerville
Jimmy Wood
Joe Kennedy
Jon Hoydic
Karen Corsi
Kathy Northway
Kelly Duncomb
Ken Ettlinger
Ken Spadafora
Kent Maxwell
Larines Rodriguez
Larry Paul
Lisa Zammiello
Margaret Feltner
Marty Shea
Melissa Wolfe
Meredith Mollohan
Nancy Futeran
Nancy Harvard
Navya Arora
Patty Erland
Paula Ross
Peg Conklin
Peter Meade
Philip Marshall
Richard White
Scott Gadwa
Shep Stone
Stephanie Carouthers
Suechu (Julie) Taing
Sweet Image
Tim Morrin
Tim Still
Tonya Barnard
Valerie A. Molinaro
Wendy Reeder
William B. Sickles
Yogesh Sheth